The Touch of the Sea

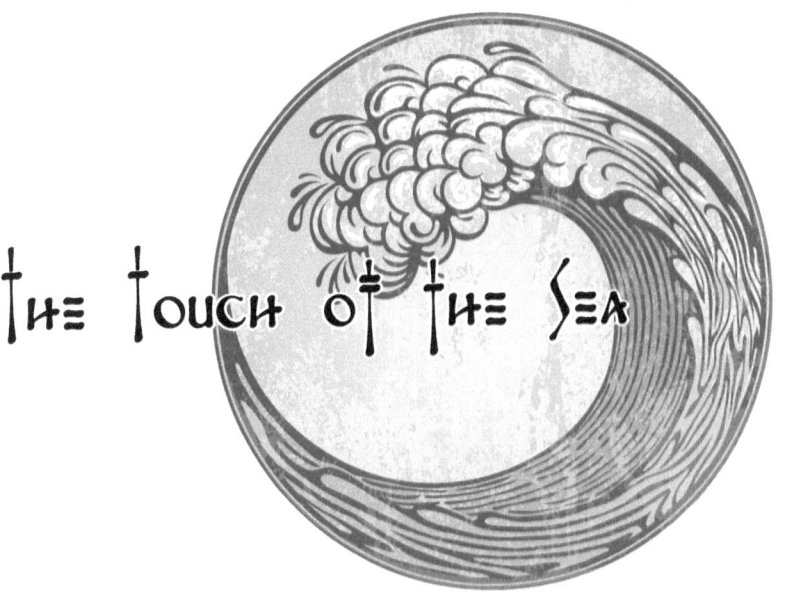

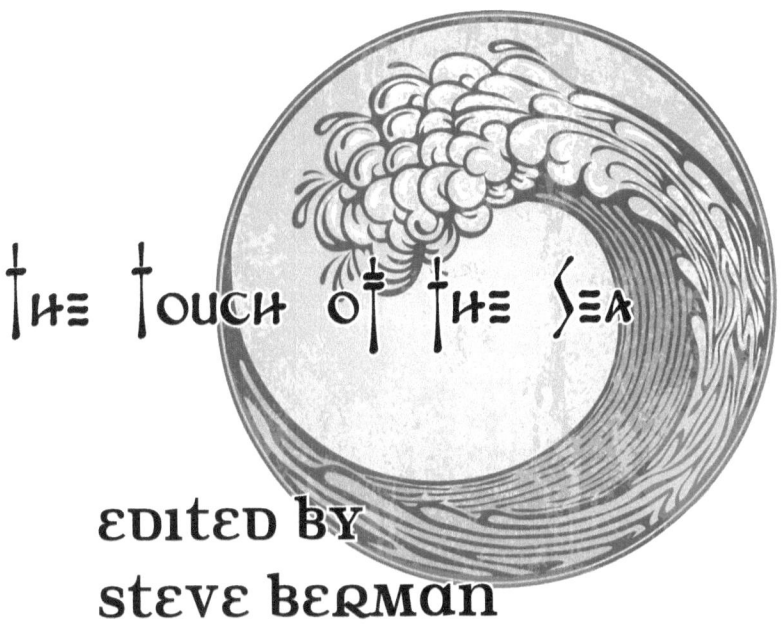

The Touch of the Sea

Edited by
Steve Berman

At sea a fellow comes out. Salt water is like wine, in that respect.
—Herman Melville

Lethe Press
Maple Shade, New Jersey

The Touch of the Sea

Published in 2012 by Lethe Press, Inc.
118 Heritage Avenue ♦ Maple Shade, NJ 08052-3018
www.lethepressbooks.com ♦ lethepress@aol.com
ISBN: 1-59021-208-8 / 978-1-59021-208-0
e-ISBN: 1-59021-418-8 / 978-1-59021-418-3

These stories are works of fiction. Names, characters, places, and incidents are products of the authors' imaginations or are used fictitiously.

Set in Jenson, Fontasia v2.0, and Water Street.
Cover and interior design: Alex Jeffers.
Cover art: Jared Pallesen.
Interior art: il67.

LIBRARY OF CONGRESS CATALOGING-IN-PUBLICATION DATA
The touch of the sea / edited by Steve Berman.
    p. cm.
 "At sea a fellow comes out. Salt water is like wine, in that respect. -Herman Melville."
 ISBN 1-59021-208-8 (pbk. : alk. paper)
1. Gay men--Fiction. 2. Fantasy fiction, American. 3. Sea stories, American. 4. Gay men's writings, American. I. Berman, Steve, 1968-
  PS648.H57T674 2012
  813'.01083538086642--dc23

        2012015324

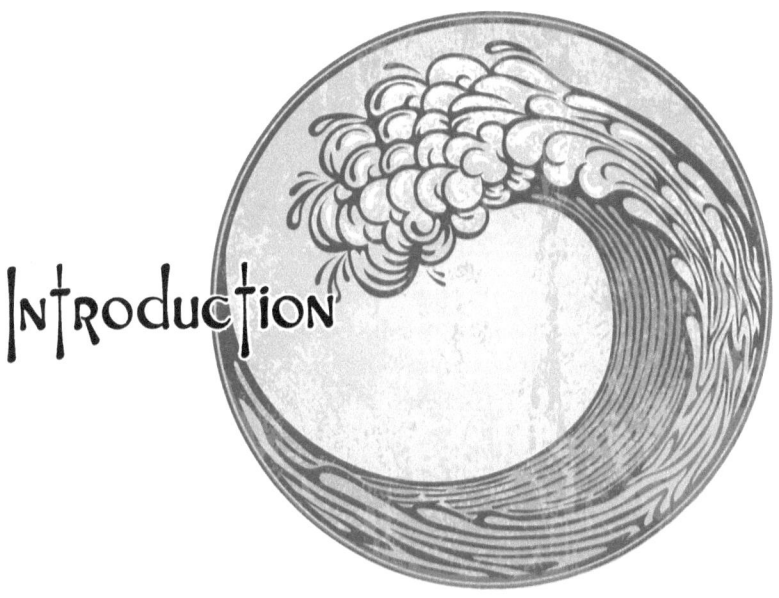

Introduction

You're sitting at a too small, dare we say intimate table, at a restaurant overlooking the coast in a seaside town. Dusk has tinted the sky an indigo but the water still captivates the eye because of its motion. The man across the table from you also captivates the eye, which is one of the reasons you are seated at said restaurant, which has far too many faux fish nets and traps and beach glass along the walls. An oar, overhead, would intimidate Damocles.

Your date sips white wine—he's a stickler for traditional pairings, except for traditional marriage, of course. You're waiting for the waiter, who is aptly bow-legged, to waddle over with the *plateau de fruits de mer*. You honestly do like raw oysters and cooked shellfish, but the true joy is in ordering and eating something referred to as "fruits of the sea."

"What are you reading?" your date asks. Does he know how much what he asked matters to you?

"*Sodomy and the Pirate Tradition.*"

He chuckles. "Really?"

You nod. "Honest. And it's even a scholarly work so I can feel erudite."

"You carry it well."

You raise your own drink in salute. After a sip: "This is my second read-through. The premise—that pirate ships are akin to prisons, keeping men isolated from women for months and months, confined in close quarters with one another so homosexual hi-jinx would *have* to ensue—is both so obvious and yet so revelatory."

"Lafitte sounds fey." Your date leans in. "So One-eyed Willy from the *Goonies*—"

"A double entendre."

The waiter arrives. He grunts lowering the silvery platter. The smell of chipped ice and salt water and fresh seafood rises over the table.

"So where are the mermen then?" your date asks.

"Hmm?"

"Sailors always claim to see mermaids. Some of those pirates must have enjoyed the lower berths more than the whorehouses ashore. So why didn't they see mermen?"

You take a tiny fork to an oyster, breaking it loose from the shell. "Remember Pelops?"

"Who?"

"The son of Tantalus. He was carved up as stew meat and served to the Greek gods. When they resurrected him, Poseidon became instantly smitten at the sight of this gorgeous youth stepping out of the cauldron."

"I thought we were talking about mermen."

"I'm getting to that…so, eat a shrimp and let me finish."

Your date listens. You are thinking he deserves a postprandial reward. Most definitely.

"So, Poseidon takes young Pelops up to Mount Olympus, to Zeus's estate and the very chamber where he used to enjoy Ganymede. Only, Pelops was not made immortal, like Zeus's boy, and so the affair between the god of the sea and Pelops ended when he started growing a beard."

"Poor Pelops. Where were all the Greek bears?"

"Oh, he didn't fare too badly. Once back on Earth, he asked his former lover for help landing a wife. Life was so Kinsey crazy back then.

"Anyway, the point is, the sea, *He* does adore men. But the tales are so little known, so little told. Pirates and sailors did see mermen and cockerel sirens, but, like so many gay stories, such sightings were hushed. Found by the boatswain's mate after enjoying the real *fruits de mer*, and you'll end up like Billy Budd hanging from the yardarm."

"So after dinner…" Your date slips his hand beneath yours. His pulse at his wrist beats beneath your fingertips like the waves breaking at the shore.

"Yes?"

"Will you tell me a story. About the sea?" His voice drifts to a whisper. "After…you know…"

You grin. The paper napkin seems to have gained weight on your lap. "I happen to know eleven."

"Isn't the eleventh sign of the Zodiac Aquarius?"

"Shhh. Pour me some of that wine. And let's finish this meal so the stories can begin."

stεvε bεαmαn
2012

Time and Tide

'nathan Burgoine

Death had made us leave Fuca, and now death was bringing me back. Stepping off the bus, the scent of the ocean was the only thing about my childhood town that seemed the same. The bus station had been completely rebuilt—it looked nothing like the rundown building I remembered. The glimpse of the town I'd had coming round the final curve of the road and down into the valley had been quick, but the mix of the familiar and the new was adding to the sense that none of this was real.

My father was dead. Holding my backpack and duffel, I stared without seeing, and just breathed. You couldn't see the strait from here, but like always, the streets seemed to deliver the scent to every corner of Fuca.

"Dylan?"

Even after a dozen years, I knew that voice. I turned, and there was Laurie, arms crossed, leaning against a shiny green cab. Her spill of curls was tucked under a beret and her curves were on display in a tight turtleneck and faded jeans. She smiled, her expression still somehow sad.

"Laurie." I hugged her and dropped my bags. Her arms squeezed once and then I stepped back.

Face to face with Laurie, I couldn't find words.

"Where are you staying?" she asked.

"The Cabins," I said, frowning. "I'm not exactly sure where that is, but apparently the hotel closed?"

Laurie nodded. "They knocked it down. There are a bunch of cabins down on the strait now. Part of the new Green Fuca." She waved a hand at the cab, and I saw that beneath the logo for the Fuca Cab Company there was a strip of text explaining the cab was electric.

"Green Fuca?" I said.

"Get in," Laurie said, opening the trunk and taking my duffel. "I'll give you the dime tour on the way. Meter's off." She tucked my bags in and closed the trunk. Then she met my gaze. "I'm sorry about your dad."

My cabin was small, but comfortable. It was built with an open concept. The kitchenette opened up on the living room and faced the open water through large sliding glass doors, with a two-seater breakfast nook built to enjoy the view. I put my bags on the counter and shivered. The cabin was so new I still smelled a trace of sawdust, but the strait looked exactly the same.

I could see the waves breaking on the beach down below. I unlocked the glass door and slid it open.

The sound—and the ocean's voice—washed over me. I closed my eyes, aware that I was shaking.

Shhhh… Shhhh… A mother's voice soothing a fussy baby. *Shhhh… Shhhh…*

Finally, I cried.

I grew up thinking of Ikuko Webster as my homeroom teacher. It was difficult to reconcile the image I had of a kind and wonderful woman in lavender blouses with the woman in the chic navy suit and steel-grey hair in front of me. Mayor Webster—as she was now known—had been at the funeral home when I'd arrived and had been re-introducing people to me all afternoon, helping me reconnect faces with names and supporting me above and beyond the call of a former teacher to her one-time favourite student. "It's good to have you back, though I wish… Well…"

I turned my attention back to her instead of watching the door. Cary Kelby wasn't coming. I shouldn't have expected otherwise. "Thank you." Then I added, because it was true, "the town looks amazing."

She visibly brightened. "Greenest town in the province."

"Laurie was telling me." I nodded to Laurie, who was standing across the room speaking with the pastor. She winked. "And the city funded the change to the electric cabs?"

The mayor nodded. "There's so much still going on. The cabins opened up last month, and they're booked solid for September and October already. The diner has a new hundred-mile menu, the local farmers and fishermen are filling the open market, City Hall has solar panels—you should have seen the hoops I had to jump through for that—and the influx of tourism has been palpable." She blushed, catching herself. "I'm sorry. Not the time or place."

I shrugged. "He would have approved."

She touched my arm. "He did. One of the voting voices." She paused, then pushed ahead. "Could I ask you… That is, the city…" She bit her lip, once again the nervous teacher with a student she was trying to mentor.

"Go ahead," I said.

She smiled. "We'd like to commission a piece from you. Local celebrity and all that. It seems so wrong that Fuca doesn't have an original Dylan Hurley of its own."

My fingers itched. It would be a very welcome distraction. "Absolutely."

"Wonderful. I'll have my assistant call you with the details. We'd like something for the centre of the roundabout. The intersection got a makeover, but it needs a centrepiece." She held up a finger. "But local materials only."

I laughed. "Of course."

She touched my shoulder again, and then introduced another one of my father's friends, whom I didn't remember and didn't know. I couldn't reconcile this grim event with my father, who had worked so hard to make me laugh and smile all my life. I surreptitiously checked my watch. Another hour and I'd be free.

My eyes returned to the door, watching for Cary. He didn't come.

Back at the cabin, I started sketching.

My ideas have always been of two sorts. The first hide and bury themselves in the deepest places of my head, where I have to flush them out and capture them and wrestle them into submission. The other sort are tenacious beasts that demand all my attention. I was pretty sure this idea was going to be one of the latter.

Before long, I had a rough sketch and an idea flushed out enough to send it to the Mayor's assistant. I snapped a picture with my phone, thumbed an email, and sent it off. Before I'd managed to unpack my duffel and backpack, my phone pinged with the reply. Mayor Webster loved it and we had a deal.

I did research on my phone's tiny screen until my eyes burned, and decided to call it a day when my stomach informed me that it was almost two hours past dinner. I tucked my wallet into my pocket and locked the cabin behind me, walking into town.

The future site of my piece was on the way to the diner. The mayor was right—the roundabout was lovely now, a small park to itself where the roads met, full of hostas but somehow not quite finished. I pictured my piece, installed, and nodded to myself. It would work. And they didn't mind the extra construction on the curbs and sidewalks surrounding it.

My stomach rumbled again.

I turned my back on the roundabout and walked down to Market Street. I considered the diner but decided I wasn't in the mood for a crowd—and I was surprised to see there was an actual crowd in the diner—and kept walking. Two blocks past was the open market where a few stalls were still occupied even as the hour grew late.

I bought some local bread, local butter, and local milk, along with some local tomatoes and local cheese. One thing was missing. I asked where I could score some coffee while the guy in the stall wrapped up my purchases. At the corner store I found a bottle of instant. I felt like a smuggler trying to procure something illegal and the cashier laughed when I said so.

I was walking back through the market with my purchases in hand when the ocean's voice started talking again.

Shhhh… Shhhh…

It was getting clearer. I hesitated, shifting the bag to my other arm.

"Already shopping like a local, eh?" His voice rolled me over, lost me in the wash, and removed my sense of up and down. I turned. "I'm sorry about your dad," Cary said.

I nodded, not willing to trust my voice.

He wore jeans and a faded Fuca High Athletics T-Shirt. He hadn't shaved today. His hair was long enough to stir in the wind and his eyes— I'd never forget that most impossible deep blue. "Where are you staying?

"The cabins." My voice only cracked a little. I cleared my throat.

He nodded. "Great idea, those were." I noticed he was carrying a package of his own. Fish wrapped in paper and some greens I didn't immediately recognize. The rest of it was buried underneath in the reusable bag.

"So I hear," I said. I wanted to touch him. I wanted to run away. *Why did you agree to build a piece for Fuca?* I thought. *You can't leave until it's done!*

He seemed to read my mind. "How long are you staying?"

"I was just going to stay for three nights. Deal with the lawyer and everything. But…" *But?* "Ms. Webster commissioned a piece." I sounded lame. I felt lame.

"About time we had a piece of you." He smiled, and the gap between his front teeth was like a punch to my stomach. "What are you making?"

"You'll see when everyone else sees." I intended to sound playful but came off sharp.

He nodded. "Right."

"I miss you." It was out before I could stop it. As always, Cary pulled things from me. He had his own gravity, even after all this time. Everything in me wanted to touch him.

"I missed you, too." Past tense, I noticed.

He looked at what I was carrying. "Are you making your sliced tomato sandwiches?"

"Yeah." The tension broke and I smiled.

"How about some salmon to go with it?"

The ocean whispered, clearer still. *Yessss… Yessss…*

"That sounds great," I said.

He used the small grill on the deck, wrapping the fish in the greens and tinfoil and butter while I sliced the tomatoes and cut the bread. I couldn't help but smile. Local bread. Local butter. Local sea salt. We had a sandwich each while we waited on the fish.

"I'm sorry I couldn't come to the funeral," Cary said. He looked at me. "How are you doing?"

"It's strange to be back," I admitted. "I remember everything but I'd forgotten it all, too. And everything is different but all the same things are there, tucked between. Does that make sense?"

He nodded.

"He never let me visit," I said, though it was embarrassing to admit I'd let my father dictate this to me. "When he moved back here, after I graduated, I mean. He visited me. Every Christmas, and his birthday. And mine, a few times. I'd call and say I'd like to see him and he'd say 'No, you stay put. I'm the retired one.'" I sighed. "I let him have that, I guess. I think he was afraid…" I trailed off. I've never quite been sure just what my father felt he had to fear about me being in Fuca.

"Memories of your mother," Cary said.

I nodded. He was right. Time to change the subject. "How's your family?"

Cary smiled. "The same. My brothers are still around. They got married, and I've got multiple nieces and nephews I get to spoil rotten. I took over the business when dad retired, but mom still comes in every day at lunch to thank the guys."

"How many you got now?"

"We downsized, actually. Just three ships, twelve men. But now we take people on tours, and we have our own fish farm." He met my gaze. "Mom's a watchdog, makes sure everyone is respectful and kind to the fish." He blushed. His mother had not been a fan of my father.

"Sounds wonderful."

He looked out the window. "Gets me out on the water."

"Do you…" I almost asked him if he remembered, but I backed out. "Do you think the fish is ready?"

He went to check. It was. We ate. Then we opened up a bottle of wine, and ate the cheese. We leaned closer to each other, and talked. The ocean whispered through the open glass doors.

Husssh… Husssh…
We stopped talking. I kissed him.
He spent the night.

While he used the shower I made toast with the last of the previous night's bread, and made us both some illicit coffee that wasn't from the same continent, let alone one hundred miles. He came out in a towel, smelled the coffee, and grinned at me.

"Coffee isn't on the approved list of local beverages," he said.

"Here. Be an accomplice in my illicit coffee-smuggling ring." I handed him a cup and kissed him again. He tasted like spring water: clean and fresh.

He swallowed some of the coffee, then regarded me over his cup. "When do you go?" There it was. The question. He might as well have asked me when I planned to hurt him again.

"I'm not sure. I have to find somewhere to stay. I need to rent a work space, too." It was an unfair answer.

"We've got an empty boathouse." Cary drank more. "And you can stay with me."

His hair was completely dry. That hadn't changed. *God*, I thought. *Nothing has changed.*

"I'd like that," I said.

He nodded. "I'd better get dressed. Have to be at work soon."

We looked at each other a moment longer. I was the one who broke. "Thank you," I said, not sure exactly what I was thanking him for.

He took my hand squeezed. Then he got up, got dressed, and left. His coffee cup was still half full. The liquid inside was spinning as though it had just been stirred. I picked it up and held it until it began to spin in the opposite direction.

Nothing had changed.

A day. Three days. Two weeks. I worked in the rented boathouse despite Cary's protests that I could have it for free, and added it to Fuca's bill. At night, we walked from the docks together to his small house. We had breakfast and dinner together. Most days I made us sandwich lunches—he claimed not to be tired of my sliced tomatoes.

The old things hadn't gone away. When Cary showered, or swam, or got caught in the rain, he'd be dry seconds later. When I held a glass of water, the ice cubes began to spin. Salt arranged itself into patterns across the counter if I spilled it. Gulls fell quiet as I walked by. And the whispers from the ocean grew louder and gained harder consonants among the sibilants.

My third week, I woke in the middle of the night to find the bed empty. Through the open window I could hear water. I tugged on my shirt and jeans and padded barefoot down the slope behind Cary's house to one of the many creeks that fed into the river. There he was, sitting beside the water.

He looked at me, and even in the night I could tell he was blushing. "Sorry," he said. It lay between us, a non-discussion. His bare feet were in the water.

"It's fine," I said.

He looked at me. "Do you still… Does it still..?" He sighed, frustrated. Not talking about it for the past three weeks had become a bad habit.

"Yes. It got less… It was less in the city, but it still happened."

He relaxed. *We're going to talk about it*, I thought. I was afraid.

Saaaay… The ocean's voice again. *Saaaay…*

"How's the piece coming?" Cary meant, *When are you leaving?*

"Pretty well." I mean, *Soon.*

"Good. Do I get to know what it is?" *You're breaking my heart.*

"You'll see it when everyone else does." *I know.*

We fell silent. The ocean whispered. *Saaaay…*

"Dylan?"

"Yes?"

"Take my hand?" He held it out. I looked at his feet, in the water.

I took his hand. I wasn't calm enough, and in moments, the creek began to roll. Waves formed, gentle at first but growing larger.

He dropped my hand, and the creek stilled. "Well, there's still that."

I meant to laugh, but I cried instead. He led me back inside and wrapped himself around me until I fell asleep.

His feet, of course, were already dry.

Mʏ moᛏᕼeᏒ waš leaninɢ on ᛏᕼe Ꮢailinɢ, ᕼeᏒ ᕼaiᏒ ᛏied bacƙ under a white cotton scarf, beside Cary's parents. My father was at the wheel, laughing about something and making her smile, chasing away that lonely look she wore on her face so often like only he could. Cary's brothers were chasing him around the boat until their mother raised a hand, and they gave him one last shove before settling in at the back of the boat.

Cary looked so frustrated, and so sad. I pushed off from the railing and sat beside him. When I was sure no one was looking, I took his hand and squeezed.

The boat lurched. My mother's head turned, and she met my gaze with a frown, then her eyes flicked down and saw our hands.

"Dylan," she said, but the boat lurched again, and water sprayed onto the deck.

"Choppy," my father called out. "Everybody take a seat. I think—"

The boat dropped and rose with a sickening lurch. I tumbled from the bench, landing hard on one knee. My head spun. There was a roar in my ears—I couldn't get past it to even think. The boat jumped again, twisting and rolling now. Cary took my hands. He was scared, eyes wide, and I saw his mouth move, but the noise in my head was too loud. My vision blurred. The boat dropped away from beneath us again and I went sliding down the deck. Cary scrambled after me, and I saw his brothers grab out for him, catching him by the shoulder and halting him. Our eyes met. I saw him say my name, though I couldn't hear him.

The boat rolled, and I was in the ocean. It pulled me under and tore me away. The roar in my head didn't abate, and I curled up into a ball. I was going to die. I opened my eyes—the salt water didn't sting—and felt my body relax. The ocean continued to pull at me, tugging me even deeper, and in some corner of my mind I realized I wasn't scared. I wasn't even cold. I wasn't struggling—in fact, I felt calm and peaceful. I was welcome here.

The water tugged and twisted around me, drawing me further and further down. I opened my mouth and felt the bubbles of my last breath rise past my face.

A hand took mine. I turned my head, and saw my mother's smile.

She shook her head once, kissed my forehead, and then she just came apart—one moment there, the next blurred as though the water were full of sediment that held the shape of her body, and then just gone. The water around me seemed to let go—and I felt myself jetting upwards to the surface.

The world returned and I sucked in a breath as sunlight hit my eyes. I heard my father's voice, and Cary's cry. Then everything went black.

I ᴄᴀᴍᴇ ᴀᴡᴀᴋᴇ ᴡɪᴛᴴ ᴀ ꜱᴛʀᴀɴɢᴌᴇᴅ ᴄʀʏ, ᴀɴᴅ ᴍʏ ᴴᴀɴᴅꜱ ʀᴇᴀᴄᴴᴇᴅ out into empty air. Once again, Cary was gone, but this time there was sunlight streaming in from the window. He'd let me sleep in. I stretched, the images in my head fading as I mentally prepared for the work I'd be doing on the piece today. It was very nearly done, and I tried not to dwell on that as I took a shower and then had breakfast. My coffee circled in the cup, and I closed my eyes for a moment, feeling the echo of its movement in my chest, and calming myself until the motion ceased. When I opened my eyes, the coffee was once again still.

On the front door, there was a note: *We're out of tomatoes.*

I grinned, and went back for one of Cary's shopping bags.

Lᴀᴜʀɪᴇ ᴡᴀꜱ ᴀᴛ ᴛᴴᴇ ᴍᴀʀᴋᴇᴛ, ᴀɴᴅ I ʙᴜᴍᴘᴇᴅ ꜱᴴᴏᴜᴌᴅᴇʀꜱ ᴡɪᴛᴴ her. She turned and smiled.

"How are you?" she asked. "You look great."

I shrugged. "I feel good."

"I'm sure that has nothing to do with your accommodations, eh?" Her lip twisted in a smirk.

"You're very funny."

"I'm also right."

I picked up some tomatoes. "You're also right."

"It's so good to see him happy again."

My chest tightened. "He hasn't been happy?"

"Cary?" Laurie raised an eyebrow. "Not since you left. You must have known that."

"I..." I bit my lip. "I guess I figured he would have moved on or something." I grimaced. It sounded lame. I started eyeing local cheeses like choosing one would be the most important decision I'd ever make.

"Dylan," Laurie said.

I looked at her.

"Are you staying?" she asked.

I breathed. "Good question."

"It's the only question," another voice added. We both turned. Cary's mother regarded me frankly. "Laurie dear, may I have Dylan for a while?"

Laurie nodded, and left us.

We didn't speak while she led me to one of the benches set around the outside of the open market, away from the crowd and any ears. Seated, we regarded each other. Jennifer Kelby had the same deep blue eyes as Cary, though none of her other sons had inherited them. Cary's gaze made me feel protected. Jennifer's made me feel accused.

"I'm sorry about your father."

"Thank you," I said. "I know you two didn't get along."

That surprised her. "You knew?

I smiled. "Cary told me that you argued. When I was staying with you. After my mother... After we lost my mother."

Jennifer pursed her lips. "Ah." Then, as though steeling herself for bad news, she said, "Do you love my son?"

"Yes." The word came out of my mouth before I could even consider it. I felt a weight lift off my chest that I hadn't known was there.

She nodded. "And are you leaving, or staying?"

I rubbed my eyes. "I don't know. It's..." I swallowed. "It's hard to be here." As if cued, a large wave crashed against the shore on the other side of the market, audible even from where we were sitting. We both flinched.

Jennifer took my hand. I felt the rush inside me, and our eyes met. She squeezed and let go. "You are a wonderful young man. Doubly so because you make my son happy."

"He's the wonderful one."

"I won't argue that." She smiled. "But I'm biased." She sighed. "I promised your father something, and I'm regretting it."

"It's okay. Cary and I talked about it, before I left. I know about the old families in Fuca. I know my mother was from one of them."

She stared at me, open mouthed. I couldn't help it. I laughed.

"But..." She shook her head. "I told him your father didn't want you to know."

I smiled. "My father wanted to leave. When you told Cary what was happening to him, he knew I was the same. We'd spent enough time together. Cary wanted me to stay so he told me. I think my father was afraid I'd feel responsible if I knew I was..." I looked at her. "Naiad, is it?"

She nodded, once. "Myself, yes. And Cary. Or at least half for me, and a quarter in his case. But you're not a naiad."

I nodded. "I know. Cary and I figured that out, before I left. I stay wet. I'm different from the two of you. Different things react to me and I can hear voices in the ocean."

"Salt water," she said. "Understand, your mother and I were very close, and we knew to watch the two of you, but we had no idea that the gifts would be so strong in either of you."

"Gifts," I repeated, scornful.

She heard the anger in my voice. "Yes. Gifts. The river for me, but the ocean for her—and you. Did you know that not a single sailor was lost or drowned while your mother was here?"

I hadn't known that. I shook my head.

"The ocean is very strong, Dylan. I'm sure you feel its pull, don't you?"

I nodded. "Sometimes. Mostly I just hear its voice."

She thought about that. "I imagine it gives good advice."

I didn't know what to say.

"She felt it every day, Dylan. Every time she went on the water it wanted her to stay, and every time she resisted. She could keep the ocean calm. You were so young. When you went under..." Her eyes filled with tears. "You have to understand, what she did, she did for you." She sighed. "She wanted you to have time to decide for yourself where you wanted to be, who you wanted to be."

I swallowed. "Is it the same for you?"

Jennifer shook her head. "Rivers flow. They don't have tides. I like the streams and rivers and they like me back, but they don't demand my attention. Though they occasionally flood," she smiled at her own joke, wiping at her eyes. "Rivers find their course, and they stick to it. But mostly they're content to be."

I smiled. "Sounds lovely."

She nodded. "It is."

We sat a moment longer.

"I'd best be going," she said. "And I hear you're almost done your sculpture."

I nodded. "Yes."

She rose, and turned to me. "I should have told you back then, your father be damned."

I shook my head. "I still felt responsible, either way."

"You weren't." Then she walked away.

I sat for a while longer, and then picked up my tomatoes and started for Cary's work. I had something to show him.

Cary regarded my sculpture with his incredible blue eyes. "I think it's beautiful."

The sculpture itself was a simple steep triangle, but I'd spent hours working on the surface, carving waves and ocean creatures both fantastical and real along both sides. Local rock had given me only the barest shades of different colours to choose from, but the subtle patterns of the various pieces, now completed into the one large shape, made an overall effect I liked. I was proud of the piece.

Cary walked around it, reaching out to touch some of the waves, and smiling when he saw a merman. "Usually those are women."

"Artistic license."

He smiled. "Is it supposed to be like a dolphin's fin? The whole thing, I mean."

I shook my head. "It's a sundial."

He looked at it again. "Oh wow."

"They're going to rebuild parts of the sidewalk and curb around it to mark off the hours—with and without daylight savings time." I watched his eyes take in the sculpture all over again. "It's called 'Time and Tide.'"

"It's wonderful." He looked at me. "Thanks for showing it to me before anyone else got to see it."

I smiled.

He turned back to the sculpture. "When will it be installed?" The casualness of his question didn't fool me. I felt my chest ache, and the sound of the ocean on the beach seemed to double.

Saaay… Saaay…

"Next week. The mayor wants to make a big ceremony around it."

Cary nodded. "So…then you'll be off?"

I thought about what Cary's mother had said. I thought about my father, sending me away where the ocean couldn't call to me. I thought about my mother, giving me time to choose with her own life. I closed my eyes, and heard the ocean.

Saaay… Saaay…

"No," I said. "I'm not going anywhere."

Cary was silent for so long I opened my eyes. He was looking at the sculpture still, tears spilling from his eyes. He made no move to wipe them.

I stepped up to him, and took his hand. "I'm so sorry."

He looked at me. I raised my free hand, and touched his cheek. His tears glistened once, then vanished under my fingers. *Salt water,* I thought.

"I love you," I said. "But we have to buy coffee. I don't care how far away we have to import it. I need coffee."

"Okay." He laughed, chest still shaking. "I love you, too."

He tilted his head forward and I put my forehead against his. We stood together, letting the shadow of the sculpture fall over us, and I held him until he stopped crying.

The ocean whispered. I wondered if I had been mishearing it all along. *Staaay… Staaay…*

I listened.

The Calm Tonight

Matthew A. Merendo

The sea is calm tonight. The swell moves slowly to shore, expiring in a glaze of foam on the sand. The spotlight moon shines on the water, lighting a straight path to the sea that tempts me to return. Beneath me, two lovers stroll hand in hand, and they stop. They embrace, their lips touch, and they fall to the sand. I cough lightly, but they do not see me. Their feet tease the tips of high tide.

My people have already returned to the waves. They travel home now, back to the depths, filled with new life and new love. This Emergence has ended, and a new cycle will begin, as it has begun every two hundred years since the Great Caress.

The couple beneath me, now half undressed, finally notices my presence here on this rock. They jump up. The woman covers her chest, and the man curses, blaming me for the intrusion. They run down the beach and then into the water, and though I should follow, I hesitate. The sea, my people, our goddess is everything I have ever known, yet still I hesitate.

I look to the moonlit path, turn to the human couple twined together, and I have no idea how I will swim again.

MY NAME IN THE SEA IS Alit Mithratin Walasha. On land, I have chosen Alex. If you saw me—and you may already have—you would catch no difference between you and me. My hair is black. My eyes are seaweed, my skin the color of clamshell. I am neither tall nor short, neither thin nor fat, neither this nor that.

But my people, they are beautiful, breathtaking and seductive. Among them, I am unique in my plainness. Even here with your people, I blend into crowds. If you took one look at me as I walked by, you would not turn to take another. If you saw a different sea-folk, you would break your neck trying to get just one more glance.

When we come ashore, we have only one thing on our minds. We do not come for your food or your architecture or your music. We do not come for the glory of the sun or the strangeness of rain or the fear of fire. We come to mate.

We sea-folk are barren without you. We are empty, useless shells, dry as the husks of chrysalis. Once every two hundred years, however, the men break the surface of the water. The air is crisp, and for a moment, it feels too thin. We spread through your towns, we meet your people. We mingle. Some of us fall in love. Some of us trip into lust. All of us mate.

When we return to the sea, there are more of us. Our love is a blessing from Yathita Alatha, and the blessed women, now sea-folk too, can return with us to the sea. We make the journey to the hidden depths, our home, where our goddess watches over us. New life dissolves into our waters, and we continue our lives, already preparing for the next Emergence.

This Emergence has passed. The sea-folk have returned to the water, their chosen women blessed with new life. But I am still here, on a rock looking out to sea. No woman has received my blessing, because I have fallen in love with a man.

ON LAND, HE IS Hunter. He HAS NO NAME IN THE SEA, because he is human. His hair is short sand, and his eyes are blue coral. He is small in stature, fragile, a self-identified "couch potato." He wears glasses. He loves armadillos. He hates Oreos. He studies the stars. His favorite movie is *The Little Mermaid*, which gives me hope.

We met at a bar. On Friday nights during the summer, the clubs and bars overflow, and this night was no different. It was the first of the

Emergence, and the sea-folk were spreading through the streets like tsunami. Considering the competition, I held little hope of finding a mate so soon.

But it happened at the first establishment I entered. I swooned from the sensations: the loud, thumping music, the sticky press of the half-naked people, the choking smoke. The only thing that kept me afloat was the moisture in the air. I could smell the ocean in it, even through the perspiration and liquor.

I saw an attractive blonde order a drink. She wore a tight black skirt, and her thin shirt hung off her shoulders. Her name was Sarah, and she was buying a round for herself and her friends. Would I mind helping her carry them back?

"Of course not," I said, trying to smile despite my disappointment. We sea-folk know immediately if the one we are with is the right woman for us. A split second will tell us about forever. For some, the first touch is all we need. Others, the first word. For me, it is the laugh. Sarah's laugh was an angry bird, a seagull cheated of his fish. She was not the one, but I had to be polite.

Her friends were sitting near the dance floor, so close to one of the speakers that the glasses on the table vibrated. I met Cheryl, who giggled like a dolphin when I shook her hand; her older sister Mika, who did not spare a smile; and Janice, who spent most of our introduction wiping away a stain on her new blouse. None of these, I knew at once, was the one.

"Sorry I'm late," he shouted from behind me, so close I could smell his cologne, a heady scent that felt like night sky. "I thought we were meeting where we always do." I did not turn around. I *could* not turn around. I was frozen in place, as if my legs already knew and were afraid to face reality. "By the time I remembered we were switching it up this week," he continued, "I had to run here."

He laughed then. It was awkward, quiet and clipped short, but he laughed, and every sound in the room faded to nothing, to drops of water against waterfalls. This was it. This was the one.

He was the one.

"You want to go back, don't you?" Hunter asks. He has snuck up behind me, so quietly that I heard nothing as he climbed the rock. I say nothing in reply. I lift my head from sea level to look at the full moon, and Hunter sits behind me, pulling my body into his. He rests his chin on my shoulder, our cheeks not touching but close enough to be felt. This is our pose.

"Don't be shy," he says. "I know what you're going to say." He pauses, waiting for an answer I do not want to give. "Do you want to go back?"

I squeeze his wrists so tightly he relaxes his grip on my waist. I hate that he lets go, and I pull his arms around me tighter as I say, "I do."

"You won't come back if you go?"

He has asked this question a dozen times, and I have answered it just as many. "I have found my mate, and I was not born to be a liaison. There is no reason for me to come ashore again."

He nods, and his chin pushes down on my shoulder, a pain that I enjoy because it is one more anchor tying me to land. His chin digs with each word—"I could go with you."—and my whole body swells into the thought, and though I want to shout affirmatives, I do not let myself respond. I look to the sea, too afraid to turn my head and catch him looking to the stars.

"I'm an astronomy grad student," he said to me as we lay in his bed after our first night together. We had met just a few hours before, but I felt more comfortable in his bed than in my own. He held one of my hands between two of his, tangling our fingers together as if he were afraid I might evaporate. "What about you? Are you in school?"

I had not been in school for two hundred years. "Something like that," I said. The post-coital excitement was dissipating, and the only thing left was the dull panic I had felt ever since I first heard Hunter's laugh.

"What are you studying?"

"The ocean," I said quickly. How had I fallen in love with a man? There was nothing about this in our history, our literature, our music. Nothing.

"Oh, what a coincidence! I'm working on a paper about tidal forces, particularly those relating to neap tides." I nodded absently. Should I leave the land once the Emergence ends? Should I stay here with him? He kept talking to fill the silence. "But I'm really interested in Roche limits."

Even distracted, I could tell he wanted me to ask. "What is a Roche limit?" He was running his fingers up and down my arm now, rippling my whole body with shivers. Maybe I should stay here.

"Every celestial body is held together by its own gravity, you know?" I did not, but I nodded anyway. "Well, the Roche limit is the exact distance that, if an orbiting body gets any closer to whatever it's orbiting, it'll get torn apart by tidal forces. Rings form like that, you know, when a moon gets too close to its planet. Boom!" He dropped my hand to simulate such an explosion.

I said nothing, too stunned to speak. Roche limits, tidal forces, moons orbiting planets, all so foreign yet so familiar to me.

He stopped caressing my arm. I felt a strange sensation where his fingers had been, what I imagine a crab feels when we pull off a leg to eat.

He spoke again, and his voice was quiet, subdued and afraid. "Are you going to get up and disappear now, like all the others?"

No, of course not, anything but that. "Consider me your moon."

He started to run his fingers along my arms again. "I'm gonna hold you to that, you know."

Please hold me tight, keep me close, be my gravity, but don't tear me apart.

You Say the Sea is hypnotic, Seductive and tempting, but I am unable to return because of what I would have to leave behind. My people have gone, their newly-blessed consorts in tow. I should be with them, my own lover behind me.

Yet I am still here, on solid ground. For six nights, I have come to this rock, praying for some sign or solution. Tonight, Hunter has followed me. He has asked if I want to return, and I have confessed. We have been sitting in silence, but now Hunter tells me why he really came here tonight.

Tonight, Hunter wants to follow me home.

I waited until the Emergence ended before I told him I might have to leave. I had waited a week for some easy solution, and I could stall no longer.

"I'll go with you," he replied without a second's hesitation. Only a week, and he wanted to go with me. I was not surprised. We sea-folk may need you land-dwellers, but you want us. No force, not even necessity, is powerful as desire.

"You cannot come with me," I said. I was not sure how to continue. Sea-folk never speak of their origins before the Return. We mate, and the blessing itself imbues the blessed with understanding. "I do not live here."

Hunter looked at me, a wry smile on his face. We were watching a film in his living room, sitting so close on his couch I had trouble concentrating if he laughed. He threw a kernel of popped corn in his mouth. "Okay. Maybe I'll move with you. Where do you live?"

"Atlantis," I said, smiling to myself at the joke. You see, we have no true name for our home. We live in the depths with Yathita Alatha, in a labyrinthine system of caves and reefs. We began to call it Atlantis in jest, but the name stuck.

"The resort in the Bahamas?" He looked confused, then grinned wildly. "I'd love to move there!"

My smile disappeared, sobered by the realization that the following conversation would be the hardest I would ever have.

"No, not Atlantis in the Bahamas." I was not entirely sure where the Bahamas were. "Atlantis is the name my people use for our home. It us far under the sea, where we live. We come on shore only to mate."

Hunter's face, so boyish, was a delicate balance between amusement and worry. "On shore to mate?" he mimicked.

"Yes," I said, taking a breath. It was such a strange sensation, breathing without water. "We come on shore to mate."

I explained everything to him then. The history of my people, our mating practices, the blessings of our goddess. My impending departure. Our inevitable divorce.

I expected anger. I expected disbelief. Mocking, yelling, possible sobbing. What I did not expect was a slow nod of the head, his expression lighting up like the eastern sea at dawn. "So that's where you're from," he said.

Dumbstruck, I stared at him.

"I knew there was something odd about you," he said. He watched the movie for a moment—the actress tripped and fell into a wedding cake, and neither he nor I laughed. "I wasn't sure what. I thought you were foreign." Another glance at the television. I had the nearly irresistible urge to wrest the remote from his hands and turn it off. What was he getting at?

"I suppose you are foreign," he said with a laugh. Not the laugh that I had fallen in love with but one without self-awareness or wit. This laugh was jaded.

"You believe me?" I did not know what else to say.

"Yes." His eyes were squinted, almost as if he had trouble believing himself. "Yes, I do. I don't know why. I shouldn't, considering your story is insane. But I do." He cocked his head and squinted more severely, as if he were trying to see something through the dark.

We sat together, neither one speaking. The movie continued to play, the silly misunderstanding that complicates every romantic comedy resolving itself in a car chase, a confession on national radio, and two security breaches at the airport.

The credits had not started, but Hunter shut off the television. He turned to me, determination in his eyes, and said the two words I feared.

"Now what?"

Now what? Now what? Now what? Those words have haunted me long before Hunter uttered them. There is no precedent in my culture for this, this falling in love with another man. Hunter and I spoke about it the day after he learned of my secret.

We woke up early after an aggressive night of lovemaking and decided to have breakfast at a nearby diner. I ordered several pieces of toast. I am fascinated by toast. I put nothing on it, no butter and no jelly. I like it dry; that's why I find it so fascinating.

"My religion hates it," Hunter said, his lips dripping syrup. I resisted the urge to lick it off, biting into my toast instead.

"I see," I said, unable to see at all. Why would a religion hate love, regardless of the form it took?

"It goes against the Bible, so for thousands of years, gays have been persecuted. It was a lot worse before. Hangings and burnings and only God knows what else." He took another bite of waffle. "There's no more of that, at least not here, but we've still got a long way to go."

He stopped chewing, hesitated, and then said, "When I told my parents, they threw me out. I haven't spoken to them since." He was not looking at me, but he was not looking at his waffle, either. "I haven't gone home since."

I thought of my own parents. They would be shocked, I knew—just like I was—but they would never banish me. No matter what, I could always go home.

The waitress came to refill Hunter's coffee and asked again if I wanted any. I declined. I drink nothing on land, considering I drink enough in the sea. Once she left, Hunter picked up the conversation. "I used to dream about going to space, flying in a rocket to some faraway star system where I'd find people who were just like me, only beautiful."

"You are beautiful," I said too loudly, without even thinking. A man at the next table scowled. Hunter blushed, though I still am not sure if it was the compliment or the contempt that caused it.

"What do your people think?" he asked.

I thought a moment. How do you respond when the answer is null? "They do not think about it."

His eyebrows slunk downwards, pointing at his nose. "What do you mean? They don't care?"

I shook my head, trying not to catch the eye of the couple who had just entered. The man was an acquaintance, and I wanted no questions at the moment. "As far as I know, this has never happened."

"Never?"

"No, never."

"In all three gazillion years of your people's existence, never?" He was grinning now, and I hoped he would laugh.

"Never. Sometimes men will return from Emergences with no mate. Perhaps they were the way we are, but none has ever returned with another man." I hesitated, unsure whether I should continue this train of thought. "I am not even sure if it is possible."

His concern was so clear I was afraid his face would crack. "So I can't go back with you, can I?"

"I—I am not sure, Hunter. As I said, there is no precedent, and I do not—"

Even through his shut eyes, I saw tears begin to well, and I could not continue spouting my grim negativity. I hung my head and stayed silent.

"I thought you could be my rocket," he said as he wiped away a tear that had escaped down the stubble on his cheek.

I took Hunter's hand—scowling man be damned!—and tilted his chin up to look me in the eyes. "I will do everything in my power to be your rocket, Hunter. I will pray to Yathita Alatha tonight for an answer."

He sniffled, but he was smiling again. "And I'll wish upon a star."

I cocked my head sharply to the side, uncertain of his meaning.

"It's something my mother used to sing to me." He chanted a rhyme about star light and the first star he sees tonight. His voice was so beautiful to me I had trouble paying attention to the words.

"Fine," I said a moment after he finished. "You wish on your star, and I will pray to my goddess. One of us is bound to get the answer we want, right?"

"Right," he said too optimistically. "Without a doubt." Our eyes met. "You want my toast?" he asked. I took it without another word.

We would be okay.

"This is not okay," I say to Hunter.

He has just told me his plan. He is standing across from me, hands on his hips. He has revealed a small bag, which he packed and sealed in plastic. How adorable, his trying to waterproof items he intends to take under the sea. But so naïve. How I wish I had his optimism.

"Please, Alex. I know you can't stay here."

"I can stay here." I am lying. "There is no reason I cannot stay here!" This is truth. I can survive on land just as well as a human. But it is partly untruth, because I cannot survive this pull, these tidal forces, that draw me back to the sea.

"Alex, I may have only known you for a few weeks, but I'm not an idiot. You don't spend every night out here on a cold rock because of the view." He sneers at the couple, who have moved only a bit down the shore before falling into love again.

I have always been a terrible liar, so I choose the truth. "There is a certain gravity here, but I can withstand it." I pause as a salted breeze brushes past us. "For you, I can try."

"And for you, I can swim." He picks up his bag as if he has won the argument and we will now leave at once.

"But I do not know if—"

"Look," Hunter says, cutting me off for the first time since we met. "You told me when your people fuck my people, my people turn into your people."

I nod, unwilling to split hairs over his terminology, since even I do not know what conveys the blessing. It may be our seed, which brings new life to both the unborn child and the mother, or it may be the unborn child itself. Then again—and how I hope!—our love alone may be enough. But I do not know.

"Well, in case you're unaware, the stuff we've been doing every night and every day for the past two weeks? It's not needlepoint, trust me."

I smile despite myself. I have no idea what needlepoint is, but if it is half as amazing as making love, Hunter will have to teach me.

"So then I'm probably a your-people now, and we're arguing over nothing, because I'll hop into the ocean in a minute and grow a tail or whatever." His eyes widen. He has just now realized we never discussed the logistics of the change.

"You will not grow a tail," I say. Of that I am certain, but beyond that, I know nothing. I do not know how the blessing works, only that it does. "We look just like you do."

"You look nothing like us," Hunter says. "Two eyes, two ears, a nose, two feet, sure. But you still look nothing like us."

There is silence. His truculence has made an impasse.

"It doesn't matter," he says finally, turning his back to me. "I'm going with you."

"I am not going anywhere," I say.

"Yes, you are. You're going back to the sea."

"Hunter, I am not—"

"Listen to me," Hunter says, coming close. He takes my hands in his, and he does not start speaking until we are looking into each other's eyes. "I used to tell myself I couldn't date someone who's bisexual, because I couldn't live with the constant fear that he'd pick up and run off with a woman."

I started to object, but he stopped me with a finger to my lips. "It's irrational, I know. But that's how I felt. And there is no way on God's green earth—or his blue seas—that I'm going to be able to live with you here, constantly worrying that you're going to pick up and swim off with the sea. It'll tear me apart."

I understand. This is his Roche limit. He is on the verge.

"So please, just let's try this. I want to see. I want to sea." He is crying now, but there's a glimmer in his eye, a grin beneath the surface. Only then do I catch the pun. I groan.

"That was bad," I say, smiling nonetheless. "Very bad."

He rushes into me, his lips reaching for mine, and we kiss. He is relentless, and my own ardor soon matches his. We fall to the cold rock. We are no better than the couple on the beach, sharing one last blessing before we go.

He is brushing the sand off his clothes now, as if the water will not wash it away in a moment. I grin, despite what is about to happen.

"So," he says, dusting his hands, "are we going to do this?" His eyes are determined, but his voice cracks.

No. No, we are not. I will stay here, with you, for you. "Yes, we are." I spend a moment studying his face. "Are you sure you want this?"

There is no hesitation. "Hundreds of years with you? Yes, of course I want this."

"You are giving up everything you have here."

"I have nothing here."

"Your friends."

"My best friend met a guy in a bar two weeks ago, and I haven't heard from her in days." He forces a smile, but it is weak. "Maybe I'll see her down there."

"Your studies," I say. "There are no stars beneath the sea."

"There are starfish." He turns to his bag, kneels down, begins riffling. "Speaking of which," he says as he pulls out something dangling on a silver chain, "I bought this for you. In case—in case things don't go the way we want them to."

It is a small pendant, a silver star. No, not a star. A starfish.

"It's me and you." It is resting in my open palm, and he puts his hands beneath mine. "The sky and the sea, yadda yadda yadda."

I choke down a whimper. "Things will go the way we want them to," I insist. "And if they do not, we will turn around." It is night. The water is cold. We will be far before we know. It may be too late...

I shake my head rapidly, like a bedraggled dog. These are bad thoughts, they have no place here. It will never be too late. I swim well. I can swim for the both of us.

"I love you," Hunter says. He has never said those words to me, and I have never said them to him.

"I love you, too."

He nods, then looks out to sea. Now is the time. He picks up his knapsack, and I take it from him. He does not argue. We walk to the waves.

It is high tide. The water stretches to meet us. Our couple—odd, how I think of them now as ours—is gone. The beach is void. The waves are flat, the sea still calm. I look to the sky and find a star. *Star light, star bright...*

We start to swim.

The Bloated Woman

jonathan Harper

It is a strange story.

They found her washed up on the beach, her body naked and spongy, bloated with salt water. She was lying face up, the left leg delicately laid across the right, barely covering her pubis. The head was bent at an impossible angle, suggesting a broken neck; her skin—the color of clay. If she had been beautiful, then it was because of her plump breasts and stomach, and the luxurious black hair that was now tangled and seeded with dirt. Her body was meticulously posed, as if she had spent her last few moments deciding how she wanted to be found.

Every fishing town has a prescribed relationship with drowning: boating accidents, storms, suicides—Amos's father had worked on the trawlers for years and brought home the news of every one of them. At first sight, Amos discreetly pressed his middle finger against his thumb, a gesture used to ward away the devil. "Let's get out of here," he said, tugging at his younger friend's sleeve. "The tide will take care of this."

Jeremiah, however, was more naïve to these sorts of things. Earlier that morning, he allowed Amos to lead him away from the boardwalk to where the beach bordered the overgrown nature preserve, where the sand hardened into coarse dark grains. Riptide posters warned against swimming; mosquitoes swarmed violently in little clouds. All Jeremiah wanted was a little blowjob or at least to see Amos naked. But instead they found the drowned body and she was better than anything he could imagine.

He shook away from Amos's grasp and leaned in closer for a better look. The drowned woman's eyes were like two streaky window panes. A scar was embedded into her chin. Sand fleas danced in the mass of her hair; she had not yet begun to smell. For a moment, he was inclined to take a memento of the experience. Jeremiah told himself later that it was a clinical sort of fascination, that he was overwhelmed with his first sight of actual death. One is lucky if he stumbles upon a mystery in his lifetime. There was bruising on the base of her neck and wrists. A body doesn't wash ashore perfectly arranged face up. And then, he poked her with a stick.

The police were summoned. They moved in quietly, as to not alert the locals, photographed her and covered her up with a gray tarp. A frumpy policewoman with her hair tied back in an ugly braid took their statements. Amos was short and curt and eager to leave. He had to be at work, he said. (He worked the night shift at the hotels.) Much later, when the beach season was over and Amos was finally arrested, Jeremiah would think of him in that moment: stubborn and angry and utterly useless.

Jeremiah had no intention of leaving: he was twenty-five years old, still vulnerable to his own imagination, and having never seen death so close, could not bring himself to leave. Every detail burned into his mind as he watched them bag her, watched the body driven off in the back of a dune buggy. Perhaps a little overeager, he recounted every detail (and added a few extra) even as the policewoman tiredly closed her notebook. "The bruises on her wrist," he said. "Did you notice the bruises?" She nodded.

"Where are you staying?" the policewoman asked. He told her the Lynch House. "Oh, the Witch House," she corrected, as if polishing off a dirty limerick. Then she was polite and insisted driving him home.

JEREMIAH WAS A SUMMER WORKER. HE HAD MET WALTER Lynch several years ago, back when he was Professor Lynch, the flamboyant co-director of the college's philosophy department. As a student, Jeremiah idolized him. But now, the title of professor had diminished and there was only Walter. Arthritis had warped his knees; dementia was warping his brain. The dazzling spark of brilliance had snuffed itself out and left behind the hollowed shell of a confused man who constantly wandered off in thought and was unable to comprehend the simplest of instructions. Otherwise, Walter was in decent health and only required supervision and patience. When Jeremiah accepted the job as his day nurse, he considered it a blessing: three months to repay his old mentor's kindness with room and board included. It would also give him space to work on his novel and enough free time for a heavy-handed affair that every twenty-five year old feels the cosmos owes him.

As for the town, it was a fractured little community. Ever since the sea bass population decreased and the regulations went into place, the fishermen worked as if clotting a wound. It was the tourists that kept the town's pulse steady. Boutique stores and crab houses populated the old wharf, a new strip mall was erected by the highway and the only good beach, the one north of the boardwalk, was littered with white trash families and their indulgent children. Every summer, they bought and ate and watched the fishing trawlers from a safe distance.

It WAS EARly EVENING WHEN JEREMIAH ARRIVED HOME. The policewoman drove without speaking, not once even to ask for directions. The Lynch's cottage was a marvel of stonework and gardening with a large porch adorned with two Japanese lanterns. It was owned by Walter's sister, who managed a tea shop in town. The officer escorted him to the porch where Nora met them at the door with her usual pleasant smile while Walter swayed in his seat at the dining table.

"Where were you? I'm starving," Walter called out. His voice sounded like the coarse whimper of a mangled cat.

Nora patted the young man on the shoulder. "Don't let him worry you. I fed him an hour ago."

Leftover pork chops sat in tin foil on the stove, a tub of apple sauce in the fridge. Jeremiah served up plates and Walter greedily devoured his second dinner in a few bites. As the young man ate his chops quietly, he watched the two women from the safety of the dining room. The officer spoke for what felt like a long time, careful to keep her voice low, while Nora's hand nervously covered her mouth. From the bureau, Nora took out a small case of tea leaves and placed them in the officer's hand.

When Nora joined them at the table, Walter stared at his empty plate in bewilderment. "Something happened. Something went wrong," he said.

"Some poor girl drowned offshore. Jeremiah found her down by the preserve this morning."

Walter puckered his lips. Half-chewed bits of pork sputtered out of his mouth and dribbled down his shirt. Jeremiah, now by reflex, took his napkin and wiped Walter's chin clean. It saddened him to do so.

"What the hell were you doing down there anyway?" Walter asked.

"He was just taking a walk with Amos Moyer," Nora replied.

"Him? What were you doing with him?"

They all remained silent for several minutes. Jeremiah cleared the dishes while Nora put Walter to bed.

Jeremiah slept in the sunroom past the kitchen. It was a tight space with a daybed, surrounded by large streaked windows overlooking the woods. There were many pretty things: lacy window dressings, shelves full of books and the half-moons of seashells, a painting of colonial ships hung on the side wall. He lay on the daybed, naked and sweating, watching the ceiling fan twirl hypnotically. He tried to masturbate, imagining Amos undressing him on the beach. It didn't work; his dick remained limp in his hand. Amos was an ideal combination of dangerous and ordinary: early forties, with a grizzly beard and shaggy hair. But he was married and that gave him a flare of the mystique. Still, Jeremiah was unable to get aroused, his thoughts too staggered, and he got up and rummaged through the bookshelves. Then he spent an hour pacing back and forth along the whitewashed floorboards.

Jeremiah's mind was laid out much like the sunroom, only a little narrower and over-stimulated with piles of junk. Walter and Nora were represented by the smallest fixtures. Amos was the daybed, awaiting later use. But the drowned woman existed throughout: in the cover art of the books, her body imprinted in the curtains and bedspread and every other fabric, other parts hidden in the overflow of papers and albums and little ornamental pieces; the amount of these only seemed to grow. She was the reflection in the large windows, on the other side of the door, until he was certain that she was everywhere, holding up the walls to prevent the weight of her from crashing down through the roof. When he finally slept and bridged into dream, he was wandering the beach, looking for her in the waves. He awoke, hours before sunrise, morbidly awake and desperate to go into town and check out the aftermath.

BEACH TOWNS ARE ARROGANT PLACES. UNBEKNOWNST TO THE tourists, each morning the wharf staged the disgruntled march of the fishermen, walking down its morose planks towards the marina. This occurred as the hotel graveyard shifts ended and the clerks stumbled out in their pristine uniforms. Both collectives never hid their disgust for each other. They were always on the edge of violence, muttering insults and empty threats. There was no peace until the end of summer.

Jeremiah, however, had no interest in such rivalries. The march passed by without his notice. He chose a little café near the boardwalk where the barista nodded a sleepy greeting and poured him an espresso. She was an almond-eyed, mousey girl and smiled graciously as he dropped a dollar in the tip jar. The morning paper was deposited in a little tin display and he snatched one up. The front-page story talked about the possible demolition of a trawler marina to make way for the country club which promised to bring in more revenue. A poorly worded editorial by one of the dock workers pleaded to lessen the fishing regulations—a small town must have its priorities. But the drowned woman was not mentioned anywhere. At first, Jeremiah was mortified. Then, he was overwhelmed by the thrill of conspiracy.

Amos stood out on the street, wearing a pair of raggedy shorts and a tank top. "You look like a hobo," Jeremiah teased and the man shrugged.

"Not working today. I can look like a hobo if I want." Amos's eyes were a pair of murky puddles, dimwitted too. He subtly removed his wedding ring and deposited it in his pocket.

"The paper didn't mention anything about yesterday," Jeremiah said. He tapped a postcard stand with his fingers and watched it lazily twirl. "Doesn't it seem odd they wouldn't put it in the crime report?"

"That doesn't surprise me," Amos replied.

"Well, it surprises me." Jeremiah's voice was defiant.

After circling the block twice, they entered a small used bookstore. It was dimly lit, with large overstuffed bookshelves that gave the room a cavernous impression. The clerk, a plump man with a sweaty face and wire-rimmed glasses, tried handing them one of the various fliers that littered the counter. While Amos walked further into the recess of the store, Jeremiah lingered up front for a few minutes. Up front, books collected dust in disorderly stacks; it smelled of old attics and cardboard-box forts, the kind that filled Jeremiah's childhood. Amos had disappeared among the corridors of large wooden cases. Jeremiah was not naïve—he was ambivalent. And then, he realized the funny little clerk behind the register was still talking to him.

"I just want to look around for a bit," he replied, cutting the clerk off mid-sentence.

He walked further back to find the shelves created a labyrinthine floor plan. It was poorly lit, too, and this caused his mind wander. It created a ghostly impression that something was watching him. Then, a mouse flashed across the floor and he yelped.

Amos stood in an alcove, gave a wicked smile and squeezed his crotch.

"Stop it. We'll get caught," Jeremiah said.

Amos observed him as if he were admiring a fancy trinket in a store window. When Amos reached for his zipper, Jeremiah nervously walked away.

The clerk watched as they surfaced from the stacks and Jeremiah plucked up a handful of books from the various piles. He settled on a paperback, a thriller about a serial killer, and placed it on the counter.

"If you like that, you should check out our local authors shelf," the clerk said. He put one of the fliers in the bag. "There's a good mystery series over there."

"I feel like I'm living a mystery. This place is like *Twin Peaks*."

The clerk stared blankly. "How do you mean?"

"Maybe not," Jeremiah said and turned to find Amos had left without saying a word.

WHEN HE ARRIVED BACK AT THE COTTAGE, NORA HAD already left for work. Lunch was left on the countertop but from the looks of the two dirtied plates, Walter had eaten all of it. Otherwise, the cottage was disappointingly quiet and ordinary. The only signs of life came from the television in the den and the coarse guttural noise of Walter clearing his throat.

However, one odd thing Jeremiah noticed: a small bowl of water was left by the front door. He hadn't seen it at first. It was a simple plastic mixing bowl right next to the umbrella stand—the water was lukewarm. Then, he found another by entranceway to the back porch and a third resting in front of the French doors of the sunroom. He picked up one of them and carried it to the den, where Walter rocked in his chair.

"Did you put this out," Jeremiah asked. Walter shook his head, eyes focused on the television. "It's all right if you did, but be careful. I could have stepped in one of these."

Walter yawned in a mocking way. "She did it," and then turned up the volume.

Jeremiah collected the bowls and cleaned the kitchen. A few moments later, Walter shuffled in. He was in a needy mood, every few minutes calling for Jeremiah's assistance. He couldn't find his reading glasses and then couldn't reach the mug he wanted; he needed assistance rearranging the conch shells displayed in the foyer. Even when the doors to the sunroom were shut tight, Jeremiah felt a flush of aggravated energy when he heard the weak tapping against them.

"Where did this come from?" Walter held up the serial killer book, his sour mouth frowning. "It's so morbid."

"This whole place is morbid," Jeremiah said to himself. He put Walter out on the front porch with the newspaper and a glass of iced tea while he mowed the lawn. He sat Walter back at the dining table while he cleaned the bathroom. The entire time, his mind was on the beach.

For days, Jeremiah wandered in and out of a state of half-sleep, that foggy space existing in the midnight route between bed and toilet. He would jolt awake at four in the morning and before sunrise, having surrendered to insomnia, took sluggish walks in town. Nothing ever changed. The daily parade of dueling hotel workers and fishermen passed him by without taking notice. By mid-morning, the wharf was animated with tourists. He considered venturing down the shore towards the nature preserve but never did. Occasionally, he sat in the foyer of a hotel and helped himself to the continental breakfast. The staff regarded him with the same polite dissidence offered to a paying guest. Amos had vanished. Jeremiah looked everywhere and couldn't find him. Without anyone else to talk to, he was careful to return home before Nora left for work. There, he fed Walter and kept the cottage in pristine condition. Still he would find the little bowls of water resting in a doorway. He resented them, eyed them suspiciously, cleaned out each one and replaced them in the cupboard. And yet they would reappear the next day. He avoided Walter as much as possible.

THE SUMMER WAS PROVING TO BE A REGRETTABLE MISTAKE. He had come to work on his novel. Distractions were inevitable, but his goal was to find inspiration and finish what he started. There it sat, abandoned on the sunroom's writing desk, nearly two hundred loose sheets of handwritten scribble. In a spare moment, Jeremiah glanced over the pages, unable to recall the plot. He had started writing it in college despite feeling he lacked the necessary worldly experience. He recalled sitting in Walter's office hours, surrounded by historic texts, and Professor Lynch handing back a handful of crumpled papers. "Are you writing about a life? Or telling the story of a life?" It was the last sensible thing Walter ever said to him. Under the twirling fan of the sunroom, he glanced over his novel-in-progress and sighed. One thing Jeremiah was certain of, it was based on his own life and that wasn't good enough. He stayed up all night rereading, rethinking, until he surrendered to the daybed and that tedious shallow sleep that never lasted long enough.

Once, only once, Jeremiah went to the police station. It was a small compact brick building with tinted windows and everyone inside was idling or eating. This added to his impression that the world was oblivious. The receptionist looked at him with a blank expression and pointed down the hall to a small office. The police woman with the ugly hair bun sat behind a large metal desk eating a croissant. She didn't seem to recognize him. "Oh yes, you're the Lynch's border," she finally said with disinterest.

"I was wondering if there was an update on the woman I found," Jeremiah said. "There's been nothing in the paper. Was she ever identified?"

The officer folded her hands together like a bishop and shook her head. There were numerous files covered with crumbs under her elbows.

"You'll keep me posted won't you?"

"Of course," she said in a flat voice. She thanked him for his concern and escorted him to the door. He left feeling pushed out.

ANOTHER WEEK OF SLEEPLESS NIGHTS PASSED AND HIS TENDONS hurt; dark rings encircled his eyes. It was past midnight when Nora came through the French doors of the sunroom, giving enough pause for Jeremiah to cover himself with a sheet. She held a large clay teacup, filled with tepid water and blossoms floating on the surface.

"I thought you might be up. Don't drink this too fast. It's potent." She sat on the edge of the mattress as he took a sip. It tasted bitter at first, but soothed with honey. Nora smiled as if wanting to stroke his hair. "I appreciate all the help, really I do. But it can't be good for a young man to spend so much time alone."

"I've had stuff on my mind," he said. Suddenly, he felt drowsy.

"Yes, Amos Moyer, I presume." She glanced back to make sure the doors were shut. "He's a very nice man. But he's been taking young men like you down by the woods for years. Never keeps them long after." She took the mug and cocked her head. She had given him a secret. He drifted into sleep and did not remember her leaving the room.

That night, when he dreamed, it wasn't about the drowned woman, but of looking for her. He walked the beach at dusk. He searched the woods, tripping through roots and thorn bushes. He finally dove out against the rough waves only to be shoved back ashore. And when he awoke, well after sunrise, light framed the daybed. It was the best sleep he'd had all summer and he felt anxious to walk into town.

THE ARCH OF THE SUMMER BROUGHT ON A HEAT WAVE THAT made the fish market stink for three days straight. Nora made seared scallops with turnip greens and baked salmon casseroles. One morning, Jeremiah caught her placing a bowl of water outside his door. She gave a little cackle and said, "Oh just a little trick to catch wayward spirits. We all have our silly habits." On occasion, she asked Jeremiah to take Walter on walks along the strip. They forced him to wear a neon-green jacket that embarrassed him. He only wandered off once but Jeremiah spotted him admiring two children running a kite, a giant glowing lime in a crowd of burnt skin. In his spare time, Jeremiah stayed on the north beach to swim or in the café working on the novel. Some days he was productive, others he was not. A happy couple from Boston shared drinks with him at one of the bars. He visited with the bookstore clerk and purchased the mystery novels he recommended.

When Amos finally reappeared, it unlocked a little door in the back of Jeremiah's mind. It was nearly dusk and Amos stood on the boardwalk waving a hand. It surprised Jeremiah enough to make him nearly trip over his own feet. There was no explanation for his absence, just his warm smile, greeting Jeremiah the way one does a beloved friend. Somewhere along the way, Amos's smile turned venomous. Jeremiah saw him pull his wedding ring and slip it into his pocket.

"Let's go for a walk on the beach," Amos said.

"No, thank you. I've already been there today."

"Let's go catch the sunset."

"Actually, I'm hungry. You can join me for dinner if you like." Jeremiah said this with trepidation, half expecting Amos to give some fickle excuse and wander off into the crowd. Though Amos frowned, he agreed as if it were easier to do than not.

They chose a diner near the highway. Nautical props were strewn about in a vain attempt at ambiance. It mostly attracted the locals who ignored the giant steering wheel at the hostess stand. In a few moments, it was evident that neither of them had anything to say, their conversation limited to their mutual hatred of country music and unruly children. The waitress brought them platters of greasy fries and open-faced sandwiches, her eyebrow raised in a knowing manner.

"Did the police ever visit you?" Jeremiah asked in a weak voice. It had taken him some time to build up the courage.

Amos slurped his milkshake. An eyebrow cocked and his hands fidgeted over his cigarette case. Then Jeremiah regretted the question. "Yes. That lovely woman came by once during my shift and asked a few questions."

"What did she say?"

"She said you and I are the prime suspects and we'll be arrested for murder as soon as she gets enough evidence." Amos presented his hands for a pair of invisible handcuffs. Then, he slumped further into the booth and sucked down the remainder of his milkshake.

"Seriously, did they ever find out who she was? I couldn't get any information anywhere," Jeremiah continued. He glanced around the diner, its tone shifting into a dreary place. A trio of fishermen sat grumbling at the counter. Their hands were ugly and lacerated. Their musky odors carried all the way to the booth. "I had trouble sleeping at night for a while. It was a strange feeling."

"When are you gonna stop being a drag and start being fun again?"
Amos grumbled. He returned a nod of recognition to one of the men at
the counter. For a moment, it seemed like their booth had been under
observation for a long time.

"She could have been anybody. Somebody's wife. Your wife."

"That's not funny."

The room went silent as the jukebox switched records. In that moment,
Jeremiah knew that if he didn't say something, something witty or pro-
found, the conversation would permanently end. A day ago, he wouldn't
have cared. Now, it meant everything. His foot lifted under the table and
grazed against the seams of Amos's thigh.

"Don't do that here," Amos said in a harsh whisper. He pushed out of
the booth with his cigarette case and sauntered outside. At another table,
a man blew a wet sneeze into a napkin, but otherwise, the diner went
quiet with the exception of the jukebox. Jeremiah counted the bills in his
wallet, hoping he had enough to cover their tab.

WHAT KEEPS A YOUNG MAN STAGNANT IN A RESTAURANT BOOTH
after he's left behind? When you feel unsettled and possess a vivid
imagination, you don't just kill time—you slay it dead. The rest of the
summer could be measured in trips to the diner. Sometimes Amos was
there, other times not. When they finally slept together, their affair brief
and unfulfilling, Jeremiah determined to rid himself of Amos for good,
but never did. They met several times, each one more like a chore.

For Jeremiah, the diner became his only place of solace. He preferred
it to the wharf because of its seclusion. He went there almost every day,
bringing his books and papers. The waitresses greeted him by name; the
locals minded their own business. It was in his booth where he trashed
the novel, that juvenile attempt at greatness. For days, he pondered over
empty pages of a spiral notebook and then began to write about a bloated
body that washed up on shore. He named her, described her and detailed
her entire history. He just didn't know what to do with her.

It seemed the drowned woman hovered over the town in ghastly morning fogs and again in the evening tides. Somehow, the insidious little
town managed to cover her up and then refused to acknowledge her existence. The policewoman never returned Jeremiah's calls. Presumably, the
body remained unidentified and was turned over to the state. Then, came

the city council's decision to convert the trawler marina into a country club and that ensnared everyone's attention. Even Walter, sitting in his lounger, was inclined to long rants against the decision. Arguments were published weekly in the newspaper and protests from the fishermen offended the tourists. It continued to escalate until one night a collective of dock workers disposed of the rotting scraps of the fish market in the public waste bins all over town. Everything stank and stores were closed for two days while the health inspector made his rounds. They made their point and the city recanted its decision. Beach season finally ended and with it went the hotels' summer staff. By mid-September, the wharf was peaceful every morning.

Eventually, Walter died from his second stroke. One night, he simply drifted off into the fog of sleep and couldn't retrace his steps back. Nora mourned him quietly, notifications sent on little sheets of ivory stationery. The memorial service as held at the cottage and for a few brief hours, it was wild with old professors and lovers and ex-students, before the cottage returned to its temporal quiet. Shortly after, Amos was arrested. He had lured a fifteen-year-old tourist boy down to the nature preserve one early morning. Though the details were vague, the whole town knew what happened, despite Amos pleading the boy had lied about his age. He was handcuffed and marched up along the wharf, giving the newspaper its front page story.

Jeremiah left before the beach season officially ended, returning back to his old job and apartment. Everything remained the same, though feeling a tad more claustrophobic. The taint of the beach town quickly faded: his body turned pale again and slightly chubby. Soon, he summarized the entire summer in a single sentence: "I spent three months in a little beach town and found a dead woman on the shore." He regarded Nora's letter with calm indifference, though his roommates, with their intuition for the dramatic, probed him for more details. He did not attend Professor Lynch's funeral (to his friends, Walter was still an exalted professor of philosophy and Jeremiah hated the idea of tarnishing that reputation). As for Amos, he claimed it was a brief forgettable affair, claimed they were only acquaintances and had no opinions on his crime. But if the accusations were true, then let Amos rot, Jeremiah said and left it at that.

It should be noted that Jeremiah met the wife. It was a brief encounter. She was tall and full figured with olive skin and long flowing black hair. What made her beautiful was her full mouth, her firm handshake, her intensity that gave all her mannerisms a sense of urgency. As Amos introduced them, he kissed her cheek as if to prove there was nothing to be suspicious of. She wasn't a fool. She knew her husband's habits of disappearing and the types of young men who kept him company. And when Jeremiah said goodbye, told her it was a pleasure meeting her, she was nothing but poised and restrained and shook his hand with a tight grip. He hoped to never see her again.

"I spent three months in a little beach town and found a dead woman on the shore," he wrote.

Whenever Jeremiah thinks of this, he relives that night in the diner, the true burden of memory. Amos had stomped out because he had mentioned his wife, his lovely wife, a plump Venus rising out of the sea foam. That night, Jeremiah assumed Amos would disappear again, perhaps for good. And if that had happened, the summer might have ended differently.

As Jeremiah prepared to settle their bill, Amos waltzed back in to their booth, the smell of smoke fresh on his clothes. He turned apologetic and cordial and even paid their check. When it was time to leave, he squeezed the young man's arm in an affectionate way.

Jeremiah knew he should have returned to the cottage, but instead, he followed Amos, back down towards the wharf. They turned southward on the beach away from the strip as the sunlight receded over the crashing waves to their left. For the first time in weeks, Jeremiah's heart raced with anticipation.

When they reached the edge of the nature preserve, Amos undid his belt and removed his pants. His cock was short but thick and it burned as he pushed it against Jeremiah's backside. The young man was bent over, staring out into the white foam flood and retracting over the dark gravel. Then, the fucking abruptly stopped. It sounded like a ferocious little animal was burrowing behind him and a few seconds later, Jeremiah felt a warm stream drizzle over him. All that anticipation for a lousy two minutes and before he could even finish himself off, Amos redressed and disappeared into the shadows.

When Jeremiah reached the wharf, the evening sky was bruised with dark purple clouds and tiny blisters of stars. Tourists wandered everywhere. His shirt congealed into a cold sticky mass against his lower back and he wondered if the stain was visible. Up ahead, a haggard woman with a leather face and tits handed out small pamphlets with her retarded son. The boy was stocky and wore overalls and waved his hands excitedly as people passed. She managed to place one of the papers into his hand before the bookstore clerk shooed her off. "Repent," the pamphlet read in large bold letters. He considered tearing it up and tossing it behind him like confetti. Instead, he bought a slice of pizza and folded the pamphlet underneath to catch the grease. Bar patios were crowded with drinkers and smokers; the boutiques changed their signs to "closed." A street performer winked when Jeremiah dropped a dollar into the opened guitar case.

It was late when he finally reached the cottage. The car was gone, but the lights were on. Inside, a note sat on the bureau—Nora was out for the evening and had left chicken tenders in the fridge. The den's television cast an eerie glow and Jeremiah took the plate of cold meat with him.

"Walter? Are you still up?" he asked. Walter sat in his arm chair facing the TV screen and did not respond. "I'm sorry I'm so late. Are you hungry?"

Walter made shallow breaths, lips puckered like a dying fish. His eyes, glazed and foggy, stared back.

At first glance, Jeremiah thought he was pouting but quickly realized he was not. "Oh, Jesus Christ," he said and the plate fell from his hands. He grabbed Walter's shoulders, gently rocking him, asking if he was all right, if he could hear his voice. Walter's neck bent over at an impossible angle and his eyes moved in rapid jerks.

Jeremiah called for an ambulance. The dispatcher's voice was pragmatic, his blunt questions almost insulting. "I don't know what's happening to him," Jeremiah said frantically. He pulled open the front door and turned on all the lights. "He's not responsive. He can't even move his head." The wet sticky mass on his back seemed to burn like a guilty afterthought. And suddenly, the words clogged in Jeremiah's throat. "He looks like he's drowning."

tHE ambulance siren wailed down tHE road. It did not care who it disturbed; its flashing lights made the neighborhood glow red. When the paramedics came through the open door, they brought in their medical kits and a stretcher. They rushed into the den, where the television was still on. There they found them: Walter slumped in his chair with the young tenant cradling him to his chest.

Walter's body was heavy. He wanted to speak to the medics but found his throat had knotted up. It felt like an albatross hung around his neck.

The Stone of Sacrifice

JEFF MANN

(FOR JOE AND CHARLENE)

I lean against the standing stone, gripping the key the landlord left. The Stone of Sacrifice, *Clach nan Ìobairt*, he called it, one of the largest in Scotland. Twenty feet tall, once the center of a stone circle long since dismantled, it's matted with moss, warm as flesh against my back, radiating heat the way sun-bathed rocks will. I stare out to sea, pulling my denim jacket tighter around me. Against my face is insistent wind off the ocean, chilly even in June, two days before the summer solstice.

I'm here at last, the land of my ancestors. Too tired to unpack the car right now. Sliding down the stone, I sit in the grass at its base. The water to the west's a restless blue-gray, rolling slowly up the rocky beach. Far out to sea bob the black heads of seals.

It's good to be alone, after the crowded plane and the noisy ferry. Alone is what I want, why I came to the Outer Hebrides for a few months' escape. Now that my long, intense affair with Thom has fallen into ruins, all I want is time to myself: time to read, write, recover, and take full advantage of a summer free of academic duties. Thus the isolated cottage

I've rented just down the hill, my new home here at the world's edge, only a few yards from the standing stone, only a few yards from the sea.

Such welcome peace. Wind rustles the purple flowers of heather, the long hair of pasture grass. Somewhere a snipe calls, a peculiar cheep and quavering. It's taken me days to get here—a plane from D.C. to Glasgow, a car to Ullapool, a ferry from the mainland to the island town of Stornaway, then a rented car down narrow, sheep-scattered roads across the Isle of Lewis to this tiny cottage by the North Atlantic.

From my backpack I pull out hoarded treats. Time to celebrate both journey's end and the coming solstice with ale, oatcakes, and farmhouse cheese bought with other supplies in Stornoway. I finish one bottle, then another, then another. I watch the sun lower over the ocean, breezes ripple purple patches of heather. I think of Thom, our last night together in Cleveland Park, his brown beard and black leather jacket, the way he sighed as I stripped him, as I bound him to that chair in the ruddy moonlight and buried my face in his chest hair. I remember how, the next morning, he did not return my wave of farewell as the Metro train pulled away. Just another warning I didn't have the sense to heed.

Too late, too late. Unsalvageable. Fuck it, fuck it. Mildly drunk, I stroll down to the beach. I pull off my shoes and step into the cold water. No sounds but wind whistling past my ears, rustling the low weeds, and waves breaking on the beach, swirling about my ankles. Relieved to be here, I lift my ale to the sea and sky. I take a big swig; I pour out the last into the lap of waves, like an offering, a tribute to the vastness before me.

By sunset, I'm drowsing against the standing stone. Storm clouds loom like gray boulders against the horizon. The rock's mossy side is still warm, as is the grass beneath me, which gleams an almost unnatural green. In the great arc of sky the light lingers, as the landlord said it would. This far north, this time of year, he explained, light never really leaves, darkness never really completes itself. Night is not night but a short-lived twilight.

I'm napping against the stone's heat when drops of rain splash my nose. Black clouds have dimmed the sky's glow, rolling in from the west. When I rise, I see, against the sea's rough gray, a pale flash, like flesh. Is someone out there? Bare shoulders cleave the surface. A face seems to stare at me—a man with long hair and a beard—then disappears behind an arching wave.

I rub my eyes and look again. Rain flicks my brow, spots my glasses. No, there's nothing. Just more slick black seals. And now the storm thickens, thunder grumbles. Gathering up the leavings of my meal, I head inside. Suddenly it's chilly enough for a fire, and the landlord's kindly left me a load of dried peat to burn.

ONE A.M. Can't sleep. Too excited to be here, I guess, plus the downpour against the roof, the gales funneling about the house, the waves beating the beach are all making quite a racket. Might as well get some work done, rather than lie here staring into the dark. The book I've been reading is still in the car, though, so I lope out into the storm to fetch it. That's when I see him, sitting at the base of the standing stone. A man.

"Hey!" I shout. Thunder sounds again. Hard wind slaps ropes of rain against my face. I hesitate, then jog up the grassy path toward the stone. It's still light enough to see, even with the storm's murk, but, as I approach, a lightning flash more clearly confirms it: the stranger's entirely naked save for a torc about his neck. He's huddled naked against the base of the stone, his arms wrapped around his knees. He's crying.

I rush up to him, gasping, "Man, what are you doing out here? You'll catch cold!"

The stranger looks up at me. His is the face I saw in the sea. Shoulder-length hair, dark eyes, a pursed and plump-lipped little bow of a mouth. Round cheeks covered with a full beard.

"Aye, here ye be," he says, wiping his eyes. "A timely trystin'."

"Here," I say, holding out my hand. "You need help?"

Nodding, he grips my hand. I pull him to his feet. His skin is as cold as the stone was warm.

Another lightning flash; a closer crash of thunder. "Come inside!" I shout. "The storm's getting really bad."

It occurs to me that I'm being reckless. Normally I wouldn't offer my house so quickly to a complete stranger. But this boy seems so harmless, so vulnerable, so distressed, standing there buck-naked in the downpour. Despite the rain-lashed dimness, I can tell he's young, only in his twenties, and only about five foot six, much smaller than I, and thus posing no conceivable threat. Plus, hell, he's very handsome, and, hell, he's beautifully built. Even in the extremity of a Hebridean thunderstorm, I gauge all that in seconds.

"Follow me," I say, with some effort tearing my eyes away from his compact little physique. "I'll stoke up the fire inside and warm you up."

He takes only one step forward before his knees buckle beneath him and he slumps to his knees. "I canna yet walk," he says.

I lift him into my arms. Glad he's such a little man. My middle-aged back would otherwise prove very unwilling to support such a movie-hero gesture.

"Guid, guid. You will be strong enough," he mutters, "for what the solstice needs doin."

"Hold on," I say. He wraps his arms around my neck. I carry him down the path to the house, staggering a little against the storm's blasts. On the stoop, I lower him to his feet, tug the door open against the wind. He stumbles on the threshold, but I catch him before he falls. I half-carry, half-drag him inside, into the dim parlor, over to the daybed by the hearth. Embers flare up, spitting sparks, casting wild shadows over the walls.

He's very wet, disheveled hair and beard dripping. It takes a while to dry him off; I work a towel over him as gently as I can. It's hard to concentrate on being a good Samaritan; my eyes keep wandering over his well-defined arms and chest before returning to the task at hand. His skin is tanned, his torso smooth—save for a few faint curls here and there—but his belly, pubes, and legs are very furry. His hair and beard are a honey-brown, edged with gold in the firelight. The torc glitters around his neck, a stained silver.

"Thank ye." He's shivering violently, hugging himself.

"Here, buddy," I say. "Lie down now." Grabbing an afghan, I wrap it around him, then help him stretch out on the bed. "How did you get out here? We're in the middle of nowhere. What were you doing by the stone?"

"Ah, I crawled there. From the water. The stane belongs to me. And the solstice is nigh."

"Where are your clothes?" I ask, positioning a pillow beneath his head.

"In the sea, in the sea," he sighs. "Lang syne lost."

"Why the hell were you swimming out there? It's damned cold. And the water's rough. You might have drowned." I add more peat to the fire, poking up the embers.

"Na, I'll not drown. The sea's kin. I heard ye, man, so I came. Didna ye call me?"

The boy's clearly dazed. His gaze roams the room, glazed with confusion, before settling on me. He stares up into my face with a vague smile. "Didna you?"

"No, I...I didn't call you. I don't even know who you are." Our eyes meet, and there's a tugging I've never felt before. His pupils are blue-gray rimmed with black, half-veiled by long brown lashes. Something inside me alters, the way iron filings shift into fine arcs about lodestones.

I shake my head. Desire's a crazy mist, a grappling hook. "What's your name?"

"Seonaidh, the folks call me round about. Shoney, to the Ingles. Or Johnny."

"That's a lot of names for such a little guy. Okay, Johnny, I'm Ewan Mc-Donald. You get warm and I'll fetch us some Scotch."

When I return from the kitchen with a bottle and two glasses, he's curled up in a tight ball beneath the blanket, fast asleep, his hair fallen over his eyes. Pouring myself a glass, I sit by his feet. The peat embers crumble. Outside, the gale continues. While I sip, I watch him sleep.

God, he's pretty. It's been too long since I've touched a man so handsome. I can't help myself. I stroke the honey-brown of his beard, ever so gently. I'd like to hold him in my arms, but I don't. Leaving him there to sleep by the dying fire, I lock the front door, finish my drink, and head into the back bedroom. Tomorrow, he should be more coherent. I'll find out who he is, where he's come from. I'll take him home.

"Ewan?"

I open my eyes. The room's gray with that endless summer twilight. I roll over onto my side. The wind's still howling about the cottage, rain lashing the window by my bed. Far off, there's the unlikely sound of music, as if someone were playing a harp in the storm. And, closer—there it is again—someone calling my name.

I sit up in bed. "Who's there? Johnny?" I flip on the bedside lamp, slide on my glasses.

"Aye, man." Johnny's on his belly on the floor, propped up on his elbows. "I canna sleep. Ill dreams. I'm afeart. And cauld. Peat's gone out. Can I snoozle with ye?"

Odd dialect. He must mean "snuggle." The proper side of me hesitates for about three seconds. The lonely side takes command after that. "Uhhh, sure. But the bed's pretty small, and I'm as naked as you are."

"Guid to hear." His plump lips purse, then break into a white grin. "Help, if ye please. My shanks are feckless yet. Unused to land."

I slip out of bed, grab him under the arms, and haul him onto the mattress. I'm pulling the blankets over his sweet little frame when I see them.

"God, kid. How'd all this happen?" I point to the cross-hatching of thin scars streaking his brown chest. "And this?" I trace it with my forefinger, a big jagged ridge of scar tissue beneath his belly's soft hair. "Jesus, this looks like a serious wound. Who did this to you?"

"My father's doing. And the priests. At the standing stane. Long syne." To my surprise, Johnny gives me a light kiss on the cheek. "The silver in your beard's bonnie. Well, my scars are a tale for tomorrow. Hold me now, Ewan. We don't have much time. Hold me while I sleep. I'm so cauld yet."

Johnny nestles his face into the space between my chin and chest, as if we'd been lovers for years. He wraps his arms around me, takes a deep breath, and soon is snoring softly. What is there to do but stroke his hair and thank whatever crazy Gaelic gods led him here, whoever he might be? I flip off the lamp, take off my glasses, and pull the boy closer. Wind sluices the house, a bass humming.

Lips press hard against mine; shaggy hair tickles my face.

It's near dawn, the short summer night already receding. The naked boy from the sea is stretched out on top of me, sighing, his slight weight pressed against me, his erection rubbing mine.

"Ah, man," he sighs. "'Tis sae guid to be here again. And *fine*-favored you are." He nibbles my lower lip. Stunned with thankfulness, I stroke his shoulders, his broad back, the small mounds of his buttocks. Everywhere my fingers roam, they brush the delicate raised parallels of scars.

"I must have a taste of you, brither." Johnny slips down my frame. He strokes my sex, brushes it with his beard, and mutters, "Ah, whappin! A blessed moothfu indeed! Been too lang since..." His mouth sheaths me. Groaning, I grip his moist hair.

The summer sun comes up early, filling the room with light. The bed beside me is wet. It smells of sea. My amorous boy is nowhere to be found.

I dress hurriedly, search the house. Awash with paranoia, I even check my wallet. To my relief, cash and credit cards are intact. I walk up to the standing stone. I return to the cottage, distractedly put on tea, slice some bannock. I wander the beach, looking for proof that last night was more than a dream. Thoroughly perplexed, I climb into my car and drive about the island.

Patches of heather; empty, blustery moors. Scraggly sheep cropping rocky pastures. Yellow irises edging wind-ruffled lochs. Light rains alternating with sudden sun. Villages of gray-brown stucco and slate roofs. Black chunks of peat drying in little heaps along peat-cuts. Beaches of sand, beaches of pebbly shingle. The Isle of Lewis is stark and scenic but devoid of what I seek. No muscular mystery boy ambling buck-naked over the pastures or along the road or hunched bereft in a circle of ancient stones. Johnny has vanished.

Why am I doing this? The kid must have been some stoned local looking for a piece of ass. I'm surprised he didn't rob me. Cursing under my breath, I give up the search. For a few hours, I work at home: a book review and an essay are both due soon. It's hard to concentrate, my memory returning again and again to the tight pull of Johnny's mouth, the feel of scars like a fine net cast over his back and buttocks. Restless, I drive into Stornoway in late afternoon, indulge in a street-vendor's buttery prawnies, watch gulls float over the harbor, buy a few Stilton-and-leek pork pies to have for snacks, indulge in a few pub-pints of Strongbow cider.

The long dusk's begun by the time I head home. On a whim, I drive to the island's northernmost tip, a village called Port of Ness. No one's around the little harbor, except for a straight couple who drive off as I park. I sit on a great boulder overlooking the sea and make a messy meal of a pork pie. The water's blue-black in the cove below, a creamy crashing and frothing when it breaks on rock. Out to sea, distant gray veils of rain move with measured stateliness across the horizon.

I've chewed the last rich bite, have brushed crumbs from my lap, and am beginning to snooze, stretched out on the boulder's crest, when I hear his voice. "Found me, eh?"

I look down, and there's Johnny, silver torc and wet shoulders glistening as he bobs in the cove.

"What the hell?" I gasp, rising to my feet. "What are you doing out there?"

"Ah, come down, brither. The sea feels like flowers." Johnny shakes the water from his hair, plucks a string of seaweed from his back, and winks up at me.

"You're one crazy kid. It's got to be freezing. Get up out of there!"

"A tease, ye are. Wait for me tonight, brither, by the sea."

Johnny waves, then dives. The sweet curves of his buttocks break the surface of the water, his feet give a sharp kick, and he disappears. A circle of foam marks the spot of his departure. I wait for a long time, expecting him to surface for air, but he doesn't. He's simply gone.

A slender crescent, the moon rises behind the standing stone. It's the night before the solstice; the sky's a deep indigo, the sun a persistent glow beneath the western edge of the world. I sit by the sea, watching waves curl, break, and wash up the shore. I think of Johnny's muscles, his tanned skin and pale scars.

I wait for a long time, go in for a jacket, wait a little longer, afraid he might not come. The thought of never seeing him again is so deep a pang it only highlights how much I want to hold the little stranger.

My eyes are beginning to droop when a sharp splash breaks the rhythm of the waves, then another, then another. There he is, floating in the summer twilight, hair a lank frame for his smile, brow gleaming beneath the double arch of a widow's peak. About him silvery fish swarm, leaping into the air in a crazy frenzy, churning the water white.

"Good even!" He swims closer, nakedness slowly emerging from the black water. First the handsome dripping face, his torc a silver half-moon about his neck, then the shoulders and taut chest, then the fur-matted belly and limp swing of cock. When he's thigh-deep, he stops.

"So many tears," Johnny sighs, looking back at the sea. "You've lost him forever, aye?" He turns to me, brushing long hair off his shoulders, wringing it out.

How the hell does he know about Thom? Despite myself, I mutter, "Yes. He's long gone. How do you—"

"Weel, I'm here now. Ye want *me* tonight?" Johnny says.

I have no words. I clear my throat. I laugh. I nod.

"Will ye carry me then? As you did yestreen?"

I have my shoes and clothes off in a trice. Awkwardly I wade in. The water's so cold I gasp. "How do you stand it?" I say. "I'd freeze to death."

Johnny smiles, wrapping his arms around my neck. I lift him, one arm beneath his back, one beneath his knees. "Ah, strang you are! Strappin!" Chuckling, he gives my shoulder a gentle thump. "Yours is the buirdly arm I've been needin."

I blush. His accent is oddly arousing. "Burly? Well, not bad for forty years old, I guess. So how can you swim so well but not walk?"

"Ah, brither, the water's been home for lang years." He kisses me, tugging gently at the thatch of time-frosted hair on my chest. Standing in the rocking cradle of waves, I kiss him back. Then I carry him up the beach to the house.

"Aye, man, hard," Johnny grunts into my ear. "Tis ridin time, and I need takin hard. Tak me hard. As Donaidh was wont to do."

I should be asking who the hell he is, where he came from, who scarred him so badly, why he's in bed naked beneath me. Instead, I hold his hands above him, pressing his wrists down into the yielding fabric of the day bed. His legs straddle my shoulders. His tousled hair fans the pillow. I ease into him, watching expression wash over his face. Discomfort, then wonder, then delight, then a glassy-eyed peace, then a grimace of pain as I slide into him deeper still. He knits his thick eyebrows, he grits his teeth, he bites his lower lip, his eyes roll back in his head.

"I don't want to hurt you," I whisper, nuzzling his beard with mine. "Tell me if—"

"Ah, brither, hurt me as ye will," Johnny says, grinning. "Gie it me rough. And make it last. Canna you tell this is my heiven and my delite?" He nods at his short, hard penis, curved back, its head almost brushing his belly hair. "Ye've made of me a standing stane," he chuckles. "Have ye not?"

His calves slip off my shoulders; his ankles cross and lock together in the small of my back. His loins buck against me; his legs tense, pulling me into him. I slide entirely home. "Ah. Ah. Aye," Johnny gasps. "There. There, man. There."

For a long time we rock together, sea rhythms, cadence of wind-laced surf. He smells of salt and sweat, his sex a restless eel, his pubic hair delicate as seaweed. "Harder, brither, harder. Ride me like a wave," Johnny groans between fierce kisses, his lips a firm suction about my tongue. At both ends his body grips mine, his mouth like a fist, his ass the tight funnel of a whirlpool.

Dimly, beyond his grunts and pants, I hear wind and waves in the distance, that eldritch harp music too. We kiss till my tongue's sore and my mouth bruised. We move together till I'm worn and chafed, he's wincing and trembling. Finally, near dawn, with a gasp and a shout, I finish inside him.

"Stay up in me, you strappin glory," Johnny whispers. So I do. Bending down, softening inside his taut heat, I finish him with my mouth. His bliss is a breaker, surging over my tongue: briny, bitter, sweet.

"Luvly, luvly. Tis not damnation but a blessing," Johnny mumbles against my neck. I hold him in my arms; he tucks his clasped hands beneath his chin, head on my chest. "Wrong they were, damn them. A blessing you are, Ewan, you strappin, fine—. If you'd ha been there, they'd never have hurt me."

I have no idea what Johnny's talking about, but he's so pretty snuggled against me that I don't care. His murmurs dwindle and trail off into soft snores. Peat-light flickers over his face. His body's like the island: grassy meadow of his belly, small hills of his chest, little cairns of his nipples, heather of his pubic bush, lean ridges of his thighs. And all these fine scars, like furrows cut in a field. I caress his scored shoulders and chest, throat tight, flooded with tenderness, till I too am swallowed by sleep.

I WAKE ALONE. My beautiful boy's vanished again. He's not in my bed, not by the Stone of Sacrifice, not on the shore. The day of the summer solstice, celebration of the sun, yet it's drizzling and gusty again. All morning, I try to concentrate, working against writing deadlines. The afternoon I waste once more driving narrow island roads. Twice I nearly hit rambling sheep. Could he be gone for good this time? He's not to be found where he appeared before, the cove at Port of Ness. I drive over to the Callanish standing stones, where pagans and hippies wander reverentially among the famous circle, commemorating the longest day of the year. No Johnny. I walk the yellow sands of Luskentyre beach, cold rain become a downpour, plastering my hair to my head, beading my glasses, soaking through my jacket and shirt as I watch the slow surge of waves climb, break, welter, and recede. No Johnny.

Something in me's seized, caught, held fast. I can feel it, as I kick sand off my shoes, climb back in the car, dry off my glasses, and leave Luskentyre behind. Only two nights together, but what I see when I close my eyes is no longer Thom cuffed and naked in my bed, begging for the paddle—the lost lover, the beautiful submissive, who's haunted me for so long—but Johnny panting beneath me, folded double, his long-lashed eyes sea-dark and wide, his hair the amber-gold of Scotch, his beard-lined lips quivering as I drive into him. I suppose loneliness has made me more than susceptible to beauty and to mystery. It occurs to me with a chill, as I look out over the violently tossing gray of waves and the sharp veer of gulls in wind, that I'll be crushed if Johnny doesn't return. You'd think a man my age would have outgrown sudden infatuation.

I distract myself as I always have when I've felt my heart threatened, unsteady, overfull: with a feast to celebrate what's been given, what's been allowed, what remains. I stop in Stornoway for groceries and liquor. Back at the cottage, I drink single malt—yes, very much indeed the hue of hair on Johnny's belly and thighs—I watch the sun break through dispersing clouds and leisurely descend over the sea, and I cook myself a fine Scottish meal. Might as well put the knowledge of my culinary heritage to good use. Smoked salmon, with onions and capers. Mashed rutabaga. Chicken and mushroom pie. For dessert, Cranachan: whipped cream, summer berries, and toasted oatmeal.

Sated, I walk the beach. The sun sinks into layers of chartreuse and orange, floats like a burning boat on the deep blue ocean, disappears. No sleek shoulders cleaving the water, no hearty shout of greeting. No silvery fish, no black seals. The wind blows sand in my eyes. I curse, blink, squint, weep. My tears dislodge the grit. Wiping my face, I head inside, stir up the fire, light a candle in the window, stretch out on the day bed, and wait.

"'tis bleedin time, brither, the simmer solstice, the light's height. Is your arm stout enough?"

I jolt awake. Johnny's nestled naked in my arms, still wet from the waves. He takes my head in his hands, kisses me lightly, and presses his brow against mine. "Ye called me, man, so ye must do it. They say bluid makes sun and soil and sea strong. I believe 'em. Do ye? Do ye understand now?" He takes my hand and holds it to his scarred chest. Against my palm, I can feel the tiny hardness of his nipple, and, beneath that, the throb of his heart. "Ye are brave enough, are ye not? To bring bluid? To taste bluid? Ye are, ye are. I feel it in ye. Have ye not duin it afore? The wounding's needful, aye? A fated, needful splendor."

Somehow it passes into me, as he holds me to him, what I must do.

"Ah, ye know it now? And ye've managed such duty afore?"

I nod. "Stay here, boy." Covering him with a blanket, I rise to fetch what's required.

The switch is willow. It leaves a long, thin, red trail wherever it meets skin, bringing blood here and there. Naked, I stand by the bed, methodically working over Johnny's chest, ribcage, and belly. He thrashes, fighting the rope that binds his wrists to the headboard. His white teeth gnash the rag knotted in his mouth. His eyes stream with tears.

When I'm tired, I lay down the switch. I sit on the edge of the bed, listening to his sobs subside, stroking his sweaty temples. I lie atop him, lapping blood from his breastbone, nipples, and gold-fuzzed belly.

"More?" I ask. When he nods, I roll him over onto his belly and start up again, covering his muscular shoulders, back, and buttocks with red welts. He struggles and cries, one minute trying to avoid the blows, the next rising to meet them. Tiny crimson spots speckle the sheets.

Now a net of red slashes joins the net of white scars over his body. Exhausted, I toss the switch to the floor. Climbing onto the bed, I soothe Johnny, licking tear-salt from his beard, blood-salt from his shoulders. We breathe together, dozing in the midsummer gloaming. His butt wakes me, bumping back against me. I haul him onto his elbows and knees, spit in my hand, grip his hips, and take him from behind. He sways and sighs beneath me: storm-tossed ship, sough of breeze in rigging. His head's

bowed, his bound hands clasped as if in prayer. The rope binding him
to the bed goes taut, goes loose like mooring; the headboard creaks like
a dock.

Indefatigable wind off the sea is rattling the windows by the time we're
finished. His wounds salved—my sadism's matched only by my solici-
tude—we're cuddled warmly beneath blankets, drifting off to sleep, his
sticky back pressed tight against my chest. "I'm going to leave you tied
and gagged till morning. I'm tired of you disappearing," I growl, kissing a
fresh welt, unknotting the rag in his mouth only to tie it in a little tighter.
Acquiescent, Johnny nods, curling against me. Fingering the sparse curls
on his breast, I fall asleep.

THERE ARE NO bloodstains where bloodstains should be. The
sheets are strangely moist—sweat and semen, perhaps—but there's no
trace of blood. The rope and gag lie in still-knotted circles on the bed
beside me. Here and there are golden-brown hairs and grains of sand.
My hot little prisoner has once more evaporated.

How the hell did he get loose? After those passionately perverse years
with Thom, I not only know how to beat a back, I know how to tie a knot.
Rolling out of bed, I pick up the rag and rope. Both are sodden. I squeeze
the gag over my palm, take a tentative taste. Salty as seawater.

This morning I don't aimlessly drive the island. I sit by the standing
stone, watch the waves, and muse on assorted mysteries. How did Johnny
let me know he wanted beaten? He never verbalized that need. Why can't
he walk? Where the hell did he come from? What did he mean when he
said he'd heard me call him? And why did he call the summer solstice "the
bleeding time"?

Like any educated twenty-first-century guy, I go online. Even on an
island this remote, there's Internet to be had. In Stornoway, in this case.
In half an hour, I'm surfing the Web in Caption's First Internet Café. One
by one, answers come up.

HE SEEMS MUCH STRONGER NOW, STRIDING NUDE AND BRAWNY-
thighed out of twilit waves without my help. The lacerations I left across
his body have already, unbelievably, faded into scars, another fine cross-
hatching to join their pale predecessors. No human skin mends so quick-

ly. He is, he must be, what my research suggests. I'm trembling despite myself as he takes my hand and squeezes it.

"Ah, ye know much now," he whispers. "I can feel it. And are ye afeart?"

"I suppose so," I say, swallowing hard. "Yes, actually. Terrified."

"And do ye want me anyway? I'm naught to fear, Ewan. Will ye lie with me tonight? Will you tak me again, brither?"

In answer, I lead him over beach-shingle and up to the cottage. Inside, I settle him onto the day bed, light a few candles, pull off my clothes, and join him beneath the covers. I fuck him on his side, cupping his hard pecs in my hands, kneading them roughly. I bite his curved shoulders, breathing in the ocean scents of his hair, thrusting into him hard. Spitting into my hand, I stroke him till he whimpers. This beautiful, well-muscled boy in my arms, what worlds has he seen? And how soon will he return to them and leave me here, listening to wind and surf alone?

Done, our heartbeats slowing, "Tell me," I say, licking his sticky-thick salt off my hand before pulling the breadth of his back against my chest. I've spooned many a man, it occurs to me, but not a Scottish water sprite, or sea god, or whatever the hell—or heaven—he is.

"Ah, weel, I must leave soon. D'ye still want to know?"

Fuck. Fuck. *Fuck*. Leave soon? "Absolutely. Are you really—?"

"What do ye know?"

"I know there were kings…pagans believed there were sacred kings who embodied the spirit of the land…and the king or a substitute would be sacrificed at the summer solstice to insure the earth's fertility." My voice has an unmanly quaver to it, so I clear my throat before continuing. "I…I've read about magical creatures called selkies and kelpies…I know there was a sea god named Shoney; on All Hallows Eve, fishermen here on Lewis used to pour him offerings of ale to insure a good catch. I know… Was that what brought you? The beer I spilled?"

"Ah, brither," Johnny says sleepily, "tak your rest by me, and I vow ye'll see. Ye'll know all by mornin." He rolls over, nuzzles his face against my chest, rests an arm across my hip. He kisses my breastbone, and suddenly my eyes are heavier than they've ever been before.

THE CHIEF'S SON. SEONAIDH. JUST AS HE IS NOW: BROWN-SKINNED, small but powerfully built, with shaggy amber hair and beard. Dressed in tartan and tunic. Kissing his comrade Donaidh when they're alone. Donaidh,

short and muscular as Seonaidh, black-bearded, fur-matted body. He pushes
Seonaidh down into straw, lifts kilts, kisses his friend's shoulders, takes him
from behind. The boys moving together, grunting together, a hushed rapture.
Meeting again and again, fearful and hungry, in byre and barn, remote
heather-clad coves. Loving in secret. Fighting battles side by side.

More and more priests on the island, in black robes moving along the
shore. The dour chapel built of wind-whistling stone. Pagan and Christian,
the power-sway. Newer, stricter moralities. Word-wars. The bonfires and old
ways called into question.

The chief, Seonaidh's gray-bearded father. Poor harvests year after year,
little yield from the sea. Clansmen huddle hungry by meager fires, muttering,
"Aging leader, aging land," remembering how, long generations back, royal
blood, lustral, enriched the earth.

The boys caught making love in the byre. Naked Donaidh's defiant struggles,
attempting to defend his comrade, to help him escape. A swift dirk in the side,
a swift death. Seonaidh's dragged from the still-warm corpse, bound, hauled by
the priests before his father. Shouts, disgust, outrage. Father's fist to Seonaidh's
face. How can a warrior play a woman's part, spread his buttocks for another
man's use? Effeminate, unnatural. Another blow, Seonaidh knocked to his
knees. Dragged off spitting blood, cursing, unrepentant.

For the old faith, substitute sacrifice in place of the king. For the new faith,
punishing sodomite and scapegoat too. "For your people's good," says the
grizzled chief, passing sentence on his son, "and for mine. And to appease
this foreign god."

Seonaidh wants to beg for mercy but, warrior-proud, does not. Seonaidh
wants time enough to avenge his lover, wriggles free of his bonds, tries to
escape, is seized by guards, struggles violently, is beaten senseless.

Summer solstice, Seonaidh grown drunk on mead. Tries to be brave, as
he's led stumbling to the place of sacrifice, where past chief-blood once flowed
to call in full fishnets and lush crops. Tries not to tremble as he's stripped, as
he's tied to the stone, hand and foot, face and torso pressed against moss. The
rag knotted between his teeth is a blessing, helps him choke back cries and
cowardice. The whips descend, and the willow switches, across his back and
buttocks. He bites down on cloth. Blood flows, tears flow. He breaks down,
sobs, cries for his father, passes out, sags in his bonds.

The blood runs down his back, is caught in sacred cups, sprinkled on the
people. The chief smears scarlet on his brow, then leaves, wet-eyed, trium-

phant, redeemed. The priests look on with solemn frowns. Not enough blood, not enough blessing. Seonaidh's untied, only to be bound again, his back to the stone. Unconscious, limp, as whips mark his chest and belly, as more blood's caught and sprinkled.

Enough. Everyone anointed save the priests. The same dirk that slew Donaidh, shoved now in Seonaidh's belly. He's cut down. Laid, naked and bloody, breathing yet, in a coracle, pushed out to sea. The clansmen and black-robed foreigners disperse.

Storm comes. Black waves rock him like a cradled child, rain washes his wounds. He wakes to the chill shock of drops. His lips tremble. Fingers fumble at the rag still knotted in his mouth, fumble and fail, hand falling limp, too weak, too weak. Clouds roll overhead. The boat bobs. So, so cold. Seonaidh wishes he had a blanket, wishes he had Donaidh's hairy warmth atop him. Seonaidh sighs, rolls onto his side, curls into a ball, closes his eyes. A strong current pulls him west.

"AH, MAN, DINNA WEEP." JOHNNY'S WARM ARMS DRAPE MY NECK AS I wake. All about me I hear that far-flung music, as if wind and humming, plucked harps and heartbeat were all intertwined. "I have a new life. Ye should see what I've seen, the leap of whales and the shimmer of fish, and *Tír na nÓg*, the Land of Youth, and mountains beneath the waves. Will ye come with me, brither? Will ye—"

Three events follow one another in the space of a second.

There's a loud knocking.

The fragile music stops.

Johnny winks out of sight and touch.

Someone's hammering at the door, and I'm naked in bed alone, curled around a pillow.

I grab my glasses, tug on a pair of shorts, and stagger to the front door.

It's the landlord, Mr. Morrison, looking rumpled and grandfatherly as usual. "Woke ye, eh? Sorry! Just wanted ye to know a big storm's on its way. The phone lines are doon, or I would have called. Power might be oot soon too. Gale force, the gusts might be. I hope ye have supplies enough for—" He stops, staring at me.

I feel woozy, addled, as if abruptly shaken from a too-short sleep. "What? What's wrong?"

"Have ye been weepin?"

Blushing, I rub my wet eyes. "What? Uh, nightmare, I guess."

Morrison nods, giving a knowing smile. He studies my face. "Ah, are ye dyein it then?

"Dyeing what?"

"Yer hair and beard, Mr. McDonald. Ye're much less gray than when I last saw ye. Keepin youthie for some lassie, eh? Our island must agree with ye." He chuckles, heading toward the driveway.

Wind swirls about my nearly naked form, fabrics of ice. I have the door half-shut when I blurt, "Sir? Did you see anyone out here?"

Mr. Morrison turns, one brow raised. "Anyone?"

"I had a friend. Visiting overnight. He seems to have…gone missing."

"No, no one oot here. I feel pity for anyone oot on this wild and gowstie night." With a wave, he scurries off to his car.

As I tug on clothes, I see that Morrison was right. The face in the bedroom mirror bears a beard far blacker than before. The fluffy mat of hair on my chest and the curly hair on my head seem thicker and darker too. But I have no time to ponder that now. I have to find Johnny. The bed's not damp as it was after his previous disappearing act, and there are no signs of his golden hairs in the sheets. But his torc is here, a stiff-twined semicircle of silver with the stylized heads of bears adorning the tips. I pick it up. The metal's still warm. As I hold it, I can feel the heat recede, the natural cool of the silver reassert itself.

I walk the beach, despite the increasingly savage winds, calling for him. By sunrise, I'm heating water for tea when the power goes out. I spend the day huddled by the peat fire, listening to wind tear at the world, fondling the torc.

By nightfall, I'm on the beach again. The gusts make me stagger, but I walk a good mile in either direction, staring out to sea, hoping to see the flash of his skin. Dawn, I'm leaning against the standing stone where he was tied and tortured untold centuries ago. It's cold against my back. I stroke the thick grass about me, where his blood spattered the earth.

I drift off to sleep. In dream, I'm pillowing my cheek on his bare buttocks, kissing them, spreading them, rubbing my bearded chin along the cleft, marveling at the softness of his skin, silky and fragile as rose petals beneath my lips and hungry tongue. "Aye, brither, luver, tak me once more ere we must part," he sighs, arching up against me.

I wake. My crotch is hard. The wind's died down. Across the western sky, a flock of gulls flies silently by. Shivering, I rise. My joints are stiff. About me, withered weeds rustle. Limping, I head down the path to the house.

OUR NIGHTS TOGETHER WERE NOT MERE dREAMS. THEY WERE NOT. Johnny was as solid as I. I could feel the fine hairs on his belly tickling my lips, I could feel his tight heat as I rode him, I could taste the salt in his beard, in his blood, in his semen. The silver torc I bear now about my neck is real, not an illusion.

No, he was no dream, but dreams surely are all I'm left with in his wake. Vague visions, smeary at the edges, watercolors left out in rain. Like caressing puffs of smoke, like fondling sea wind. The wind touches me; I can't touch it. Johnny's always naked, always at a distance. Smiling, waving, beckoning. His muscles are moonlit, beaded with sea-spume. I wake in bed, weary, sweating, painfully erect. Stroking myself, stroking the twisted silver around my neck, I bring myself relief.

The summer's ending. The sunlight dwindles, the dark grows longer. I sleep later and later. It gives me more time to dream. Every day, I drive the island, walk the hills, moors, and beaches. My time's nothing but search. Earlier and earlier, I start the peat fire, turn on lamps against the night, pour out Scotch. Into the sea I pour out ale, as I did before. In the windows, I light candles to serve as welcome, hoping to lure my lover home.

I should return to America, but I can't, I can't. Instead, I take sick leave from work, decide to stay in Lewis and live on my savings. Every time I try to get work done, reading or writing, I remember Johnny's body—compact, bare, brown, scarred—and then everything I am and have ever done crumbles like cold peat-ash.

It's early September now, the rain-wet grass still a bright green, but the bracken ferns back of the cottage are bright orange, the heather clumps a rusty blood-brown. Mr. Morrison arrives with a new lease for me to sign. He stands in the doorway, staring at me. He opens his mouth, shakes his head, then steps inside. I should offer him some tea, but I'm too tired.

Here's the new lease, for another six months. I sign it, hand it to him. "Thank ye," he says, folding and pocketing it. There's an awkward silence.

I used to have the energy to carry on trivial conversation. I don't any longer.

"Well, Mr. McDonald…" Morrison's brow crinkles up.

"I'll show you out," I say, heading for the door.

His hand falls on my arm. "Son, I have to ask. Are ye ill?"

"Sir?" I'll drive to Luskentyre beach today, walk the water's edge, whisper his name. Today, perhaps, instead of seals, gulls, ospreys, the occasional breaching whale, I'll see his beard again, his bare shoulders. "No, I'm not sick. Why do you ask?"

"Ye…ye're so, so thin, man. When ye came here with the simmer, ye were stout-framed and strang. But now, ye're sickly thin, lookin whitely, pale as bap-flour, and your hair's all gone gray, gray as burr-thristledown it is."

I open the door, mustering what feels like a smile. "Not much appetite, Mr. Morrison. Too busy to cook. But thanks for your concern."

"Is it money ye need? For the doctor? For food? There's a job cutting peat over in—"

"I'm just fine, sir. Now I'd better get back to work; I have a writing deadline. Thanks for bringing over the lease."

At the threshold, I shake his hand. I wait till his car's disappeared over the hill before climbing into my own vehicle and heading off to Luskentyre.

All Hallows Eve, the Celtic festival of the dead, the night fishermen strode into the waves and poured out their libations of ale to the sea god Shoney. The moon's nearly full, rising over the Stone of Sacrifice, slipping in and out of cloud-rack. It's very cold, with heavy flurries coming and going over the sea, but I strip nevertheless. Naked save for Johnny's torc, I wade, teeth chattering, out into the waves. Up to my knees, up to my waist, shuddering as the cold envelops my genitals. I call for him, I pour out ale. Shaking uncontrollably, I stagger back to shore, stand on the freezing sand, and wait.

Long minutes pass. Cursing myself for a deluded fool, I'm pulling on my jeans when the splashing begins. There, out there, in the black heave of sea, is the churning of fish. And a tiny boat, moving into shore against the slant of snowflakes. It drifts closer; it runs aground with a grinding sound.

Barefoot and shirtless still, I approach it. It's very old, made of animal skins. It's empty, save for a wood-hewn paddle. The hull's stained with spatters of rusty brown.

I stand by it, shivering, hugging myself, for a long time. Sea-spray dashes me, wind-blown sand blasts my bare back, icy water laps my ankles. Then I hear a voice.

"Ewan!" A few yards beyond the breakers, a floating face. Even from here I can make out in moonlight his wet hair, widow's peak, white grin. "Come, brither!" he shouts, shaking water from his locks. "The sea feels like flowers!"

"Johnny!" I shout. "Come to land! Stay here with me! Please!"

"I canna stay. Na, Ewan, ye must come wi' me. I've missed ye, man. I'll care for ye well. Come with me, luv, to the Land of the Living!" He beckons, dives, disappears.

A fated, needful splendor. What else can I do? There's nothing true and faithful left but the salty taste of him, nothing left but death or the Land of Youth.

"Wait for me!" I shout. I push the craft out to sea, leaping in as billows catch and carry it. Snow falls steadily about me. I start to paddle. There's that music again, very faint but audible, and there's his form in the distance, pale against the inky deep. He waves again, then begins swimming steadily out to sea. A strong current seizes the coracle. I steer as best I can, following my lover's wake into the west.

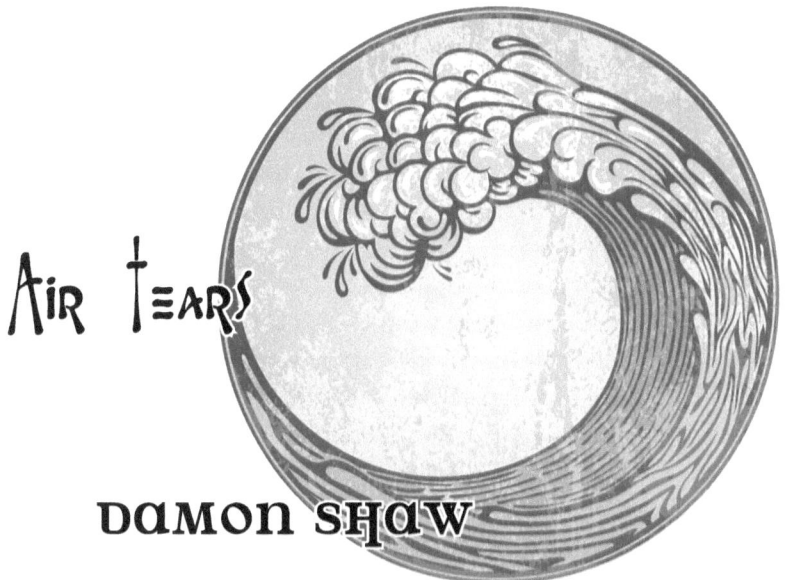

Air Tears

Damon Shaw

My lungs ache, full of water. Under the ache is a sparkling burn that I love already. I need it like I needed air.

I pull my head from the waves. The sounds of Brighton beach hiss, tinny and sharp. Music from the fairground at the end of the pier, seagulls, children squealing. Water streams from my nose and the acrid tang of traffic stings my nostrils; underneath it, the sweet smell of candy floss, and underneath that, the sea.

I want to run up the pebbles in my sopping jeans, cross the street, oh God, find a café and have something normal. Breakfast. Full English. But I can't leave the sea. My eyes bubble and sting. With a gasp that sends lukewarm seawater down my tee-shirt, I realize I am crying air. Gas tears pop and mix with the traffic smells.

I need to breathe. A wave folds around my waist and I duck under again. Something flickers over my eyes, and the turquoise water focuses, crystal sharp. Every stone distinct, the gravel sea bed slopes underneath me, from turbulent white foam to depths tiger-striped by the shadows of the incoming swell. Pushed around by waves, I pull cool water into my lungs, loving the burn, feeling tiny air tears detach and float up to the surface. I'm stuck here. I can't leave the sea. Who would have thought that one kiss could cost so much?

A shoal of silver fish shivers through the cloud of my hair. They brush my skin, ice cold, like tiny bells. My heaving chest slows. I breathe the sea and the dull panic fades.

For the first time since I woke, hours ago, tumbled in the breakers in the darkness before dawn, I start to feel in control. This morning, only the fact I couldn't stand stopped me wading out of the water and drowning in the thin air. Instead I thrashed, fell, choked and tried to scream. I passed out at least twice, and woke to find myself naked, submerged in the breakers, even more bruised, and still trapped. The sun rose. I hardly noticed. When people passed with their dogs, or jogged over the shingle, I hid in the water, only my eyes showing.

After hours shivering with fear on the edge of land, I saw my jeans rolling in the surf. Further along the shore, I managed to scramble three steps, grab my tee-shirt, and roll back into the waves without being seen. I was shocked at how heavy I was without the sea's support. I had to rest before tackling my clothes. But even after I had snugged the wet denim around my hips, and draped the translucent tee over shoulders that seemed wider than before, I still didn't dare speak to anyone.

I was torn. I still am. I do want to grab someone, babble, get help. But a dread of sharing this nightmare and finding it real, embedded in normality, would break me, I'm sure. And somehow I feel ashamed. Like this… change was my fault. I don't want to be caught out in this embarrassing situation.

When I surface, a dog walker has waded thigh deep into the sea towards me. He bundles off his jacket and throws it towards the shore where his terrier yaps on the dry shingle. His face is creased with worry. I try to speak, hiccup, and drool sea water.

"You all right?" he asks. "Need help?"

I shake my head, nod and shake my head again. I've been thinking about being discovered all morning but have no idea what to do now. My mouth is full of sea water.

"Thought you was dead," the man says. He rubs his chest and winces. "Got my wallet wet."

This is my chance to beg him to get help. To call an ambulance, quick, and make sure it is full of seawater. But I can't speak. Can I ask him in mime without scaring him away? He is looking at me with obvious mistrust already.

Instead, I nod and grin, and stand tall as if my feet were on solid ground. He doesn't look convinced, so I mime swimming and try to look like an eccentric health freak on a normal, Sunday morning, fully-clothed lap of the bay. The need to duck under and breathe again builds in my chest.

"Hmm." The man looks at the sky and shakes his head. He wades out of the water and strips off his wet socks, glaring at me as he wrings them out. His terrier bounces and yips at his side. It does not let the waves touch its paws.

I turn and make a show of diving into the water and swimming in a sporty way, faking lifting my head to take breaths. What can I do? Where can I go? If I stay on the beach, I'll be discovered soon. I should go deeper, but the thought of being alone out of my depth fills me with dread.

I swim into the shadows under the pier and clutch a barnacle-scabbed column. Slanted blades of sunlight slice through the gaps between the planks above. This is where we kissed last night. This is where I stumbled upon you, stretched out on the shingle, lithe and sleek. Were you asleep? Were you dead? No, your chest rose, held, and fell on an out-breath, almost a sigh. Your armpit winked up at me in the moonlight. Shadows pooled, defining the spilled hollows of your ribs, your hips, your long thighs. Taut as a seal, knotted like seaweed, the muscled length of you pulled me to my knees. Only two minutes earlier, I had left my hotel room, looking forward to a night out in the seafront bars. Two minutes later, I was dreaming a sea dream, with your hips hard against me, and the waves were drowned out by the song of our lust.

In between was the kiss. I stole it. I couldn't resist. Your lips called me the way the sea calls me now. They were soft, and hard, and cool. They tasted of salt. I'm sorry.

I would do it again.

There's a big, white, plastic bottle floating near me. Could I fill it with water and get back to my hotel, nonchalantly swigging and drooling as I go? But what could I do there? I've lost my mobile. I can't even speak. I would have to fill a bath, quick. Can I even breathe fresh water? Panic overtakes me again. I push away from the wooden post and beat the water, letting the waves lift me and drop. Lift and drop. Duck under to breathe. Face the shore.

I haven't looked at the horizon yet, I realize. It has been lurking there behind me: the boundary between sea and air. I spin slowly and it slides into sight, chopped up by the pier's supports, interrupted by two yachts and a windsurfer, but wide and unmoving and utterly terrifying.

Blue sky shades to silver, and there is the no-line, the nothing between, and then the shifting planes of the sea. The nothing between is too thin a line to walk. I teeter, my bare, sea-wrinkled feet balanced on its blade. I will have to fall one way or the other.

I want my job and sitcoms and drinks in the theatre bar, and shagging and nightclubs, and trying to find out if Derek fancies me at work. I want internet shopping and holidays in exotic but comfortably normal places. Inland.

But the sea calls. There are gulfs where the ground has no hold, and water stretches from my armpits to Africa. There are blue shadows, blankets of rippling fish, white spray and oil slicks. Boat engines chop whale song into staggered stanzas of loss. There are toxic dumps and many, many corpses.

I drift from under the pier. Looking back, I can see my hotel, stacked ten stories high against the shore, as if the whole town wanted to wade in but didn't dare.

I slip under the skin of the water. Its pulse booms in my ears. I stretch and pull, feeling muscles pop in my shoulders. The seabed flows past beneath me. Seaweed darkens the stones as I slide deeper. It brushes my ankle. I freeze, my shoulders clamped near my ears. What the hell am I doing? I coast to a stop, and hang there, teetering…

And then I remember your smile and I tip, fall over the far side of the horizon to where the water shades into the clearest blue.

I dare. I do. Loss washes me, fear, relief, all threaded with a current of dark joy. I swim onwards, further out. Bladderwrack turns to black kelp beneath me, and my skin thrills as I slide into a shelf of colder water. I'm coming. Perhaps I'll meet you in the space between the surface and the earth. Perhaps your arms will wrap me from behind. Perhaps we will kiss again, and follow the deepening sunbeams into cobalt twilight, while above, cupped in the dry palms of cruise ships, tourists dream and almost dare, but never jump.

The Grief of Seagulls

Joel Lane

The fish will fly and the seas go dry
The rocks will melter in the sun
The working men will forget their labour
Before I do return again
—TRADITIONAL

THE QUAY WAS NEARLY DESERTED. ONLY A FEW OLD MEN standing outside the pubs, gazing out to sea as the evening light faded. One of them looked familiar. Maybe I'd seen him at the Duthie Park memorial, though I didn't go there much. Here was where I went to be with Andrew. When I looked across the metallic water, the image was still there: so clear I could believe it was imprinted on the landscape, not just on my memory. The crimson fireball of a burning oil rig.

I walked from the station to the harbour, which was choked with steel Halliburton ships and grey oil tanks. At least the company had changed. Further on, the oil vessels thinned out until I could see across the harbour to a finger of bare land where temporary buildings stood behind wire fences. The pebble beaches were mostly pink granite, as if they had soaked up blood from the water. Out at sea, I could just make out a line of black rocks like burial mounds. Seagulls flew out and back again in long swooping arcs, crying like weans.

Andrew had been working on the Piper Alpha rig for three months. He'd told me the American oil company was trying to make workers leave the union. They'd stopped safety training because it reduced productivity. *We don't believe in red tape*, the site manager had said. He didn't like it, but jobs were hard to come by. We were saving for a flat. It still wasn't long since they'd changed the law—we had to be furtive, but at least we weren't facing jail for sharing a bed.

That day, I was working in the shop when the news came through that Piper Alpha was on fire. I had to wait until my lunch break to run down to the quay and see the rig in the distance, wreathed in flames. A carpet of burning oil surrounded it. Helicopters were circling above the fire, looking for a place to land. I walked back to the shop. Half an hour later, I heard a dull boom, felt the walls shake. I walked slowly to the staff toilet and threw up, then went back to the till.

That evening I was one of hundreds of people waiting at the Infirmary. Some were praying or greeting, but most were silent. Of a hundred and sixty men only a few dozen had come back alive, and it was rumoured they were terribly burned from the oil: crippled, faceless, blinded. Andrew's parents were there too, and his sister. She knew about us but they didn't, so I had to keep quiet. But I didn't have to hide my tears in the middle of so much grief. Ambulances were coming back with only dead men inside, or none at all. I went home at three in the morning. It was hard to walk. I'd not have believed emptiness could weigh so much.

It came out in the enquiry that after the fire had started, the site manager in Aberdeen had twice decided to keep the oil pipe running because the risk of an explosion didn't justify losing a day's income. The company escaped prosecution because too little evidence had survived the wreckage.

Tears were blurring my view as I turned back towards the quay. There wasn't much to look at anyway: distant streetlights in the town, a few vessels out at sea. Once Andrew and I had walked out here, hand in hand, and seen a twisted blue-green shape hanging in the night sky. But tonight there were no visions. Only a small dark figure on the quayside, making its way towards me.

It was the old man from the pub by the station. Had he followed me all the way out here? I wondered if he'd seen me in Oh Henry's some time. If so, I wasn't in the mood. There'd been other men since Andrew—it had been twelve years, after all—but tonight belonged to him. The seagulls cried louder as I stood and waited. So near the sea's dark mass, the night was chilly. I could smell oil on the pebbles.

He stopped a few feet away from me. I couldn't see his face clearly, though I remembered it: white hair around a clean-shaven, rather gaunt face, a man of sixty or so. "I'm sorry to intrude," he said.

"It's a public right of way," I answered. "You're not intruding unless you bother me. I'd recommend not."

"I lost someone too," he said. "In the disaster, the fire. I wondered if maybe we could talk."

"I'm not big on support groups." But as I spoke, I could feel the story's weight inside me. Could it be shared? "Look, if I tell you—whatever you hear, it stays with you. Understood?"

"Of course." He touched my arm gently. Close up I could hear a faint wheeze on his breath. Maybe he was ill. We walked back to the quay and I told him about Andrew. How we met, how we became lovers, our plans. And then that long day. The burning rig on the horizon. The night at the Infirmary, waiting. The funeral with an empty coffin.

By the time I'd finished, we'd walked past the station and onward towards Balmedie. The old man was silent; so were the gulls. "What's your story?" I asked.

"It's late," he said. "I'm older than you'd think. Need to rest. Meet me here tomorrow and I'll tell you what happened. Nine o'clock on the quay, outside the Moorings. Can you make it?" I nodded. He looked fit to drop, and I was worn out from the long walk. His thin hand gripped my shoulder. "See you."

It wasn't closing time yet, but I was too tired for a pub. The sea twitched and shook restlessly, a blanket over a sleeping body. I walked home, poured myself some whisky and fell asleep with the glass still in my hand.

The next evening was brighter: the sky held a faint glow, like granite. I was in no mood for company, but the old man had listened to me. There were a few men standing outside the Moorings

on Trinity Quay, smoking, but he wasn't among them. I went into the
pub, bought a dram of Laphroaig and drank it straight off. It tasted of
ashes—but then, it always does. There were pictures of old sailing ships
on the walls. When I walked back outside, another man had arrived. Not
the one I was waiting for, though he looked vaguely familiar. There were
faint scars over his face and neck.

Then he looked at me. "Callum?" I nodded, wondering if the old man
had sent him. But we hadn't exchanged names. And this stranger could
be my age, though the scars made it hard to tell. It was like a fine pale
cobweb over his skin. He held out his hand, which was similarly marked.
"Good to see you," he said. Not wanting to be rude, I shook his hand. His
thin fingers tightened their grip, and suddenly I knew.

"Did he send you?" I asked. He nodded. "What the fuck?"

"We don't have much time." His eyes were dark with pain. "Let's go to
the harbour. I've got things to tell you." The same voice, but quieter—and
flawed, as if the scars were internal too. I was shaking as we walked together along the quay. A dull red flame was spreading on the water, but
it was only light.

There was nobody at the harbour, where tall grey oil tanks almost
blocked out the view. He took my hand again and just held it. I could feel
the warmth of his skin. And the scars, a faint Braille I had no idea how to
read. "The oil companies won," he said. "They always get what they want."

I turned to look at him. Then our faces were together and the taste
of his kiss was in my mouth, the same as before. His hands on me, our
bodies pressing together. He kissed my neck and bit gently, not breaking
the skin. I reached up to his chest, slipped my hand between the buttons
of his shirt. More scars.

Seagulls were crying above the oil vessels. I stepped back, staring. "How
did you survive?"

He just shook his head. "Where have you been?" I asked.

"Under the water. In the stone. Nowhere." He raised his damaged hands
towards me and I stepped forward, let him touch my face. "And you, Callum? Did you stay here?"

"I moved away. But I had to come back. This is where I belong." My eyes
were blurring. "God, I've missed you. You don't know...."

"I do," he said, his mouth almost touching my ear. "Missing someone
can be a place. The city of without." His hand rested on my belly, moved

down. "Callum, we don't have much time. Is there somewhere we can go? I mean near."

"Shall we have a look?" I said. We'd done that before, a few times, but not here. We walked out beyond the harbour, to where the quay turned back towards the city. I could see the line of rocks in the water. Most of the buildings were locked up, and some looked derelict. A passageway between two houses was unlit, but didn't smell bad. I touched his arm and stepped backwards into the darkness.

He followed me and pressed me against the wall. I could hear his breathing, louder as I unbuttoned his shirt. His thin hands pulled at my shoulders, gently taking control. I knelt and unzipped his jeans, went down on him. My lips found no scars. His fingers gripped my hair. "Callum," he said quietly. I felt him tense, shudder and spurt in my mouth. Twelve years, but his taste was the same.

I stood up and reached for him, but something was changing. The scars on his chest were denser, and they gave way under my hands. I reached up towards his face and could feel only a web of scars, as if that was all that held him together. Glad that I couldn't see anything here, I gripped his torn arms and we pressed together against the wall. I felt a cool breath against my lips. And then my hands and my face were crushed against cold, damp brick.

When I walked back along the quay, night had fallen. A frail aurora was glowing above the black water: a ragged veil of blue and yellow like bruised skin. As I watched, the colours melted into each other and the night. Near the station, I saw the old man sitting asleep on a bench. He looked worn out, as if after a hard day's work. Then I realised what his work was.

I SAW HIM AGAIN—THE old MAN, THAT IS—A FEW WEEKS later. By then it was autumn, and a bitter wind was blowing in from the iron sea. He and a younger man were walking towards the harbour. As they passed me, deep in conversation, I avoided catching the old man's eye. I didn't want to interrupt his work. Or make him think I was jealous. Or, to be honest, know him.

Ban's Dream of the Sea

Alex Jeffers

Some time after the fierce, out of season tempest had passed, Ban woke to hammering at the door. He started and lifted his head, perplexed to discover himself slumped over the desk rather than in bed. A thin whine of wind pierced through intervals in the banging. A loose shutter rattled, wanting to break its latch. Wiping the drool from his lips, he called, "What?"

"Ban!" came his brother-in-law's voice, hardly muffled by the door and thick walls. "Banto!"

On the surface of the desk, Ban's candle had guttered down to a puddle of cold, hard wax in its chipped saucer, wick twisted and bloated with black carbon. A sliver of daylight made the water-filled glass globes and polished steel mirrors positioned around the candle shine dully. He had fallen asleep reading.

"What?" he called again. "I'm coming."

Stiff and chilled, he pushed the chair back and levered himself to his feet. The storm had got into his bones and tendons. Pulling the robe tighter over his chest, he crossed the room, fumbled at the overcomplicated Akkatese lock. The city's original builders had not bothered themselves with locks—or doors. All their portals were always open, if not welcoming, until people from the far side of the world came to block them up.

Keron gave him no time to speak, hammering the door inward immediately the tumblers fell. The lower edge struck Ban's slippered foot. "Your sister!" Keron yelled over Ban's yelp, storming in wild eyed and windblown. "Is she here?"

Biting back irritation and the pain in his toes, Ban said, "Of course not. She disapproves of me, where I live. Why would she climb my stairs?"

Keron was out of breath from climbing those stairs himself: Ban rented rooms at the top of one of the ancient towers, cheap because of the laborious climb. "She's gone," Keron gasped. Mottles of red and pink mapped unknown archipelagos on his cheeks above the patchy, greying beard. "Into the night—into the storm. We quarrelled."

"Sit down," said Ban. "You woke me—I'll make chocolate."

Keron knew as well as Ban there was no comfortable seat. Agitated, he pulled the brocade cap from his head and passed it from hand to hand. "Banto," he began but went no further. The brocade was threaded with silver. His drab black casaque was likely of more value than his brother-in-law's entire wardrobe.

"I disappoint my sister," Ban said, his tone light for he was no fonder of her. "Etkass sees little use in me and resents the small demands I place on Father's estate. I'm the last comfort she'd seek after a quarrel." Turning to the battered iron brazier in the corner, he stirred the coals under the kettle, coaxed up a flame. "Doubtless she has confidantes…."

"I do not know them."

Shaving chocolate into the jug, Ban half saw Keron reach toward him. Curtailed, the motion looked clumsy and shy. "I disappoint you," Keron mumbled.

It was an old plaint of which both were weary. "Don't speak nonsense, my dear," said Ban, scrupling to look up and embarrass Keron. "Tell me about this quarrel."

Keron paced. "She woke me. I was dreaming. The dream had made me amorous and she took it as for her."

"Keron…."

"No, Ban. You know full well I don't favor your sister, any woman, but my father will have grandsons so I do my best. I *did* my best, once I understood it was Etkass, not my dream, but it was neither enough to satisfy her nor to make sons. So we quarrelled before she slept. Her dreams too were amorous. When she woke, she asked why it was I could not pleasure her as the man of her dream did. Bitter, I said it was possibly the same man in both our dreams."

"Keron," Ban said, aware of a heat in his cheeks. The water had nearly reached its boil. "Do you have these dreams often? Does she?"

"Etkass? I wouldn't know. Myself? Not of such…intensity, no, not often."

"Was it a man? Truly?"

For an instant Keron's expression was offended, before he became thoughtful. "For my purposes, in my amorous delirium, surely he was, but…perhaps. It's difficult to recall. Until your sister woke me, he gave me such pleasure as I have not known for some years."

Ban lowered his eyes from the accusation of his brother-in-law's regret, poured steaming water over spiced chocolate in the jug. They had agreed—Ban had bullied Keron into agreeing—it would not be fair to continue carrying on as they had while boys once Keron wed Etkass.

"He had no hair, none at all, on his head, on his body, no beard, no eyebrows. His skin was oddly cool, oddly…thick. Resilient, rather like rubber. So somehow not human, perhaps you're right. But a man, equipped as a man, that he was."

"I…." Peering into the jug as he whisked the chocolate, Ban watched foam form and break, froth up again. "I have had such dreams. Recently. Not last night, but the night before, I think. On earlier occasions as well. He is a very great lover, yes, that creature, but not a man. Did you notice, were you in your own bed?"

"Of course not! How should I take a man into your sister's bed? I was—"

"Under the sea? Were there bones, human bones, strewn about the sands below as you…cavorted, suspended in deep waters?"

"Banto?"

"Did my sister say she meant to find him, the *man* of her—of your, of our—dreams? I fear you are widowed, Keron."

"You—" Keron paused. "You are saying things I don't understand."

Without speaking, Ban rose to fetch cups. He poured out the chocolate, handed a cup to his anxious brother-in-law. The bitter fragrance from his own unsettled him: chocolate was a drug Akkatese had not known before they discovered the New World.

"People disappear often, have you noticed, from our city."

"How could I not notice my own brother?" Keron demanded. "Stupid boy—the promenade's no place to stroll in a storm."

Ban had forgotten the fate of Keron's brother. That was long ago. "Not always the promenade. Not always a storm. Often after a peculiarly vivid dream, the records suggest. The admiral was the first." Sipping, calmer but not calm, he moved toward his desk. "Perhaps you didn't know that."

"The admiral?"

The book Ban had fallen asleep over was old but not terribly precious, with multiple editions since the work had been discovered in the viceroy's archive half a century before: *A Narrative of Admiral Saro, His Voyages of Discovery*. Intended for the common reader, this twenty-year-old edition boasted no scholarly apparatus beyond its preface and was illustrated with fanciful engravings. Ban had it nearly by heart for the moment—merely glancing at the open page he recalled the passage he had read as sleep overcame him:

> We came upon this marvel from the east, late in the afternoon when the sun dazzled upon the sea beyond so we believed it no more than a rocky island spired and chimneyed in natural stone. Wary of submerged rocks and reefs off an unknown coast, the admiral chose to drop anchor until morning. Happening to wake in the night when the great moon was high and full, I peered across the waters toward the undiscovered island some furlongs distant.
>
> "It appears a mighty castle or city, alone in the sea," said the sleepless admiral, joining me at the gunwale.

On the following page, a fine engraving depicted that vision of admiral and chronicler: the city rising sheer and high from moonlit waters, the admiral's *Pearl of Akkat* and the two smaller ships of his flotilla, the *Ruby* and the *Sapphire*, becalmed at a distance along the moon's path. Although Ban knew well his own ancestors had built the Admiral's Spire more than a hundred years later, steepling above the builders' halls and towers, he felt the engraving's effect was not spoiled by its depiction outside its own time. The artist had drawn the admiral's vessel as a modern galleon rather than a carrack of the era.

Closing the book, Ban ran his fingers along the top edge where cloth had frayed against the board. The same anachronistic galleon was blind stamped at the center of the cover. Turning to his brother-in-law, he said, "The admiral spoke to his secretary the night before he vanished, complaining of dreams in which a devilish woman attempted to seduce him. There was no storm. No women had yet come from Akkat—it was only men, a tiresome thing for those who preferred women. The admiral was not the last of his men to disappear before the queen's viceroy brought wives, maidens, whores across the ocean. Afterward…not so many vanishings, two or three a decade in the records for three hundred years. But the number has been increasing lately, the last half or quarter century. Ten years ago it might have been two or three a year. These days—" Ban shook his head. "Not people you would notice for the most part, two or three each great month."

"What?"

Ban walked away, toward the shuttered window that faced north, toward the distant mainland. "As I said, not people you would notice. Young people, sons and daughters of fisherfolk, ferry tenders, small merchants and traders, laborers, clerks. I began to look into it some time ago, after my first dream. Did you not feel a powerful urge to join your lover?"

"A…wistfulness. I knew it was a dream, he was not real. I knew I could not survive beneath the waves with him."

"You were awakened early, untimely." Slipping the shutters' latches, Ban pulled the heavy wooden wings wide. Fresh, clean air boomed in, instantly banishing the human smells of chocolate, spices, ink, coal smoke—fresh, invigorating, heavy with salt over the faint, probably imagined fragrance of pine from the mainland's forests. Ban simply breathed for a moment before looking down. "The causeway is gone," he said, faintly shocked.

"Broken in the storm. It often happens."

"Not broken. Gone. Vanished, like your wife."

"That cannot be." Keron's voice was sharp, his hand falling heavy on Ban's shoulder. "You're imagining things, Banto."

Turning toward the door, Ban did not look through the window again, paused only when his brother-in-law implored him not to appear on the public street uncombed, awry, in stained house robe and slippers. On another day, Ban would have joked his fairest attire was not much more presentable, his reputation as tattered as his slippers. Throwing aside the robe, he dressed hastily, mindful only after, when he glimpsed the longing in Keron's eyes, how long it had been since he allowed himself to appear so defenseless, so intimate, in his brother-in-law's presence.

The fact of it, the lapse in the fiction between them, irritated him, so that he pulled the door open with unnecessary force. The hinges protested, the wooden jamb shuddered and creaked against the ancient stone to which it was clumsily fastened. "Come," he said brusquely, not looking back as he ducked under the lintel.

The stairs were also wood, steep and creaky, jigsawed onto the builders' spiral ramp, which men of the admiral's time had found treacherous to climb or descend in that age's high-heeled boots. Over his own footfalls, Ban heard Keron drag the door closed and jostle the latch but did not pause. Without the key, Keron could not lock the door but Ban possessed little that would tempt a burglar. There was no particular market for thirdhand volumes of dubious scholarship, outdated maps. A thief who required Ban's aimless manuscripts to kindle a sad fire was, in the end, welcome to them.

The odors of old cooking rose to meet Ban from his neighbors' kitchens on lower floors, the myriad stenches of the city at the bottom of his stairs. Soles clattering, he plunged down, one hand trailing the stone of the ancient builders' walls.

When the sun rose behind the Pearl in the morning, we saw the admiral's night vision had been true. A mighty, fantastical city rose from the waste of waves as if some deity had plucked up one of the great towns of Akkat or the old empire or another of the countries about the Home Sea and dropped it here, well offshore of these new lands half the world away.

There were cries of anger, of amazement, among our men. The few peoples we had encountered on this side of the ocean were rude savages who spoke no civilized tongue nor recognized the true gods, built no great structures, whether of stone or wood. They boasted no architects or engineers. Nomads, they packed their dwellings of leather and withe on the backs of strange hairy camels as they moved from one hunting or foraging ground to the next. Their canoes and rafts were scarce seaworthy, so that only a madman would trust them to bear him across the wide, treacherous strait from mainland to this islanded city. In any event, as we voyaged west from our first landfall, we had met no people at all since the last waxing of the great moon. The men at the final slapdash encampment shouted at us from the shore, as if in warning, when we turned the Pearl to follow the sun, and the fellow we had taken aboard in hope of teaching him to speak intelligibly and guide us became agitated, broke his bonds, and threw himself into the sea.

Immediately the master at arms saw the city across the waters, he called his marines to order. The guns were rolled into place, creaking across the deck, matches lit. Men grown lax in all this time checked their powder was dry, the bores of their calivers clear. Yet the admiral on the foredeck said, gently but firmly, "I see no threat."

Indeed, no banners flew from the city's tall towers. The sharpest spyglass could pick out not a single person on the wide esplanade that circled the town instead of defensive walls, not a face at any of the myriad open windows. In the grand harbor rested no ships or smaller vessels. More astonishing than its being a city in the sea far from civilized shores, then, it appeared to be deserted.

ONCE THEY EMERGED ONTO THE QUEEN'S HIGH STREET from the tangle of dim, narrow alleyways that made up Ban's sestiere, he paced faster where pavements were swept clean and refuse hidden away. It seemed to him he noticed aspects of his city that had never seemed important before. Was it peculiar to see so many images of women and men? More, it almost seemed, than living persons. In Ban's neighborhood, the night lanterns were simple white-glass globes or guttering open naphtha flames where globes had broken. On the high street, gem-colored blown-glass busts of grandees stood on plinths down the center of the avenue. Caryatides and atlantes upheld the wooden porticos attached to quite unimportant establishments. Frescoes of dubious quality encrusted the unwindowed lower floors of buildings now warehouses or manufactories with garlands of brightly attired dancers or processions of heroes.

Ban set too hard a pace. By the time they reached the waterfront and its stenches of spoiled fish and produce and humanity, Keron was lagging, as breathless as if he'd climbed the tower stairs all over again. His call for Ban to wait was nearly a whimper.

Distrustful crowds milled about the piazzetta. Ban had to edge between agitated grocers and wholesalers, scholars, marines, sailors. Luminously pale bondsmen and freedmen of mainland heritage formed troubled groups, speaking their own barbarous languages in low voices. A cabal of grandees had accumulated around the toll station. Rumor had it two centuries of tolls had long since paid for New Akkat's greatest feat of engineering, though the holders of the concession (Keron's father among them) never hesitated to impose new levies for extraordinary repairs.

The brothers-in-law had nearly reached the colossal pylons that had anchored the final link of the causeway between island city and distant mainland, where crops were grown and cattle raised, metals and coal mined, stone quarried, lumber cut and sawn. Between the massive shoulders of a pair of stevedores, Ban saw that the pylons had changed. He stopped dead, grabbing Keron's hand to halt him as well.

Keron looked back, eyes wide. "What is it?"

No longer plainly utilitarian piers of brick-faced concrete, the pylons had become monumental statues, each seemingly sculpted from a single outcrop of native stone, one hunkered into a crouch, the other kneeling. They were…not men but masculine, figures as like as brothers, one to the other and each to the lover of Ban's dreams. Barnacles like pox and tumors of coral marred stoney skin, garlands of blue-grey mussels and small pink-grey clams clung to the fissures where muscle folded into rocky muscle, skeins of iridescent rotting seaweeds draped tensed limbs as the statues attempted to lift the sea into the city.

Between one blink and the next, Ban discovered himself to be alone with Keron on the desolate piazzetta, though the agitated echoes of the crowd's voices lingered for moments and the stenches and fragrances of their commerce seemed still to overwhelm the clean scent of the sea. He uttered a sound, a moan. Releasing Keron's hand, he turned about. The city looming was recognizably the same but no longer New Akkat, for it was flensed of four centuries' alien accretions. The Admiral's Spire did not steeple above older towers. Lower Akkatese buildings, brick or stone or wood, had likewise vanished. The builders' stark walls were stripped of foreign ornament, whether carved wood, molded plaster, or simple paint. Doorways and windows gaped darkly without the wooden and glass barriers bracketed on by folk who valued privacy and distrusted weather. No people at all marred the ancient architecture.

"I—" Ban felt heat rush back to the surface of his skin when he blinked a third time and saw his familiar, resplendent mongrel city once more. The Spire bisected the sky as it had all his lifetime.

"What, Banto? You look frightened. What is it?"

Over Keron's shoulder, Ban recognized the brick pylons, sturdy, eternal. "I…. Nothing. I felt faint for a moment." Pushing past his brother-in-law and the arguing stevedores, he reached the piazzetta's ruled edge, where bollards and iron chains presented no real barrier to one who wished to risk the rocks and reefs and treacherous waters below.

The pylons remained, but their great cables dangled limp as if they had never supported the causeway's first segment. In the open waters beyond, a few of the huge, roughly squared logs that had formed the roadbed bobbed on rough seas between waterfront and the artificial islet to which that segment had led. The gate that was half garrisoned fort stood up from its foundations in the submerged reef, banners flying, though storm had tattered the banners and no bridge now reached the great arched gate ten feet above the waves. Under the arch stood soldiers of the garrison, who seemed not terribly concerned, and below a party of marines was hauling a small barge from the sturdy boat house.

"Broken," murmured Ban, "merely broken, not vanished."

Moving closer, Keron studied him. "You haven't eaten. Knowing you, you didn't eat last night."

Ban shook his head. "I don't recall." Could hunger cause such visions? He blinked again, squeezing his eyelids tight for a moment, but the fort remained.

"Come." Keron had decided. "Back to my house. Perhaps Etkass has found her way home from her wander. At any rate, there will be food."

Within ten days of our landfall in the deserted city, most of us had come to take the place for granted. The admiral had raised our flag on the waterfront of its fine, deep, sheltered harbor and claimed the island in the name of our distant, indifferent queen and the merchant-adventurers' company which had financed the expedition. The rough, gross prelate who accompanied us at our sponsors' insistence performed a rite meant to cleanse the place of native demons and ghosts; as the admiral would not countenance sacrifice of our last hog or laying hens, priest and gods must needs be satisfied with one of the hairy camels

intended for the queen's menagerie. We had already determined the
beasts were not good eating, less wholesome than horse even.

I do not know who among us first called the place New Akkat. Not
the admiral, I believe.

Etkass had not returned. Her bondswoman, a mainlander
in Ban's family's service longer than he could remember, extending the
term of her bond again and again to buy freedom for one child after
another, only cringed and muttered in her own language when asked of
her mistress. She prepared a small collation for Keron and her mistress's
scholar brother, which Ban could not recall eating after it was gone.

Then—imported from the Old World, more precious than silver—
coffee instead of chocolate. Ban savored the rare bitterness of the drink
and permitted himself not to think: of his vanished sister, of the broken
causeway, of his inexplicable visions. Across the parlor, Keron had laid
aside his own cup and drawn up his feet, leaning back into the settee's
corner, contemplating nothingness with his chin up and eyes downcast.

Ban regarded his brother-in-law for some moments. Keron had never
been handsome, the beard he had allowed to grow in the last year did not
flatter plump cheeks and thick neck, but he was comfortable and...dear.
Ban had been appalled when his boyhood friend (*lover* was not a term
either ever used) first paid suit to Etkass—not because Ban loved his
sister so much but for the suit's cynicism. Not a trait he had previously
ascribed to Keron.

"You truly believe she is dead?" Keron asked, speaking to the high back
of the settee. "My wife?"

Ban shook himself. He set down the coffee cup. "I believe she won't
return."

"I treated her unfairly."

"I feel you did. But she was no kinder to you."

Liquid glimmered in the margins of Keron's eyes. "It was you I loved."

"No."

"Yes."

"No. We pleased each other, for a time."

"We must leave. If you're right about the dreams." Turning tragic eyes
on Ban, Keron set his feet on the floor. "We should go far away. I can't
lose you too, Banto."

Ban hardened his heart. "You chose to marry."

"I had no choice! My brother...."

"Where would you go, Keron? Your name means nothing in Akkat. Nowhere in the Old World. You haven't enough fortune of your own to make a new name."

"I—" Keron wept openly now. "I'm frightened. What you tell me—I cannot think about it."

Reaching again for his coffee, Ban declined the invitation to comfort his friend. "Then don't. Forget it. Wait a suitable period, then find another girl. Sire sons and raise them."

"How can you—"

"Or follow your dream lover into the sea."

"Banto!"

Ban rose to his feet. "Thank you for the coffee, my dear. I must go. If my sister should return after all, please send word."

After some weeks, the prelate demanded to see the admiral. Two men-at-arms and I stood attendance, for nobody—the admiral least of all—trusted the priest or his distant, luxurious masters. As the admiral's amanuensis, I sat to one side with my ink and pens, while the soldiers stood behind and to either side of his chair. The priest was displeased to see us but endeavored not to reveal his displeasure. "My lord admiral," he said without hesitation, "this is an evil place."

"In what way evil?" inquired the calm admiral.

The elder man-at-arms, a person one had not known to be pious or righteous, muttered, "The men are forever buggering one another."

The admiral dismissed his concern. "As they will on any long voyage or campaign, deprived of women. Unfortunate, perhaps. Not evil." He turned his hard eyes again to the priest.

"It knows not the gods and the gods decline to know it. We must destroy it, crumble it into the sea, and depart."

The admiral smiled coolly. "But, sir, one might say the same of all the lands we have discovered on this side of the great ocean. None of the people we met on the mainland recognized the gods. Indeed, the same might be said of our own home. Was not the great temple in Akkat first built for worship of the old empire's false god?"

"The great temple and all of Akkat were cleansed of that taint long ago."

"As you cleansed this place the day we made landfall, no? Here there are no men or women to know the gods or not. It is, it would seem to me, a blank page on which we may write a new history to the glory of the gods and our queen."

"You persist in misunderstanding, my lord," the prelate said, anger mottling his face. "The builders of the great temple, the men of the old empire, mistaken into evil though they were, were men. This place was raised by demons. It is unholy and cannot be cleansed except by destruction. It must be thrown into the sea."

"Demons?" It was apparent the admiral, an educated and well travelled man, did not credit their existence. "An intriguing theory. It is true we have not met men on this side of the ocean who appear capable of such architecture." Pondering, he leaned back in his chair and regarded the high vault of the audience chamber.

Understanding he was being toyed with, the prelate became more angry. "You have no standing, my lord," he said, "to quarrel with the gods' commands."

Irritated himself now, the admiral sat forward, peering into the priest's small, piggy eyes. "Sir," he replied in measured tones, "I will answer to the gods when that time comes. Until then, I answer to the queen. This place, this readymade port and fortress, answers very well to the queen's needs. I will not abandon it, still less destroy it, on the suspect demand of a minor prelate who has been hounded out of every temple he served and who fetched up on my ship because his influential relations preferred he—you, sir—cease embarrassing them at home in Akkat." He gestured over his shoulder to the younger man-at-arms. "Please, escort this gentleman into confinement. He will speak to nobody without my permission. I believe he has been fomenting treason."

Across the avenue from the door of Keron's house stood the sole remaining temple in New Akkat of the old Akkatese gods, who had not prospered in the New World. Built of brick and stone to traditional design, it appeared somehow more out of place than even the Admiral's Spire. Ban could not recall ever seeing woman or man climb those steps between wolf-headed warrior gods to step under the lintel

carved in high relief with other gods, owl and stork and bear and spi-
der headed, feasting in their palace atop the cloud-wreathed volcano far
across the ocean. Once he had known their names—the names of the
greater seventy-seven, at any rate—but more compelling knowledge had
long ago crowded them out of his head. Now and then he glimpsed the
middle-aged priest or his elderly acolyte sidling about the town in their
robes more threadbare than his own. Both, he knew, were unwilling ex-
iles of the Old World, inspiring as little confidence as the first prelate in
New Akkat.

As he studied the temple's statuary, Ban recalled later passages of the
Narrative. That prelate had been permitted to poison himself rather than
endure the excruciation and execution due a traitor. Before that, he had
dictated a screed on the unholiness of New Akkat—it did not survive
but the admiral's secretary provided an epitome largely unintelligible
to one not familiar with the histories and heresies of the old faith. The
point Ban remembered, the prelate's damning proof, was the deserted
city's lack of images. Demons, he claimed, were incapable of creating art.

"Ban."

It was only a few moments, surely, he had lingered on the steps across
from the temple.

"Please. I'm sorry. Please don't abandon me. I shall try not to be foolish."

Ban didn't turn. "I meant to go to the watch, to inform them of Etkass's
disappearance."

"I'll send the bondswoman. It's not your place to deal with the watch."
Keron's hands grasped Ban's hips as he laid his cheek against his brother-
in-law's shoulder. "Please stay with me. Don't be angry."

Knowing he would give in, Ban waited another moment. "Have you,"
he asked, "ever visited the temple?"

"Why would I?" Keron sounded perplexed, his breath tickling Ban's
neck. "Does anybody? It's all nonsense."

"Like inhuman lovers that call to you from beneath the sea?" Turning in
Keron's embrace, Ban kissed him roughly. He felt Keron's prick harden
up, pressed to his thigh. "Come, bring me indoors."

Keron scrupled to take his wife's brother into his wife's bed. After sending the bondswoman out to the watch, he led Ban to the study where he
managed the few accounts his father allowed him. There, the door locked,

he stripped his old friend, exclaiming that Ban had not changed at all, unless for the better, in the three years since last one saw the other nude. "But I have grown flabby," he admitted sadly, "in body and mind."

In turn, Ban removed Keron's garments and laid him down on the narrow couch. Keron was eager, too eager, reaching his climax early, before he was ready. Ban was self conscious, regretful, clumsy. He hurt Keron, who cried out, spoiling it for Ban, which caused Keron to weep again.

"No," murmured Ban, petting him, soothing him. "It's nothing. We'll try again later, learn the way of it all over."

I had seldom seen the admiral troubled. When one great month's sailing into the wastes of the ocean had not brought our flotilla to the new lands he had predicted, he was merely disappointed, then irritated he must persuade the captains of Sapphire *and* Ruby *to continue on. In the event, it was merely another five days before we sighted land.*

But when he woke me that night nearly half a year after dispatching the Sapphire *back across the wide ocean to Akkat with news of the queen's new dominions, I knew at once he was not himself. "Old friend," the admiral said after I dressed and he pressed on me a cup of wine from nearly the last cask. "Old friend. Perhaps that man was right."*

"That man?" I did not understand whom he meant.

The admiral sighed. "The traitor prelate. Or perhaps I have simply been away from my wife too long." He glanced at me with a sardonic glimmer of his usual temper. "It would not do, of course, for the admiral to bugger a common sailor, and one's hand becomes tiresome."

I believed I knew what he was saying. Though the prospect revolted, terrified, perversely excited me, I was ready to offer.

"No, old friend," the admiral said gently. "I would not ask it of you. I value too well our friendship—as well as my marriage vows, of course." He sighed again.

"How was the prelate right?" I ventured, at once relieved and disappointed.

"In the nights—" the admiral began. "In the nights, I am visited. Nights, you understand, my hand has not done its job. By a...woman who wishes me to give her the delights of the flesh. A kind of woman. I feel they are not dreams, these visitations, for I have often, away from

her, dreamt of my wife and other women I have known, though those dreams ceased when we landed here. It is unlike those dreams and she is strange, this person. She seems more a creature of the sea, where I meet her, than of the land, and when I am with her I too can breathe beneath the waves. And yet, too, I know somehow she belongs to this strange city, or the city to her. And so I wonder if the priest was correct that this place was not built by men like ourselves but these seductive, terrifying sea dwellers. As a lure or trap, perhaps. Is she a demon? I know not what else to call her. Have—" The admiral hesitated. "Have you been visited? Or heard of peculiar dreams from any of our men?"

I had not. I nearly wished I had.

"Well, after all, it must be a dream. I have been too long from my wife, as I said." Rising from his seat, the admiral bade me goodnight and left me with troubled thoughts.

In the morning, Admiral Saro was not to be found. In the night, I was myself visited by a strange sea-dwelling person, a kind of man who wished me to act upon desires I had always feared. Two days later, the Sapphire *returned from Akkat across the ocean, accompanied by more ships bearing more cargo than the admiral had requested, and I must inform the admiral's wife she was widowed.*

THE LOVER IN THE SEA WAS FAR MORE ABLE AND LESS CLUMSY than Keron, and it seemed that Ban's own stamina and powers of recuperation were magnified beneath the waves. Their lovemaking went on and on, unwearying, ever changing. When they were restful or nearly, Ban gazed upon his lover and marvelled that he had ever found men—fragile spindly men like himself, like Keron—beautiful. Then he worried his lover would soon tire of him, imperfect man of the world of air, until he saw the reflection in his lover's great mirrored eyes and saw that he, too, Ban himself, was a magnificent creature of the sea, handsome as a seal, mighty as a whale. And they fell to pleasuring one another again.

He was far from weary when his lover took his hand and together they swam over coral gardens, through kelp forests, among shoals of brilliant fish, for a very long time. At last they came to a place that appeared somehow familiar. The stone colossi on the promenade had succeeded in pulling the sea into the city that had briefly been New Akkat, or drawing the city into the sea.

Familiar but strange. Strange. Of course the Akkatese additions that had spoiled the city's peculiar symmetry were gone, but it was more than that. Ban found himself able to understand the buildings' odd proportions now, for the sea people were considerably larger than the vanished usurpers, more apt to swim than stride upright. Every bracket or cornice that had appeared incomplete now was intricately carved, every empty niche or pedestal filled, every breadth of naked wall mosaicked. Everywhere he turned were images, statues, depictions of the people of the sea.

Everywhere he turned were the people of the sea themselves, calmly going about their day-to-day business. He glimpsed a monumentally beautiful woman sorting kelps in the market whom he believed to be his sister Etkass. Two great men passed overhead, swimming in the wake of the school of tunny they tended, and Ban felt certain the stranger who saluted him was Keron.

His lover urged him beneath the open arch of one of the city's towers. In dim undersea light, they followed the long spiral like the interior of a conch shell that had once, briefly, been deformed by the land dwellers' stairs. Up and up they rose, through turn after turn, until—still within the tower's nacreous walls—their heads broke through the ocean's comforting grasp.

For an instant Ban could not breathe, until he followed his companion's example and painfully coughed life-giving water from his lungs. The air that replaced it was thin, burning like acid, and he must take great, fast gulps of it to sustain himself.

Clumsy as seals out of their natural element, Ban and his lover clambered onto the damp floor of the tower's topmost chamber. Rolling from belly to back and back to belly, Ban peered about, his eyesight strangely dimmed and altered. Though all the possessions of his former, land-bound life were gone, the walls encrusted with barnacles and mussels and wizened anemones awaiting the tide's return, he recognized the place.

Flopping like a landed fish with the hook still in his mouth, he rolled into his lover's arms, who gazed long and wisely into his eyes, then propelled them both off the landing, back into the embrace of the sea.

Gasping, coughing, unable to breathe, Ban woke thrashing, alone, falling from the damp velvet of the narrow couch to a slick of wet, a puddle, on the hard stone floor of his brother-in-law's study. He smelled salt, nothing but salt, felt salt brim in his eyes.

Night of the Sea Beast

Brandon Cracraft

I never thought I would work again after Harry Ipswich and his team of self-righteous sleazes exposed me as a homosexual. Senator McCarthy convinced the public that all gay men were the bastards sons of Stalin and Lucifer, so good Christian patriots boycotted my movies and burned my underwear ads. The only time producers or photographers called me was to tell me to stop calling them. Less than a year ago, the papers touted me the next Johnny Weissmuller.

Even though I paid my rent on time, my landlord gave me an eviction notice. He told me that he didn't think it was safe to have me live there. The coward kept his screen door locked and carried a baseball bat. "Your kind can't control themselves," he said. "I heard Harry Ipswich talk about you on his radio show. I have to give you until the end of week, but I don't want to see you again after that." The old scarecrow looked on the verge of panic. "You have until Friday. If I see you after that, I'll call the cops on you. I swear."

For the next couple days I saw mothers grab their children whenever I walked out to the beach to swim, and grown men cross the street so that they wouldn't catch my homosexuality. I finally wised up and agreed to meet with a photographer who wanted to use me for some gay men's publications. I didn't want to do it, but I didn't have a choice. I couldn't even get a job as a short-order cook.

When I heard someone knocking on my door at the crack of dawn, I haphazardly pulled on a robe and expected more bad news. I stumbled over yesterday's clothes and threw open the door. "What do you want?" I asked angrily.

"Are you Hughie Wildsmith?" the man on my doorstep asked. He casually pulled up my robe and smiled when he saw my briefs. "I would recognize those legs anywhere. My boy used to demand that he wear nothing but your underpants. Most of the high school and half of the junior high refused to wear anything but your shorts."

"Thank you," I said, my stomach starting to flutter. "Are you a fan? Do you want me to sign a picture?"

"Trevor Trecaman," he said, extending his hand to be shook. "Not exactly a fan, Mr. Wildsmith." He shook his head. "Not Mr. Wildsmith. You're just Hughie, aren't you? When you did those ads, you looked like everyone's brother or son. You call a boy like that by his first name. He's an honest all-American boy, not some arrogant celebrity. I bet you played baseball, Hughie."

"No, sir." I stepped back so that he could enter my apartment. "I was on the swim team, won at least one medal a year since I was ten. My dad used to tell people that I was born with webbed feet."

Trevor raised an eyebrow. "So you're a good swimmer? I figured that you were. I saw you last night swimming against the current."

"Yes, sir. I signed on to the Navy as soon as I graduated. I worked underwater construction until the war with Korea and then I was drafted into the UDT. I would've still been in the military, but they started to suspect I had a boyfriend. The Navy convinced me to leave before they had to throw me out."

"And now Hollywood has thrown you out for the same stupid reason," Trevor said shaking his head. "I'll be honest with you, son. I'm not your biggest fan. I'm even wearing boxers. I can't imagine wearing something so vulgar. I'm getting to be an old man, fifty years old next month."

"You don't look it," I said honestly. He barely had any wrinkles, and his Roman nose gave him a slightly royal quality despite his short, squat body.

"Flatterer. I'm afraid that I don't bat for your team, Hughie." He thought a moment. "How tall are you? You look like a giant."

"Six foot three, sir. How can I help you?"

"You can start by getting dressed, son. I know that you're used to walking around in just your shorts, but I don't think it's proper for two men to discuss business like that." He went to the closet and chose a charcoal suit, white shirt, and pink tie. "You like coffee, son? I know this great place by the pier."

"Business?" I asked, hastily pulling onto my pants. "Are you a photographer? Do you need me to do some fetish shots for you?"

"I'm pretty handy with a camera, but I wouldn't call myself a photographer. I'm a filmmaker, and a darn good one. I'm working on casting my next picture."

"I'm a homosexual, sir," I said. "Are you sure that you want someone like that associated with your films? I could—"

Trevor's face flashed with anger. "I might not be your biggest fan, but my boy adores you. He was wearing those fancy underpants when he met his boyfriend, a rich fellow and handsome to bellow. Do you know what the American dream is, Hughie? It's having a kid that never has to ask you for money. His boyfriend's a redhead, just like you are." He reached up to straighten my tie. "My son is my pride and joy, I love him more than any of my ex-wives. I'm not ashamed of what he is."

"He's a very lucky boy. My parents stopped talking to me when they found out."

"Don't let that get you down, Hughie," Trevor said. "The world is changing. Just a couple years ago, everyone was looking under the bed for Communists. Most sane people know that Senator McCarthy was full of crap." He gave me a wink. "I predict that in 1958, just two years from now, everyone will realize that gay folks are the exact same as regular folks outside of the bedroom."

"You really think so?"

"Even the worst bigot knows that Harry Ipswich is an idiot and a gossip monger. Once the world wakes up and realizes what they've been listening to, they'll turn against him."

Trevor opened the door and led me down the pier. A couple people gave us a confused look, but the older man's polite smile and confident wave prompted them to wave back. "Hide in plain sight, my boy," Trevor said. "With you walking down the street with such an obvious hetero-sexual, they think you're just a normal guy." He motioned to a college girl riding her bike. "That little lady can't keep her eyes off you. All she sees is one hot dude." He made a face. "I think that's what the kids say. I should ask Arch. You'll like Arch when you meet him. He's a great kid."

"Who's Arch?"

Trevor trapped his foot with impatience. "Arch Hunter. He was in my last movie. I guess you didn't see him." I thought I upset him, but he quickly cheered back up. "It wasn't the biggest role. The next one is a huge. Takes to water like a fish. I'm sure you two boys will have a lot in common."

"Are you trying to set me up?" I asked.

"I'm sorry to tell you, Hughie, but I don't think Arch likes boys the same way that you do. He's just a nice kid, barely out of high school."

"I would love to be in a movie again," I said. "I'm just afraid that people will recognize me. I don't want another situation like what happened with my last movie. A crowd in Toronto literally pulled the film off the reel and burned it. Some kid in Chicago claims that he went gay after seeing me in a loincloth."

Trevor nudged me in the shoulder and laughed. "You're an attractive man, Hughie, and you certainly fill out a loincloth, but even you aren't that pretty. That boy just needed to explain to his daddy why he was kissing the quarterback."

"I know that, but a lot of people—"

"Won't care that you're in my movies. I make monster movies and not very expensive ones. I spend a little money, and I make a lot of money. You ever see *The Necromancer?*"

I nodded, remembering a little of the film. Some high school kid who was the son of a mortician finds a book that brings the dead back to life. In the end, the zombies bring a demon back to life.

Trevor's face puffed. "That funeral home was my parents' house. Hell, that was my mom playing the corpse. It was the role that she was born to play. She has to be the worst hypochondriac ever, always sick and dying. I've been digging her grave since I used a Boy Scout shovel." He snapped his fingers. "Remember that character of 'Charlie,' the kind of mean kid that gets killed by the zombies early?"

"I guess," I said, honestly trying to picture him.

"That was Arch," he said. "I saw that kid in his high school's production of *Hamlet*. He was playing Laertes, and he stole every scene he was in. The rest of the play was pretty crap. The girl who played Ophelia started burping after she kissed Hamlet."

"I'm sure he's a great kid…"

Trevor leaned closer and offered me a second cup of coffee. "The reason why I'm talking about good old Arch so much is I know all about your problems. That landlord of yours wants to kick you out and pocket the money. I can't have one of my actors sleeping at the YMCA."

I blinked. "I couldn't ask you—"

"You're not asking me nothing, Hughie. I've already asked Arch if you could stay with him. He's got an apartment on the beach. You've probably seen him surfing. The boy was born with the board in his hand."

"If he's a straight kid, I doubt he'll want to share a room with a gay guy," I said. "I don't want to make him nervous."

Trevor slapped the table. "You won't make him nervous. When I told him that you were going to be his co-star, he practically insisted. The kid did some modeling when he was really little. He sees you as sort of a hero."

"This is all very incredible, Mr. Trecatan—"

Trevor let out a long sigh. "I hate when people call me that. It means that they plan on telling me no. I don't take rejection well, just ask any of my ex-wives. I need you for my movie."

"My face is pretty famous," I said. "I'm scared of ruining your film. Harry Ipswich made sure that everyone knew what I looked like."

Trevor laughed again, munching on his cookie. "You still don't get it, do you, kid? I make monster movies, Hughie. I need you for the title character of my next horror extravaganza." He smiled and pointed at an imaginary marquee. For a second, I saw it as well. "You will play the title character in *The Sea Beast*."

Arch Hunter looked like the picture-perfect Southern California boy with his tanned skin, wiry muscles, and wavy blond hair. He extended his handshake, but he pulled me into a hug. I felt like a giant next to him, he barely stood five feet tall. "Sorry," he said, breaking the embrace. "I loved your movies. I saw all three of them, even the last one."

Goofy grin on his face, he shook my hand again. "I can't believe that we're going to be roomies."

I whispered, "You know that I'm gay, right?"

"Of course he doesn't," a familiar velvety voice said. "He spent the last year living under a rock."

My own celebrity fanaticism caused my heart to stop when I saw one of the greatest femmes fatales of the Saturday morning serials walk up and give a trademark sinister, grin, complete with black lipstick. Zipporah Bloodgood played alien princesses and jungle queens better than anyone else. Even as a gay man, I was fascinated by the raw sexuality she portrayed with a single tilt of the head.

"I just don't want to cause problems," I said, speaking to Arch while keeping my eyes glued on the satin floor-length gown with rabbit collar that Zipporah wore, oblivious to the heat. "I mean, if he lets a gay guy stay with him they might think that he's gay." I felt nervous, like I was about to become the victim of a practical joke.

"Dietrich Albrecht," he said, pointing to himself. "That's my real name. My sister changed both of our names after we came to America. Freja joined the League of German Girls when she was fifteen, so she could play the part of the obedient Hitler youth. Our brother, Dierk, had been captured by the Nazis when they raided a gay bar. They took him away, and my parents told us that we would never see him again. They told us never to even talk about Dierk. Everyone condemns the Nazis for what they did to the Jews, but no one wants to talk about what happened to all the queers." He shrugged, and gave me a crooked smile. "My sister didn't smuggle us to the United States so that I could act like a Nazi."

Zipporah raised a perfect eyebrow when she saw a man stumble his way onto the ship between sips on his flask. It took me a few moments to realize where I knew him from. Five years ago, he played a string of fresh-faced fighter pilots and eager Marines. Alcohol aged him far older than his actual thirty years and a gut that spilled out over his belt.

"Is that Yancy Cole?" I asked.

"The one and only Yancy Cole," he drunkenly slurred. "Not as pretty and never as sober." He let out a whistling laugh than glared at me. "If it isn't the skivvies queer." He let out a whistling laugh. "I used to want to get into your underwear so bad, and I don't mean the ones that you were selling." He fell over and choked.

"Trevor told you to clean yourself up," Arch said.

After a couple failed attempts, Yancy made his way back to his feet. "I'm not drunk." He motioned to the point. "We're in a marina. Isn't it obvious? I'm just seasick."

Zipporah scooped up some seawater in a bucket and splashed Yancy. He choked for a few minutes, blinking and forcing his vision to clear. She walked over to fill her bucket again, but Yancy threw up his arms. "I'm all right, I swear," he said. "I'm going to put the booze away." He shoved his flask into his belt.

Everyone stared at each other in silence. Arch began drumming his fingers against the side of the boat. "Beautiful ship," I said, trying to break up the tension. "I'm used to going out to sea on battleships. This'll be the closest I probably ever get to a pleasure cruise."

"A couple hundred men in white uniforms," Yancy said. "I figured that would be your idea of a pleasure cruise." Zipporah motioned to the bucket, and he started to cough. "Relax, I'm a sissy, too." He walked over to me and took a cigarette out of his pocket. For a brief moment, I saw the cocky young fighter pilot instead of the lush. "Any chance I can get you to put out tonight?"

The reek of beer sweat and his rancid breath returned to me to reality. "None. I plan on living like a nun until I get my career back."

"Later then," he said, strutting away. When he played a character, the drunk seemed to vanish. "You get your career back, and I'll work on getting my girlish figure back." He looked back and winked. "I'll save myself for you, but don't hold your breath for me." He took another swig. "Rum is the best kisser on the planet."

Trevor arrived twenty minutes late with a young brunette in a white bathing suit in the passenger seat. She giggled and held onto him, acting like the leisurely drive was more suspenseful and dangerous than a drag race. "I would like to introduce you to the lovely Ginger Prentiss."

Arch let out a wolf whistle as she stepped into some open-toed heels and slinked her way onto the boat. She moved with such measured grace that I knew she had to be either a runway model or a beauty contestant.

"Mr. Trecatan found me at the Miss San Diego Cookware competition," Ginger Prentiss said, confirming my suspicions. "I didn't come in first but I was the lucky lady that got cast in his movie."

I extended my hand to be shake but Trevor stood between us with a huge box. "I have a present for you," he said. "Actually, it's a present for all of us. I talked to my sculptor, John Fukada, and he finished monster's costume." He shoved it into my hands. "Why don't you get changed in the cabin? I want my stars to get a look at the monster."

"Sure," I said with a shrug. "Sounds exciting."

I expected a rubber suit like in *The Creature from the Black Lagoon*, but the monster outfit was little more than a kilt made of fake seaweed, fake claws that slid over my hands and feet, and a mask that looked more like a snake than a killer fish. Fukada cut strips of scaled fabric to cover any spot where a zipper or button would be exposed. I took a look at myself in the mirror and thought the costume looked ridiculous and haphazard, anything but scary.

"You're the actor," I reminded myself. "It's up to you to make it scary." I saw Ginger Prentiss giggling with all the boys. "Time to scare the pants off that little girl. Maybe get her to jump into Arch's arms. I owe the guy for letting me stay with him." A part of me was a little jealous. Arch was a pretty man, the kind of boy that I would have chased after in the early days. Those were behind me. I wasn't looking at some cute little queer who would jump into bed with me for the chance at catching some residual fame. Arch was an actor, a friend, and he was straight. As I got the perfect growl, I said, "This is for you buddy. You better not kick me out of the apartment so you can make a salami sandwich with her tonight."

I burst out, crawling on the ground, slithering on my belly, and gaiting like a dinosaur. When I let out my growl, both Arch and Ginger screamed. The blond actor went into character, shaking as he put a protective arm around his girlfriend. His eyes locked with mine, and he took his first brave step toward me.

"What is that thing?" Ginger yelled, honestly afraid. Zipporah tried not to roll her eyes too much. "If that's really an actor, I don't think it's funny. It's not funny to scare people. I hate being scared."

Trevor made a confused face. "This is scary movie. It's a blast to scare people." Ginger glared at him, and Trevor shook his head. "Take the head off. It's not a monster. It's just a man. You might have even heard of him."

"Don't be upset if she hasn't," Zipporah said before taking a drink out of Yancy's flask. "She didn't know who I was."

"Hughie Wildsmith," I said, extending my hand to finally get shaken. "Before I was an actor, I was a model."

She recoiled from me. Ginger looked more terrified of me now. "I heard about a model and actor named Hughie Wildsmith. He was a *homosexual*." She then looked around, expecting everyone else to be shocked.

"He's a nice guy," Arch argued. "He's going to be staying with me, and I'm sure that he's going to be a perfect gentleman."

"You're gay?!" she said, pointing to Arch.

"Ginger," Trevor said, his tone revealing a growing frustration, "he's not some kind of serial killer." He forced a smile. "Gay people are just like everyone else. I'm sure that Hughie likes going to football games and having apple pie. It's really not a big deal."

"If you want me in this movie," Ginger said, stomping her foot, "you've got to fire him. I won't work with someone like him."

"Should I leave?" I asked Trevor.

Trevor shook his head. "How about we take a vote? Who's in favor of letting Hughie Wildsmith play our monster."

Arch never hesitated, just threw his hand in the air. "He's a buddy. And you don't turn your back on a buddy, especially for a girl with tiny boobs."

Ginger let out an exasperated sigh as she pretended to hide her chest. "I can't believe you would say that kind of thing to me."

Zipporah walked over and started to push Ginger toward the side. For a moment, we all expected to hear a splash. "I'm quite a hit with the queens. I've seen a couple of them perform as me. I think gay guys are the only people that ever bought my album of torch songs." She turned toward me. "I have to side with my queens over a wicked, spoiled princess."

Yancy looked at both of us. "I'm a bit of a switch hitter. I bat for both teams." He pointed to me. "Hughie's got the better can." He walked over and slapped me on the butt. "He's got my vote."

"I'm afraid that it's unanimous," Trevor said. "And I'm going to have to find a new leading lady. Maybe I should look up the young woman who actually won the beauty pageant."

"You can't be serious." She was enough of an actress to attempt tears. "What am I supposed to do? You told me that you were going to make me a star! You lied to me. I don't even have a way home."

"You can always swim." And with that Zipporah pushed Ginger overboard.

"I THINK I SHOULD SET A COUPLE GROUND RULES," ARCH SAID
as he opened the door to his studio apartment. "No skins." The room was
even smaller than I thought it would be. Arch decorated the house with
posters of baseball players and a couple cheesecake pictures alongside
posters that advertised all of Trevor's pictures and one of mine.

"I'm sorry," I said, still marveling at how tiny of space we were in. "What
do you mean?"

Arch jumped onto the bed and patted the space next to him. "No skins.
I sleep in my skivvies, and I don't mind if you do." He laughed. "I've already seen you in your underwear. The whole world has seen you in your
underwear. Some of the swimsuits that Trevor's having me wear for this
movie are smaller than underwear." He reached over and gave me a swat.
"I just don't want to turn over and touch your sausage. We're buddies. I
hope that you understand that."

"Sleeping like scouts," I told him, stripping off my suit and carefully
folding it. I jumped on the bed in my briefs, and I felt like I was a thirteen
year old at a sleepover.

Arch looked at me nervously. For a moment, I thought I did something wrong and came across as too casual or flirtatious. "Before I take
my cords off, I should probably tell you something." The younger boy bit
his lower lip and started to blush. "I'm not wearing briefs. I really do love
your underwear, but I saw these things in a European catalog."

He slowly took off his belt and kicked his pants onto the floor, letting
them fall in a crumpled bundle. They were very trim, lighter and less fabric than briefs. They were as colorful as boxers. "They look comfortable,"
I said. "Makes me wish that I was still modeling. I could help bring them
to America." Arch took off his teddy-boy collared shirt and slid under
the cover in his undershirt and European briefs. He gave me a smile and
good night hug before settling into the bed.

"Can I ask you a question, Hughie?"

I shrugged and lay down next to him. For a brief moment, my mind
lingered back to his muscular, freshly shaved legs. When I made eye con-
tact, all pretense of Arch being a sex object melted away. He was just a

friend. "Ask away," I said. "I don't think Harry Ipswich left me a lot of secrets."

"How many guys have you been with?" he said. "I mean, actually been with? According to the officers that arrested Dierk, he had been with a couple people. Some of them were even Nazis."

For a moment, I thought about lying and giving him a locker room answer. The truth came out before I stopped myself. "Four guys," I said, "plus one in high school that barely counted." I laughed at the memory of Whitey Blaylock. "Neither of us really knew what we were doing. It was more kissing and petting than anything else."

"I lost it on prom night," Arch said. "I don't think I did anything right. Probably she started dating another guy the day after junior prom. I bought a hooker later that summer, hoping that she would teach me pointers. I'm not sure if hookers count as real women. After that, I met this colored girl named Amelia Jones at the church picnic. We did a bunch of stuff I'm pretty sure Jesus wouldn't approve of."

"I had a boyfriend when I was in Navy," I admitted. "All of my friends knew but they pretended they didn't know. When we were in Korea, I never got to see him. The life of a combat diver is pretty intense. I did something stupid, and I ended up going to bed with another diver. As soon as my tour was up, our commanding officer encouraged us to go home before the Navy threw us out. The last two were after I started to become famous. Neither of them would really count if the last one wasn't hired by Harry Ipswich to seduce me."

"Do you hate him?" Arch asked.

Without hesitation, I said, "Yes, I honestly wish that the bastard was dead. People like him are nothing but scum."

"Do you mind if I turn on the radio?" Arch said. "I'm used to going to sleep that way. It soothes me to hear music. I've got a pretty early morning tomorrow."

"I'm a pretty deep sleeper," I lied. "It won't bother me." Arch fell asleep before Earth Kitt finished her song, but I was still wide awake. I buried my head into the pillows and wondered how long after Arch was asleep it was safe to turn the radio off. I was about to shut it off when I heard the news bulletin.

Any bit of lethargy left my body the second I heard, "Local girl, Ginger Prentiss, was found dead this evening in the marina. According to friends, she was visiting a man who claimed to be a movie producer and wanted to put her in the film. The cause of death is still unknown. She was found severely mauled. According to authorities, her injuries could be the result of a boat propeller or a wild animal attack. Foul play has not been ruled out and according to an eyewitness the eighteen-year-old girl looks like she had been stabbed nearly a hundred times."

The phone rang, and I tried to wake Arch up to answer it. He just turned on his side and stuck the end of his thumb in his mouth. When it wouldn't stop ringing, I picked up the receiver. "Hello, this is Arch Hunter's house?"

"Did you hear the news?" Trevor said enthusiastically. "The police just interviewed me about the death of that little trollop, Ginger. I guess she decided to hang out on the pier or something."

"Are we suspects?" I asked. "We were the last people to see her alive."

"That's the best part," he continued. "This is great publicity. It was rumored that she was trying to shut us down, but no one knows it's about all the gays and foreigners I hire. They think it's because the movie is too gross and scary. The executives gave me more money. I'll be able to get John Fukada to sculpt a better monster costume. You were great in the lousy one."

"Trevor," I reminded him. "A girl died. We were the last people to see her alive. We should make a statement or something."

"You're not listening to me, Hughie. We weren't the last people to see Ginger Prentiss alive. She called Harry Ipswich. She spent the day with him trying to figure out how to shut us down."

"They think Harry Ipswich killed her?"

"Yes," he said. "We are completely off the hook. The maniac who carved her up didn't leave much skin left. It takes a real lunatic, a man like Harry Ipswich, to commit that horrible of a crime."

"So they determined that it was murder?" I asked.

"With the way that girl was sliced up, it would have to be murder." Trevor let the information sink in for a moment. "This is San Diego and that was a lot of cuts. Do they think some kind of tiger or polar bear swam here just to kill Ginger Prentiss? It had to be a be a sick person. What else could it be? Unless it was our sea beast, it would have to be Harry Ipswich."

THE NEXT day WE MET A young platinum blonde NAMED Dorathea Marie Smith who looked so much like Mamie Van Doren that people would probably mistake her for the actress in the production stills and poster. She was another beauty queen, and Dorie conducted herself like she was at a debutante ball. Arch, just like half of the film crew, was smitten with her. When her equally young and attractive husband showed up with her two-year-old son, most of the men on set sighed in frustration.

Eugene Smith ended up taking off his shirt and filming a couple scenes as a whistling deckhand. Instead of being jealous or freaked out when she saw Yancy start to flirt with her husband, Dorie seemed to think it was cute. Yancy told me that he would have both of them in his bed before the production was over.

The weirdest part of the next few days of filming was that Dorie and Eugie seemed perfectly comfortable leaving their son in my care. They even taught me to how to change a diaper. Arch started to joke that I was a great father and should try the other team if only to have a family.

We loved all three of them, and we were shocked when we came to work on Friday and found Dorie dead on the boat. Arch had some lifeguard training, and he tried to save her but she refused to breathe. The police had to pull him off of the unconscious woman and sedate him. The poor kid was convinced he just wasn't trying hard enough and that there had to be away to bring her back.

They found Eugie and their son in the lower decks, both wet and shaking. Her husband was too far in shock to answer even the simplest question. He couldn't even remember his name.

"What happened to her?" Trevor asked the police.

The overweight man thought about dismissing him, but his eyes kept trailing to the slit in Zipporah's dress. "We think she was murdered," he said, "just like the last girl."

"But she wasn't cut," Trevor said.

The police officer checked his notes. "We're not certain that she was murdered. It could've been an accident. The young woman had been drowned. The thing that makes us think it was foul play is that you normally don't find drowning victims on a boat. Someone pulled her back out of the water."

"Do you think it could be some kind of animal?" Zipporah asked. "The same thing that killed Ginger?"

"There wasn't a mark on her, ma'am," the police officer said. "She had a couple bruises, but she probably got that from trying not to drown. No animal drowns its prey before eating it."

"So it could have been a killer?" Zipporah looked at the water. "Could a man have purposely drown her?"

"It could've been Eugie," I said. "I don't think he killed her, but he loved her. He would've dove into the water to save her. I doubt he's ever been a lifeguard. He probably pulled her out. That's why he's freaked out."

The police officer shrugged, completely emotionless. "Hard to say. I don't think we're getting any answers from the husband. When they look like that, you just drop them off at the booby hatch."

They started to move Eugie off the boat and he was crying and screaming. Five cops had to hold him down. He finally managed to say an actual word. "Monster!" he screamed. We all jumped. "There's a monster!" He looked over at Trevor. "You were right! There really is a sea beast!"

JOHN TUKADA BASED THE FINAL DRAFT OF THE SEA BEAST costume after pictures of the Fiji Mermaid, a well known hoax that used to be dragged around circuses. The head was a modified monkey's face with an eel's jaw and shark's tooth. It had scales running down the back, arms, and legs, and the seaweed kilt was created to make it look like the beast was both masculine and ready to mate. He couldn't sculpt a tail that I could swim in, so he added fins to the claws on my hands and feet.

As I lay in bed, I kept hearing Eugie's words that the monster was real. I tried to put that out of my head. John didn't even base it on a real creature. Only the most naïve schoolboys would be fooled into thinking the Fiji Mermaid was an actual creature.

"Trouble sleeping?" Arch crossed his arms behind his head. "I don't want to have nightmares tonight." His blue eyes trailed over until they met my green ones. "I mean, Trevor gave us the week off. We really don't have to go to bed."

"Do you have something else in mind?" I asked.

Arch sat up, one leg already out of the bed. "I know it might seem kind of stupid after what happened with Dorie…" He leaned back down and told me to forget about it as he stared at the ceiling.

"What is it?" I prompted.

Arch turned toward me. "I don't suppose you want to go to the beach? I mean, it's what I do to cool off. Everything just seems so peaceful and simple when I'm surfing." He let out a disgusted growl. "That probably sounds stupid. The killer might still be out there."

He was right, and I knew that I should've told him he was being foolish, but I saw how he was looking at his surfboard. If I fell asleep, that kid was going to ride the waves without a chaperone. Even without a killer on the loose, that was dangerous.

I changed into my swim trunks and grabbed my mask and flippers. "I could use a good skindive myself. We'll just watch each other's backs."

Arch gave me a smile even though I could see that he was still aching inside. "Thanks," he said, giving me a playful punch in the shoulder. "I really appreciate this, Hughie."

I expected the beach to be deserted with the recent murders, but it turned out a bunch of Arch's old friends were there, and had started a bonfire. Arch stiffened when he saw them, the blood rushing out of his face as he let out a quiet gasp. "I just wanted to be alone," he whispered.

His old girlfriend, Amelia Jones, smiled at him as she danced close to the radio. Her breasts jiggled and threatened to break free of her too-tight gold swimsuit. "Come on down," she said. A bunch of guys started jumping and letting out some kind of primal whoop sound. "We're having a party."

Even though I was still a month away from my twenty-ninth birthday, I felt ancient next to these kids. Most of them were still in high school, and were far more concerned about whether they were going to get spanked or grounded for being out past curfew than the killer on the loose.

I looked over at Arch, who played the part of the normal, carefree teenager. "Do I smell hot dogs?" he said, running up and engulfing Amelia in a hug and planting kisses on her cheek. He slapped palms with several of his buddies and delivered bear hugs to all the girls. Arch was such a good actor I almost forgot how shaken and scared he really was.

"I want to introduce you to my best friend and roommate," Arch said. Amelia stared at me, something sad and angry in her eyes. "This is Hughie." I shook some hands, and they stared at me as the outsider.

Arch introduced me to Bud Caplan, the de facto leader of the tribe since he was twenty-one and still a senior in high school. "Been to several reform schools," he bragged. "My philosophy of life is that it isn't worth living if you don't risk dying." The beach bunnies nodded at his wisdom, and I tried not to roll my eyes.

"Enough with all this heady stuff," Arch said. "Let's go catch some waves." He gave me a scared look and then turned toward the ocean defiantly. "Save me a hot dog, Amelia."

"He idolizes you," Amelia said, standing next to me. "Don't break his heart. A lot of people have let him down." She took a large bite out of a roasted marshmallow. "I should know. I'm one of them. The way he talks about you, I know that he's thinking about his gay brother that died."

I nodded, staring at the boys as they became dots against the black water. "I kind of figured that."

"He lost his sister when he was sixteen," she continued. "He hasn't really had anyone since then." She let out an exhausted breath. "I tried to be there for him, but I'm not ready to settle down."

"Do you love him?" I asked her.

Amelia thought a moment. "I thought I did. I really wanted to. I guess I would be with him if I did." She looked out to the water. "I'm going to go for a swim. It's a nice night for a swim."

I stared at the kids for a while, before I donned my goggles and snorkel. I told myself that I needed some time alone, just me and the fish. The reality was that a feeling that something horrible was about to happen.

Whenever the waves crashed, I heard Eugie's voice. "No such thing as a Fiji Mermaid," I said, putting the snorkel in my mouth and diving into the silence with my flashlight.

I surfaced after sixteen minutes and looked around. My flashlight caught a shadow moving closer to Amelia. I tried to convince myself that it was just a trick of light and the reason why I was rushing toward her was that it could be a some kind of shark about to take a bite of her leg.

The closer I got to the shadow, I saw a human shape. A scaly hand reached out from above the surf, and I saw the glint of long claws. I chewed on the snorkel, spitting it out and screaming to her. She couldn't hear me over the roar of the ocean. The monster got closer and closer.

My naval training taught me how to swim quickly and silently. Within seconds, I was almost up to the girl. She looked over at me, shocked. "What's going on?" she asked.

"There's something in the water with you," I told her.

Amelia was so nervous that she could barely tread water. The shore looked like a mile away to her frightened eyes. "Help me," she whispered, slowly looking behind her. "Is it a jellyfish?"

I prepared for a fight when the monster surfaced. My fist stopped just a few inches short of its face when I realized that it was Arch. He started laughing, and Amelia gave him a mouth full of salt water. "Not funny, Archie," she said. "You scared us both. It would serve you right if Hughie clobbered you."

Arch started to apologize but Amelia headed to shore. "You're not funny," she told him. "I can't believe you did that to me."

He made a frustrated face as he followed her. Arch looked over his shoulder at me. "I'm sorry," he said. "I just wanted to make fun of it. Maybe it would seem less real that way."

The sound of someone screaming caused all three of us to freeze. I looked over and saw Bud panicking to the point that he was drowning himself. Between my naval training and Arch's experience as a lifeguard we managed to get him onto shore safe and sound.

Bud wouldn't stop crying. "I want my mom. Someone call my mom. I need my mom." Amelia screamed and pointed at his leg. "What's wrong?!" Bud sobbed, nearly in hysterics.

I looked at the wound. Something had clawed up Bud's leg, tearing through flesh and muscle and exposing bone. It looked like whatever attacked him did that damage with one attack.

"What was it?" Amelia asked. "A shark?" She started to breathe heavier and heavier. "Was that what you saw Hughie? Was it a shark?" She started crying. Arch held her even though he was as spooked as she was.

"Whatever it was," I said before I could stop myself, "it wasn't human." I took one last look toward the ocean, and I swore something was staring back at me.

We were all surprised to find Eugene Smith waiting for us on deck when we returned to filming. He looked a little tired, but he wasn't a raving lunatic like the police thought he would be. Eugie gave us a nervous smile. "I wanted to thank you," he said. "Thank you for finishing this movie. This picture meant a lot to Dorie. I'm glad that people will get the chance to see it."

Trevor waited for us to stop hugging Eugie before his enthusiasm returned. "I've got great news for each of you. I talked to the executives, and they think that *Sea Beast* could be a franchise. They want me to work on at least two sequels: *Son of the Sea Beast* and *Bride of the Sea Beast*."

"What's with kids these days?" Yancy clapped me on the shoulder. "Shame on you. Having kids before you get married."

"I've got another announcement," Trevor said, raising his voice. "Dorothea was irreplaceable. I'm keeping all of her footage. I split the lines between all of you. Most of them are going to Yancy."

"Should I practice my screaming and fainting?" he asked in a falsetto.

"I am also bringing in two of my actresses from previous films. I created two characters. I'm bringing in a lady to play Arch's mother, a scientist turned housewife. All of the screaming and fainting is going to be handled by Suzee Shang. She would be playing a naïve assistant to Zipporah's mad scientist."

"Thanks for giving me the extra lines, Trevor," Yancy said in a rare instance of actual humility.

"You're a good actor," Trevor said. "I wish you would get off the sauce. You're too young to look like an old man. You start taking care of yourself and lose some of those extra pounds, I'll cast you in the sequel. I could always give your character a brother or have the mad scientist figure out a way to bring you back."

"What's the sequel called?" a familiar, irritating voice asked. "*Boyfriend of the Sea Beast*?" Harry Ipswich's nasal laugh caused me to shake. He lit a cigarette. "That's too subtle. Maybe you should just call it *Undersea Sodomites*?"

"This is private property," Trevor said. "If you don't leave, I'll be forced to call the cops."

"I know that's Hughie Wildsmith under there," he said, starting to walk up to me. Arch stood in his way. "The public has a right to know that this film that will be seen by children has known perverts in it."

"That's the sea beast," Trevor said, his smile fading. "If you approach him again, I won't be responsible for you. He might bite your head off."

"That's the lunatic that approached Dorie," Eugie said. "He tried to get her to take pictures of the sea beast without his mask. I remember him. He was the last thing I remember seeing before blacking out."

"If your little slut had taken my money," Harry Ipswich said, "she would probably still be alive."

"Did you kill my wife? Eugie asked. He looked like wanted to rip the man apart. His tone was calm and anger flushed his skin to fire red. "If you hurt my wife, I'll kill you."

"I didn't touch your wife," he said, starting to take a few steps back. "I'm a moral man. You need to look to those perverts. Everyone knows that gay men hate women." He pointed to me. "He probably killed her. That's why you thought you saw a monster. It was that maniac in a mask."

"I didn't hurt her," I said, feeling scared. Eugie looked irrational, and I didn't blame him. "I swear."

"I know that you didn't hurt her, Hughie."

Harry Ipswich starting cackling like a witch. "I knew that was Hughie Wildsmith under that horrible costume. You're all ruined. I'm going to make sure that your film never gets released."

"You are not a very bright man." Zipporah lit her cigarette. He started to say something, but he took a mouthful of salt water when she pushed him overboard. "Never stand that close to the edge, especially in a room full of people that hate you. That's just common sense."

Harry Ipswich began screaming and cursing, demanding that we let him back on the boat. "I'll sue you," he yelled between gulps of water.

"You really are not very intelligent, Mr. Ipswich," Zipporah continued. "Didn't your mother teach you that you can catch more flies with honey than with vinegar? Why would we help you out if you are just going to sue us?"

"We'll help you," Trevor said, "but you've got to agree to leave us alone."

"Avert your eyes," Yancy told Zipporah, who turned away smiling. "I feel like taking a manly piss." He undid his fly, and we heard Harry Ipswich start to scream. Seconds later, Yancy stumbled over his feet in an attempt to get away from the edge. He tried to say something, but horror tied up his tongue. Urine spilled into his pants, a loud feminine scream left his throat.

"The sea beast," Eugie said. "I didn't imagine it." His body began to shake and then he fell into unconsciousness. Zipporah ran to him, pulling him away from the side of the boat and trying not to panic herself.

The real sea beast studied with me its gigantic eyes. It looked like a twisted mismatch of an octopus, shark, and man. I recognized the long six-fingered hand from its attempts to attack Amelia Jones. Stinging tentacles held fast to Harry Ipswich, infecting him with neurotoxin.

As much as I hated him, I couldn't let Harry Ipswich die. I let my instincts take over, and I jumped into the water. The sea beast moved closer to me, slime drooling out of its mouth. Arch dropped beside me, but the sea beast only cared about me. Its claws prepared to strike, but it moved slow and unsure.

I slammed my fist into its teeth, knocking out several of them and then started pummeling its soft skull. It let out a pained sound and dove under the wave. Arch managed to untangle Harry Ipswich and pull him on the boat.

"What are we going to do?" Zipporah said. "That monster is stalking us. He thinks that Hughie is a rival or his lover or I don't know." She started to hyperventilate, so she forced herself to calm down.

"You've got to kill that thing," Eugie said, still only semi-conscious. "It deserves to die."

Arch looked at the surface of the water, a slight smirk curling on his lips. "I think I have an idea how get rid of it." He walked over to me and put his arm around my shoulder. "I'm going to need your help, Hughie."

WHEN I MET ARCH AT THE BOAT IN THE MIDDLE OF THE NIGHT, he was wearing my swimsuit, goggles, snorkel, and flippers. He smiled around the mouthpiece. "I think he's attracted to you, Hughie." I blinked at that statement. "That monster likes the way you smell or something. I figured if we both wear stuff with your scent on it, we can confuse the monster long enough to kill it."

"Should I go get some trunks on?" I asked. He shook his head and handed me the sea beast outfit. I changed as quickly as possible.

Arch jumped into the water and began dog paddling around.

"Are you sure that's a good idea? I think that monster is following you to the surface. If we don't kill it now, it's just going to murder more people."

"Maybe if I just left?" I scanned the black water around my friend. "Maybe it will forget me and go away."

"This isn't a stray puppy," Arch said. "This is a monster. It's getting to be more dangerous. It was always around. I bet it's been killing people for years, maybe even centuries."

I shook my head. "Someone would have seen it before now, maybe even caught it."

Arch thought a moment. "Not if the creature is smarter than it looks. Maybe the creature is acting like it doesn't know what it is doing. It seems to be targeting you directly, Hughie."

"The monster is just more active since it's trying to get my attention." I hoped that Arch was wrong. "It probably wants to mate with me."

Arch winked. "You can do a lot better."

We waited around for hours, long after Arch started sneezing and I forced him to come onto the boat and wrap up with some blankets. "I really thought that would work," Arch said, trying not to cry. "I keep seeing Dorie."

Before I could respond, I heard the sound of something slither onto the boat. I got up and picked up a spear gun. I didn't need to see the monster to know where it was. For a moment, I hesitated, scared I was about to kill a human. The figure was too big to walk; its tail propelled it forward. I held my breath and fired.

The monster let out an agonized yell, and I saw the harpoon sticking out of its scales. I ran to the spear and drove it through even further. I gasped when the monster's skin melted off.

"No need to hide myself anymore," he said, his voice little more than a series of hisses and gurgles. The creature underneath the monstrous chimera form was covered in blue-green scales and had a decidedly human torso connected to an eel's head and long piscine tail. "Bow to Lord Triton, mortals."

Arch rushed Triton, and he swatted my friend away like he was nothing. Triton's mouth opened, revealing venom. "Did you really think that would work, mortal?" He looked back at me. "You thought you were my mate?" He let out a primal gurgle and snapped at the air. "You offended me. I am the prince of the ocean. Your form was disgusting. You humans portray mermaids and sirens as beautiful women but your mermen are always monsters."

I fired a second spear. Triton dodged to the right but I predicted that move. It hit straight in the right eye, and I drove it forward with a swift kick. Triton broke off the shaft and tried to use it as a weapon. Blood oozed out of the wound and stained his shiny scales a dull brown.

"How dare you?!" Triton yelled.

Arch jumped on the beast's back with two machetes. He dug the blades deep within Triton's hide and twisted. More blood erupted onto the boat. Triton spun and convulsed, knocking Arch off. "How dare you attack me? I am the son of the god of the seas!"

"*Son of the Sea Beast*," Arch said, smiling with a split lip, "is our sequel." He forced himself onto his feet. "You're not going to live long enough to see that." With one great lash of the tail, Arch was back in the water. I told him to swim for the shore, because I would take care of Triton.

"Do you worst, man-lover!" Triton taunted.

The spear left my gun and this time it tasted nothing but open air. Triton charged on me, believing that he could catch me before I reloaded. A spear went through his hand. While he was screaming in pain, I swatted him with the gun.

The agony must have knocked Triton out of it for a moment or two, then he counterattacked with a swipe of his claws. "You humans wanted a monster." He circled me. "I hope you liked what you got."

My chest burned. Triton's claws turned the monster suit into scrap fabric. I pulled off my mask and swatted the monster back with it. On the fifth swipe, Triton ripped open my arm.

"Looks like you are losing, mortal. I was going to keep you alive as a pet. It's too late for that now."

When Triton dived for me, he caught nothing but air. I jumped on the monster's back and pounded his neck and back with my fists. It hurt Triton more than he wanted to admit.

The tail whipped me off, and I scrambled throughout the boat looking for any kind of weapon. I finally found a gaff hook. I taunted Triton into attacking, and then leaped onto his back.

Triton started laughing, about to easily buck me off his back again. I shoved the hook into his mouth and pulled until his jaw started to snap. Blood and bubbles escaped his throat and then silence. Triton was dead.

"You killed the sea beast, Hughie," Arch said climbing back onto the boat and sitting next to me. "I was worried—"

I gave him a knowing smile. For the first time in a really long time, I actually started laughing. I gave him a playful pound on the shoulder, and the boy began laughing as well.

HARRY IPSWICH LEARNED A LESSON ABOUT SUSPICION AND RUMORS.
After years of accusing people of being communists and homosexuals, he discovered that people turn against you the second the word "murderer" is whispered. The law locked him away in the funny farm on the day of the premiere of *The Sea Beast*.

Arch and others convinced me to go to our opening night even though there would be reporters there. Zipporah picked out a suit that made me look like a gangster and wet down my hair. "You shall hardly be the first gay man that I accompanied, darling," she teased.

"Besides," Arch said. "It's not like a B-Horror movie is going to make the front pages. They normally send an intern or two to snap pictures."

Zipporah took my arm. "You are an actor, Hughie. Roll with it."

Arch grabbed me by the other arm. "You owe it to your fans. If someone asks if you are Hughie Wildsmith, just say no." He leaned closer. "You fought a monster and killed it. I think you can handle this."

The first thing that happened when we got to the showing was a pretty blonde intern wearing a cheap knock-off gown running up to me and asking, "Aren't you Hughie Wildsmith?"

Zipporah laughed. "Of course not, darling. This gentleman played our monster." She flirted at the camera to take the attention off me. "Let me tell you. He can be a real beast some times." Everyone laughed along with her joke. "Keep your eyes on him. He is going to be the next Bela Lugosi."

The young reporter flushed with embarrassment. "I'm so sorry. You look just like him." She played with her skirt nervously, trying to recover. "He is an attractive man. He is just..." she let her voice trail off before taking her breath. "So what is your name?"

"Dirk Hunter," I said, saying the first name that came to mind. Arch stopped and looked back, his trademark smile growing on his face.

"Dirk Hunter, huh?" the reporter asked. "Any relationship to Arch Hunter, the lead actor?" The camera shot quickly to Arch, then back to me.

"Yes," I said, walking over and putting my arm around Arch, "I'm his older brother."

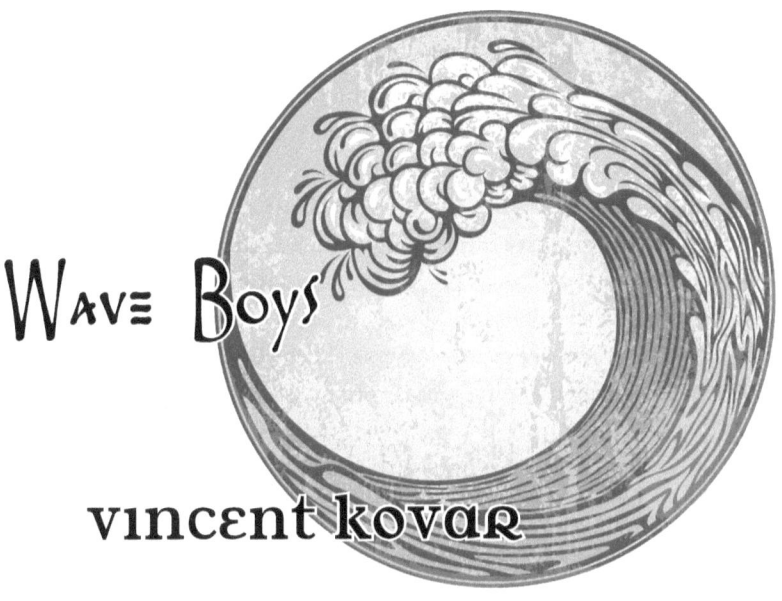

Wave Boys

vincent kovar

Item Catalog #0455-A
Translations made with omnilingua.3.1

----------FRAGMENT BEGINS----------

The boats and barges, junks, single-sails, skitts and catamarans tied up on nine-night, making the third city of the big moon. This city is smaller than the second and third 'cause man o'man the Rooskies are poor losers after a fight. Poor losers until it comes time to sell their stinky Voka or fuck-trade.

This city-time was fighting too. Wattabee and Tat-Tat, his skin all painted over with blue paintings nobody can read, are wrestling on the deck of our boat. Wrestling and punching and sometimes biting so as you'd never know they loved each other like brothers and sometimes something more too. Doobie made a necklace of a pearl drilled through and strung on whale leather that he said he'd tie on the Wave Boy who won.

We's all Wave Boys. Most of us anyway except the oldsters but they keep mostly to the barges and slow-movers anyway. The eight of us: me,

Doobie, Tat-Tat, Wattabee, Gem and Ki (they's the green-eyed twins; the only real brothers), plus Sparks and blind-Zef—we's the Tunder-Boys. We's called that on account of the drumps Tat-Tat's pa taught us to make. He was a thin-eye like Tat-Tat and painted the blue on his skin. He painted some of us too but only pictures of real stuff. Only pictures that we can read. I got a kraken-eye on each ass cheek. Zef's got stars all over his low belly. Most of the other guys have stuff too.

It's part of what makes us the Tunder-Boys though most people don't know that as we usually make clothes to cover our pictures when the cities get made. People see them of course, during Oyo when nobody wears clothes and during market if we want to fuck-trade but that's not the...

----Section damaged/illegible----

...like me an...

...sacred to all Wave Boys...

Tat-Tat throws a good punch and Wattabee spits blood. Not on the deck of course. He spits into the sea, so as to maybe draw the fish. Wattabee has Tat-Tat by the hair see, and pulls him in too close. Should have put him face down but didn't. So Tat-Tat throws two, right into Wattabee's lip. Gem and Ki and Sparks all let out a big whup and I'm laughing. While Doobie and Zef pound the drumps as hard and fast as they can.

We's always having fun like that. The other Wave Boy clans know we's at city. They hear our drumps drumpin and want to play and maybe they will but not now. Now is when we just drump and cheer and fight and let 'em all know the Tunder-Boys are here and we's the best.

Three of the Sea Feather boys come up to the rail to watch the fight. I can't tell if they want to fight or trade or if they just can't pay the pass fee to walk across our boat to the next in city. But I know Sparks has his bow up in the rigging and everybody can see the bone knives the twins got strapped to each arm. Then I see the lead Sea Feather boy giving me the eye and so I give him the eye back.

He's a tall, lean one, with a gandy face and black hair spiked up on his head but none on the rest of him. He smiles at me. A big wide smile. I can see one of his front teeth has a little chip out of it and under his left eye is a bit of purple-brown so I know he likes to fight. All three of them are slicked up with oil. They're out looking to be looked.

I don't smile back. Not yet, though my eye likes him. Instead, I look over the other two, real obvious so I show him I'm looking to look. The other two is neither so tall but they're both hard. The oil and sun makes bright-shine all the grooves in their muscles. Only the lead boy is wearing a loiny. Oily lines carve diagonal down each hip and duck beneath the hide, making a secret. Yeah, he's definitely looking to look 'cause most Wave Boys only cover when they don't want to show their true feeling.

Even over the drumps I can hear Wattabee and Tat-Tat chumping each other. I stare down the Sea Feathers then turn my back. I'm not afraid see, 'cause my boys is watching and Sparks has his bow.

When I turn to look, Tat-Tat is lying on the deck with Wattabee's head on his chest. There's blood in Wattabee's blond hair. His head is bouncing 'cause Tat-Tat's breathing so hard. Wattabee has Tat-Tat half in a hold, one arm around the neck, one arm going between his legs but he's given up trying to lock his hands. They're all worn out now.

Doobie and Zef stop drumping.

"So who won?" I look up at Doobie who has the necklace and his face is all tight with thought. Gem and Ki and Sparks all start shouting their votes but they keep changing their minds and don't make no sense.

From behind me I hear one of the Sea Feathers say, "the yellow-haired one is the winner. He's on top and has the most blood on him."

I didn't have to turn to know it was the smiley one. I know 'cause I got eyes painted on each ass-cheek and it's like they can see even from under my loiny. That's what I like to tell boys anyway. Gem and Ki and Sparks all start to argue but they's just making noise. So, like always, Blind Zef comes down from the roof of the deck house and makes the decide.

"How's he gonna choose?" I know it's the smiley one talking again, trying to get me to turn around so he can look to look. I talk back without moving.

"Zef's the best wrestler. Watch."

Sparks makes some jokes about Zef being a better archer than Sea Feathers too and that makes us all laugh. Blind-Zef though, real serious, runs his hands all over knot of Tat-Tat and Wattabee, seeing with his fingers where our boys touch and where they don't. He feels the blood too, in Wattabee's hair and running out of Tat-Tat's nose.

His fingers are so light that the blood barely leaves a mark on em. Sometimes his touch is so light he can walk on the waves without sinking. That's what we tell the other clans anyway. Blind-Zef also cops some good feels and that makes Tat-Tat and Wattabee giggle a little. Because his light fingers tickle and 'cause he looks to look with his fingers. He knows 'em already. Both of them. He's hammocked with both apart and both together and his fingers remember every inch of skin that's ever been at any Oyo. He probably would know the boys behind me if he touched them. Maybe even if the wind turned and he caught their smell.

Zef says they should share Doobie's necklace and everybody gets real serious then. I know without looking that even the smiley one behind me isn't smiling no more. Sharing a thing somebody made with their hands makes ---WORD UNTRANSLATABLE--- like Oyo only a little bit at a time.

The Sea Feathers respect that and pay their toll to walk over. They pay in feathers that we'll make into stuff or maybe we'll trade on. Who knows?

As he walks past me I snatch one side-glimpse of the smiley lead boy. He feels it and looks over. He smiles again. This time I smile back. I tell him my name.

"I'm White Cloud," he says and tells me it's because he was born with white hair. I look real close and yeah, all up and down him. I can see his hair is colored black because down deep in the depths it's coming out of his head white.

He says, "It's one of our totem-ways. We all make it black with octo-ink."

He lets me touch it and it feels very soft. His skin gets red under the brown when I do.

His boys don't like me touching him though. It ain't Oyo and my own are starting to whistle so I take my hand away and the Sea Feathers pass over to the next ship. I wonder if he's got his own eyes painted under his loiny 'cause though he doesn't turn around, I can still feel him looking.

A few more pass-over and pay up. Some oldsters drop a couple reed mats. One brings a net from some Wave Boys who wear them like clothes. We also get three shar tooth-tip arrows for Sparks from the Hawkers. They's always good with the sharp things like the blades they made from blackrock to shave the sides of their heads. They leave a strip down the middle that stands up like a shar fin. The oldsters call that hair a Mohawk.

Pretty soon we got enough that we can pass-over ourselves. It pays to make city early.

Sparks stays back to watch our ship. Wattabee too. But the rest of us is itching to look and be looked so we gather up strings of shells with holes carved in 'em for trade and head to center.

City always catches my wind but I never let it show. All the masts gathered together like a crowd of skinny giants makes me think there's never been anything so gandy in all the world. There are four junks in a line out from center that the skinny-eyes like to use so they don't have to pay pass-trade. Sweating, big-bearded Vice-Kings, all wearing their fight-shirts of whale bone, are pouring weed-wine for cheap on their single sail oar-ships. We see a dozen jangada and there and here some skip jacks.

I even pay our pass-fare to walk over one of the big clippers— the Spana Boys boat—even though it's not on our way. As we pass, they sing down from the rigging and everybody around stops to listen. Their songs don't make words we Tunder-Boys know but the sound rolls down in loops and dances in my head.

"We shoulda brought some little drumps." Doobie sounds frustrated 'cause nobody is looking him. Everybody is looking the Spana Boys.

Tat-Tat is walking Blind-Zef, they each got one arm around each other's waist to make Zef look like he can see. Ki and Gem walk that way too. It makes Wave Boys talk. Sometimes they say we all got a twin or sometimes they think one of us is blind that ain't. We keep 'em guessing and talking. I try to put my arm around Doobie's waist but he is cranked about the drumps.

He snaps, "I'm going off to get some weed wine."

"We'll come too. Wait," says either Ki or Gem, nobody is sure. They talk sneaky like that. Sometimes they talk together or finish what the other started.

"No."

"Not a Wave Boy without your clan, Doobie." Blind-Zef says it and even if it wasn't the totem-way they'd respect him. Part of me is thinking that maybe I'll see White Cloud again and maybe my boys won't be around when I do. Maybe his won't either.

"Yeah, take 'em with you. Bring back some star fish before Oyo," I say, knowing they will even if they swear about it. They will because I'm the Tunder-Boys bull see?

Doobie stomps off. Walking a gangplank over to an Ice-Bear barge and then on to the next boat.

Ki and Gem walk after him, not too close, 'cause they know he'll be fighting soon. The Tunder-boys never fight alone and they don't want to miss out.

Every clan has their sails tied up and oars stowed but the sun is getting high so they're putting up their shade cloths. Lots of green. Lots of blue. Some gots paintings on their shade cloths, big hawks, octos, many fish in nets. Some gots paintings to read that shout colors about how they think they the best.

I know back at our boat, Sparks and Wattabee are putting up our own shade cloths. Ours is green with a big drump painted over a cloud. It means the sound when the clouds drump and make lightning.

We pay to cross over three more boats. We see Tooney and Fat Bru on one of the Ice-Bear barges in a big cloud of smoke. They's always cook up good food. I trade out some shells so we all can gobble up three sticks of their fry. I have the shells 'cause I am the bull. Ki and Gem and Doobie only got pass-trade. Too bad for them.

Fat Bru ask, "you boys finding Oyo yet?" Fat Bru loves Oyo even more than most. You always find him at the center of the pile and even when he does try to leave he always has Wave Boys holding on like barnacles.

We don't know about Oyo yet but we talk with Tooney and Bru while we eat our fry sticks. The Ice Bears is one of the friendliest clans but they don't playfight like us. When it does come to a fight-fight you always want Tooney and Fat Bru on your side. Just ask the Rooskies.

Us three keep going to center. Over Hawker boats, other Ice-Bear barges and skinny ships of the Vice-Kings. With the Rooskies gone, the Afro-Chan boats are closer to center: the Barbars swinging clubs, the Gold-Teeth and the Zulu-Zannies in their drift-wood hats.

Now that Doobie is off soaking in weed-wine, I can spend the drilled shells without hims moaning. I want to get the Zannies to carve us a big-tittie for the front of the boat.

They say they got plenty made up so I can get one now.

Tat-Tat shakes his head no.

"What you shaking no at me for?" I say and I breathe in deep to make my chest big. "I'm the bull I say when we spend it."

The Zulu-Zannies just stare. Their eyes are like pearls hammered into wood man o'man and their bodies is big fish strong. I don't want to look weak in front of them so I tell him to get down so Blind-Zef can sit. He drops on all fours and Zef sits on Tat-Tat's back. That'll keep him quiet for a while.

I'm looking over the big-titties they got. They got three and trying to haggle it out. They all looking to look Tat-Tat so we might be able to fuck-trade and save the shells but they playin' coy. It's hard to haggle in hand-sign. The Zulu-Zannies all cut their tongues out. Story says that they hate the lie so much they cut out the tongues of all their new boys to keep always the truth. Also, if you lie to them in hand-sign or if they lie to you, they'll cut off the hand that told it.

The lead Zannie is got gold rings in his ears and they bounce as he taps his hand in the air twice. I think he means two shells but when I start to pull them off the string, they all laugh. They laugh with a gargling blow-hole sound as they got no tongues. He taps again to say, two strings. I tap and flip my hand upside down to say two is too much but the Zannie keeps tappin two, two, two.

Tat-Tat lifts his head and shows off his lip which is all nice and swollen by now, but they know Oyo is close so I guess they figure they'll wait. I wished Wattabee had come with his bloody hair. Zannies like blond boys.

We close on two 'cause he knows how much I want the big-tittie. A big-tittie on your boat sees the wander logs that smash open the hull. It sees the sun when you sail east and when you sail west. You got a big tittie and you never go down. Never get lost.

The Zannie and me shake. His hand is bigger than mine and dry. Mine gets surrounded by his, like they is hammocked up. I am sweating a little. While our right hands are locked, I use my left to slide the two strings of shells down my arm and up onto his, up to his big, big bicep. He rolls it the rest of the way, up to the diagonals between his shoulder and arm. Those diagonals make me think of White Cloud's belly. Some Wave Boys would try to reach for another string but not the Zannies. They bargain hard but they honest like the sun.

The big-tittie is the best. She's got hair carved real nice down over the tops of her shoulders and it's stained dark brown. The rest of the wood has gone to a real nice fade and makes her skin parts lighter. Her eyes are painted blue and when I bend down to look, I can see there's little chips of shell in the paint that makes 'em sparkle like they wet. She also has beautiful big lips like an Afro-Chan boy.

Zef stands up to finger-see the big-tittie. He says good things which I like because he is the

---SHAMAN? PRIEST? LITERAL TRANSLATION IS: HOLY-BOY-VOICE-OF-THE-SEA---

With Zef off his back, Tat-Tat stands up and starts touching the big-tittie's lips like they real. Reluctantly, he goes, "yeah okay. She's a gandy one," but I don't need him to say so.

And the titties are big. Man o'man. That's the power of the big-tittie. They gotta be big to keep away the shars and cross waves and kraken. They make the rain come too if you rub the nips with fight-blood. She's the pretty best of all of 'em and I would have paid three strings just to get her.

I feel good about the Zannie boy and I think to look to look for him at Oyo but then I remember White Cloud and decide maybe I'll do with him instead.

The Zannies sign that they will keep our big tittie for us until we come back from center but after Oyo we'll be tired, drunk on weed-wine and walking funny so I decide we'll carry her back now. Passing home never costs. I figure we can wait on our boat until everyone has gone center for Oyo and then pass-over again for free.

"You boys strong?" I ask. It's a taunt.

"Stronger than you." Blind-Zef is probably right. He's as big as Doobie in the chest only not so soft and he's got bigger arms too. At clan Oyo, he's wrestled us all down and I think sometimes if he weren't blind he'd be bull and not me.

Tat-Tat gets insulted. Probably because he's feeling snubbed by the Zannies so he spits on my feet. I look down and he punches my nose hard enough to stagger me. Before you knows it we's wrestling and all the Zannies are looking. I know Tat-Tat is just showing off. So I give him an elbow in his fat lip to make it fatter. He sweeps my feet out and I fall to the deck but kick up fast so as to make his eggs sick in his stomach.

We fight for a while and make it a good fight but I also want to get the big-tittie home and don't have all day to give the Zannies a show.

Zef is hot and tired of standing around so he follows our noise and starts kicking. This sets the Zannies up making hoots in the back of their throats and pretty soon the Gold-Teeth are watching too. Yeah, city is a lot of fun boy.

He may be blind but Zef lands plenty of kicks on us both. He don't care which he hits, he just wants to move us on. I get his toes in the ribs twice and Tat-Tat gets it in the big part of the thigh.

After a while, we're all fighted out so we decide to leave 'em wanting and stop. Zef struggles up the big-tittie on his own but he don't know where from where at city and is as like to fall into the water as get home. I don't want to have to pay Afro-Chans flotsam fee for losing the big-tittie in the sea so Tat-Tat and I get up and help.

Tat-Tat's limping and I am breathing rough. Man o'man. Everyone waves us bye and though we didn't bring our drumps, everyone knows the Tunder-Boys are at city for sure!

The big-tittie is heavier than I thought. It's good wood too. We's so pleased that Tat-Tat signs to the Zannies to come by our boat and we'll give 'em a drump and make ally. They don't sign yes or no. The Bull taps his headdress twice. I can tell he's the bull because his hat is woven in with red and blue reeds. The tap means he needs to think about it. Two times means how long he's gonna be thinking.

I'm not mad at Tat-Tat. I'm the Tunder-Boy bull but his pa is what taught us the making of drumps so it's like that.

Though Blind-Zef can lift the big-tittie all by himself, it takes two of us to carry it as it's so big and awkward. That and Zef can't see where he's going. We lift it over the rails between the Zulu-Zannies and back toward the Vice-Kings.

I think again maybe to send my boys away so if I meet White Cloud they won't be around to hoot and whistle. I think maybe to send Tat-Tat home with Blind-Zef but don't want to leave my new big-tittie. That and nobody's a Wave Boy without their clan. Even so, I keep looking for White Cloud.

Lifting is thirsty so we trade Tooney and Fat Bru six shells for three hits of weed wine and they tell us a story about how they stole their own big-tittie from the Shellies in a fair fight. I lean out over the prow and look down. Their big-tittie is good but theirs don't have the blue shell paint in the eyes and one tittie looks bigger than the other. Even looking upside-down I know ours is better.

After a while I can see Fat Bru's beady little eyes starting to stick too long on our big-tittie and he's wiping the fry on his hands into his beard like he's thinking so we lift off.

It's when we walking along the barge of the Ice-Bears, who wear their white furs even when it's hot like today, that I hear the conch horns of the King's parade. So we all fall down on our knees and faces. Everyone one of us on all the boats grouped around in city. Even the big Vice-Kings, the hair-proud Hawkers and the Gold-Teeth put their faces right down to deck.

As we hear 'em coming close, Tat-Tat and me and Zef all try to block the big-tittie with our bodies so the king don't see it and decide to take it as his Oyo gift.

I peek up and see-tell by the marchers' ink-stained hair that it's the Sea Feather Boys who's won the election. The clans is parading to Oyo. They's all painted the big kraken eye on their chests in bloody red and the oil they put on their bodies is mixed with fish-scales so their skin sparkles in the sun. The king is up on his fancy chair, carried by reps of all the Wave Boys. The mantle of shiny fish-skin and shell is around his shoulders and the crown of feathers is on his head. In between, there's the smile of White Cloud.

Nobody told me he won the election and it's not good to wish it on any other boys except your own but somehow I'm happy. He looks down from the carved and painted chair and I can tell he's looking at me, not our big-tittie, and I am thinking man o'man this is gonna be a good Oyo.

I look for Gem and Ki or even Wattabee but don't see 'em. Then my face gets all hot with shame man because none of the Tunder-Boys is helping carry the King's Chair. I'm the bull but Doobie is the one who usually remembers that kind of stuff and he's off drunk on weed wine and fighting.

White Cloud don't seem to be minding none though. He's still smiling and the carrier boys is waiting. I can't look him in the eye though so I look him over, respecting the knife scars and bruises that say why he's king today. I want to touch them scars. I want to follow them with my fingers and see-touch him like I'm Blind-Zef.

Then comes a thrump, a big thrump, bigger than our tunder and a Afro-Chan junk jumps up in the air before flying to pieces. The boys that been flung up in the air flop around and even from across city you can sense their faces is all confused like, why we flyin' in the air and the boat coming all apart?

The waves makes city ripple, masts and rigging popping up and down like somebody is shaking the rag of the ocean. He is though. We all know who. It's a kraken, come to claim his due from city.

Sunna, everybody is hooting and hollering, running for their home-boats. The King's Chair goes down as every Wave Boy but the Sea Feathers drop it. White Cloud's boys turn, kraken eyes all turning with their chests and looking as he goes down. They none fast enough so I spring up and he crashes into me and we both go down a tangle of skin and crown and noise.

"Take the big-tittie home!" I shout at Tat-Tat and Blind Zef but the next boat, an oldster barge, has a kraken tentacle wrapped around its middle. It don't move so much as it just gets smaller all quick-like and it folds the boat in half with a sound like the time Doobie broke my nose. Only this time everybody hears it and it hurts my ears it's so loud.

Ki and Gem come over a pile of nets carrying Doobie between 'em. He looks like he was drinking then fighting rather than the other way around. There's blood all over his chest and his head is lolling forward. Every time it bobs up I can see his face is all red-wet too. I'd be real proud only now's not the time.

The barge we're on pitches port-ward real fast then back and everybody goes flying down in a pile like me and White Cloud. They're on the other side of the King's Chair and as it slides it scoops a bunch of them off the deck, smashes them through the rail and into the gap between us and a boat of Gold-Teeth that's untied and trying to pull out.

White Cloud and me is pulled out of our knot as we slide down on top of the whole mess then we fall downwards as the boat pitches the other way. The chair and the nets is above us now but goes flying over. White Cloud grabs a ring in the deck and I grab his leg and for a second we's floating over the water watching the King's Chair splash into the foam.

The deck bucks and leaps, trying to get away from the Kraken, trying to get away like the Gold-Teeth boat that tried but didn't make it. Then the two boats clap together like wood hands man. They clap and every Wave

Boy who's holding onto the port side is crunched between the barge and the Gold-Teeth boat. They're not hooting anymore. They're screaming like gulls over and over. Some ain't moving anymore at all.

A mast comes down from behind us, thrumping onto the deck and more boards fold in half, their ends fly up like the hands of Zulu-Zannies signing. The deck swings out toward the water again, not so much this time, not so much the mast comes down on White Cloud and me but enough we can see.

In the waves I can see Sheller Boys face down. They's no friends of the Tunder-Boys, except during Oyo, but some of them is handsome and it's all us against the kraken right?

Now we're not Tunder-Boys anymore, not Sea Feathers or Afro-Chans or Vice-Kings or nothing. We's all just Wave Boys fighting the kraken that's come to city.

There's fire climbing up the masts North Northwest and I can tell that Tooney and Fat Bru's fry has spilled and is making their boat go to char.

City is broken and boats are heading out to all the compass. I see some Wave Boys pull Ki out of the water by his long hair. Some others got Gem too but they see his right leg is torn off leaving insides dangling like red weed. So they drop him back into the water. Ki is screaming because he and Gem is real brother-twins but there's nothing to be done. The Hawkers is got Ki now. He's flotsam and I know they'll do him like they do. If I ever see him again he won't be a Tunder-Boy no more but a Hawker. Outside Oyo that's what make a Wave Boy part of his clan, the other boys doing to him like they do.

There's still a bit of city left. The boat we're on and fish skeleton of others branching off the main line. Blind-Zef is three boats down now and holding up bloody Doobie by the chest. Doobie's feet are dragging and his knees are bent. I yell again at Tat-Tat to take the big-tittie home.

"I'll go give Blind-Zef some eyes," I say and I start to clamber-climb over toward them when there's sharp in my thigh. I look down and see White Cloud has stuck me with his knife. Not all the way in, not so as to hurt but to mark me. I's pissed off as I'm the Tunder-Boys bull and nobody marks a bull except in a fair fight. As I am looking down at my body though, I see a smear of fight-paint from where the kraken eye painted on White Cloud's chest has rubbed off on mine and I know how he's thinking.

Fast like, I rub my hand in the blood on my thigh and put a hand-print of it on White Cloud's face. Now he's black hair, white smile and red print of me—his brown eyes shining between the bloody fingers I've left. Yeah man. Now I am sure sad there's no Oyo as city is all breaking up.

That's when the big bastard lifts his head out of the ocean and gives us a look at his face. It's not just a kraken, it's big Dagon himself. I swear boy. Dagon himself.

His face is like the back of your hand, tentacles hanging down like your fingers only bending every which way. And he's big. Man o'man is he big. He's his own island of greeny suckers and wet fish belly. That's when another junk flies clean over city. Clean over. Scattering screaming handsome boys like a shitting bird dropping its gunk on your deck.

Then I mark White Cloud one more time. I grab the hair on the back of his head. I do it as hard as his black hair is soft and plant a kiss on him. Our teeth crack together and one of us is bleeding. We both taste it I know. It's not a fuck-trade kiss. It's a mark that says nobody is his or mine until we fight at Oyo and decide if who gets the claim. Maybe we both do.

Dagon makes his rattling tunder and everyone is clamping their hands over their ears because it's the loudest racket ever. The sound makes your brains bleed into the back of your throat. The sound smells like sea weed left too long on still water. The sound smells like fish guts when you cut 'em open and throw 'em at your mate. It's everywhere and Dagon's not just chewing fish, he's chewing up Wave Boys. Then he dives back into the deep-deep and a wave slaps us down.

After that White Cloud goes with his boys. Back to find their own home-ship. There's only four of them left so they gots to move before they get claimed as flotsam or their boat does. I get back to the Tunder-Boy boat right as the last branch of city cuts its lines behind me.

Tentacles are springing up like flying fish and splashing back down. Bits of boats is flying behind. Bits of boys. A foot flying naked of its leg. A bit of rib leaving shiny strings of red air behind it.

In between the tentacles shooting up and down is the horizon of sails. To all the compass, until next city. I think, bye-o Ki. Bye-o. The next time I see you, you'll be walking funny and wearing Hawk-hair. Tat-Tat is there with the big-tittie. She's sitting on the deck and her shiny eyes are looking back at the churn we're leaving behind. I'm at the wheel and am wrestling it west. The sails is up and we've got wind but we aren't going too fast. Not yet.

Wattabee is yelling and pissing off the bow to show we're not afraid, not even of Dagon. The boat is pitching and yawing and he's using his hands to hold onto the boat rather than to his thing so the piss goes as much on him as on the ocean. But he don't care and we don't care 'cause after the churn, at the next city, we'll tell 'em all that Wattabee pissed right on the head, right on the very head of Dagon because Tunder-Boys aren't afraid of nothing. I turn around, bend over and yank up my loiny to show Dagon I got kraken eyes just like him. I show him my ass-eyes to say he's nothing and that I ain't scared of him behind me.

Behind us, the sea makes three big thrumps and masts of water spurt up after each one. Some oldsters are dropping their tanks of sod-yum, the water lightning that they make we don't know how. It's all cloud powder that wants to get back to the sky if you try to drown it. Man o'man does it thrump big.

Two Narrow-Eye boys climb on board. They're scrubbed by the sea. Nothing to mark 'em so when we get clear we'll fight 'em and do them like we do and then they'll be Tunder-Boys. They wrap themselves in each other and stay real quiet on the deck against the rail.

Over the side, I hear somebody yelling for help.

Wattabee yells back to us, "I see the beard of a Vice-King and he's crying."

And though everybody is dying all around we laugh 'cause no Wave-Boy should cry in battle.

"What's he say?" I shout back.

"He say nothing. He sink real fast is all."

We know that a tentacle took him from below. Tat-Tat starts to drump on the big drump, the one with our Tunder-drump and cloud painted on it. The passing ships look at us like we're crazy for drumping while death is up from under but we shame 'em all. Far away, a Narrow-Eye boat gets the brave and blows its horns back to us. I turn to the two on our boat, the flotsam boys and tell them to get up and drump and drumble. Pretty soon we's all making a racket and hooting our Tunder-Boy cry out as we head to horizon.

I look around and take a count. I see four Tunder-Boys and two flotsam. "Zef?" I shout out. "Where's Blind-Zef?"

"He's with you." Wattabee says and his words are sharp. I see he's wearing the pearl Doobie drilled. The one he now shares with Tat-Tat.

The other Tunder-Boys stop drumping and are quiet. The flotsam boys stop drumping. They're not made yet and they don't know our rules so they're smart to go still. There's just the waves and the creak and, farther and farther away the horns of the other ship. Tat-Tat looks storm clouds at me. His face says he remembers me saying to haul the big-tittie when we should have been giving eyes to Blind-Zef. And they all remember me hanging on with White Cloud instead of my own boys.

Spark says it also. "He's with you," and I know the vote's being taken. I lost our holy-boy-voice-of-the-sea. When we clear the churn they'll elect the Wave Boy who'll knife fight me to be bull of the Tunder-Boys.

"Where's Doobie?" Wattabee asks and touches the string around his neck.

I know what I have to say but I don't want to. "He was with me, but now he's not."

"Where's Gem?" It's Sparks this time, from up in the rigging. I look up. The sun is behind Sparks and he is a shadow with edges of fire. I can't see it but I know his bow is out. I know a bone-tipped arrow is pointed down at the smear of White Cloud left on my chest.

"He's with Dagon." I shout this, as though it makes it better. Though it don't.

"And where is Ki?" Tat-Tat keeps the ritual going.

"Ki is not with us."

"Who is he with?"

"The Hawkers." This is maybe the worst thing I got to say besides losing Blind-Zef. Dagon taking a Wave Boy is one thing. Another clan doing what they do to one of yours and making him theirs is crime man o'man.

Doobie, Ki, Blind-Zef all dead. Gem is flotsam, so dead to us. Just like the flotsam boys we salvaged is dead to whatever clan that lost 'em.

Wattabee knows the way of things. So does Tat-Tat. So does Sparks is up in the rigging with his bow, honest as the sun. The flotsam are watching us. Their narrow-eyes real wide now. I can see they're not scared of us doing what we do and making them ours. They's scared for me.

I spit at their feet to show them I'm the bull and I ain't feared, though I am.

The challenge is gonna come from Wattabee or Tat-Tat, Sparks don't like to come down from his rigging and he often only fight with a bow. The challenge comes by knives. I make my face grey clouds and look between them. Wattabee is brave and fast but not so good. Tat-Tat is deadly, man o'man. They vote.

Wattabee say, "Tat-Tat."

Sparks calls down, "Tat-Tat."

Then the boy bends at the waist with his legs straight. He shows me the top of his head and then lifts back up.

I figure I got a half-chance of living and a half-chance of dying today.

Hand to hand they pass the long, bone knife. Each Tunder-Boy but me touches the challenge knife. It's as long as Tat-Tat's forearm. It's spotty with tan where the blood of past challenges has sunk into the blade and turned brown and pale. That's the knife I used to beat Chandro, who was bull before me and tough as a kraken. That's the knife my brother Ivan tried, and my brother Otumbe tried, and my brother Brogan tried to stick into me and make them bull instead. I beat all three and fed their blood to that thirsty knife. Then I pushed what was left into the water to chum the fish.

Now my brother Tat-Tat comes for me and even if I beat him I know I'll face that knife again in Wattabee's hand. Because they're sharing the necklace Doobie made and Blind-Zef tied between them.

Sparks asks, "Who will take your stories?"

We argue about this for a while. Sparks can't make the word pictures. Wattabee can but he's not very good so Tat-Tat and I decide we'll take each other's stories. That's the right way of it.

When we hammock up together, we realize how cold we are. We got deep water in us so we put the heat back into each other first to show we have no hard feelings. I stroke my hands over him and he rubs up on me. We wait until we're good and warm then he goes first. I listen to the maybe last story I ever hear and watch his face.

He's older now than when I proved him two years ago. He's got a proud scar from below his starboard ear to his chin that wasn't there in the beginning. Others too. The marks is all good ones though, fight lines. No oldster folds and wrinkly-wrinkles. I run my fingers through Tat-Tat's hair and look for strands like White Cloud but they's all still dark as dark can be. He's a good Wave Boy. Beautiful and wild and strange and keen to fight or hammock equally. His plumpy lip gives his story an extra whisper as it don't always go where he tells it.

He tells me about his pa and making drumps. He tells me the best ways to stretch the skin over the circle and how to make each drump have a voice different from the others. He tells me about all the great cities we been to and how we dreamed about making city ourselves one day. About the Tunder-Boys at center and how all the pass-fares would flow into our boat. He tells me about fights he had with our boys and fights we all had with other Wave Boys. The time we sailed up to a Shellie boat at dark moon and threw fish guts all over them as they hammocked on their deck. The time the Hawkers set our main-sail on fire trying to make us to jetsam but we put it out and we set them paddling away bloody.

He tells me about the fuck-trades he made and times we all got drunk on weed wine and voka. It's gandy to hear it from his eyes. It's like living it twice man o'man. I hear how he dreamed of being elected King of Oyo and being bull of the Tunder-Boys too.

"But not like this," he says soft.

He tells me his story of how I brought him in and how we the Tunder-Boys did what we do to him until he was us.

"I was scared at first," he whispers, so the others can't hear and I know he don't mean the knife fighting but the other thing.

We each take a turn telling it all. We each listen. Then we each write. I look over and see his pictures for reading dance like knife points and I see the ink of my death. I'm not as good at writing it as he is but I do like Tunder-Boys do everything, the best. I'm the bull man. I'm the bull until I die.

Tat-Tat waters out his eyes a little bit and there's not shame in that. Not when you're telling your story and letting the words out all at once. Not when I drink up his story into my bones and he breathes up mine into his. I put my lips on his tears and taste the salt of his water.

Our stories both are almost written when the moon is all the way up. We hammock a couple times, quietly, not to wake the others. This is not like Oyo. This is quiet. Then we took a rest from writing and get up to walk a circle around the deck. Him with arm around my waist. Me with arm around his shoulders.

The other boys are asleep. Blond Wattabee is curled up on top of the pile of nets, the flotsam boys cuddled up on either side of him. Sparks is still up in his sky, in a lump like stowed sails. It looks lonely with just him and his bow but he likes it that way.

For a while, Tat-Tat and me stood at the wheel together and put our hands together on the wood circle, talking. I look at our hands on the wheel. In the dim, our skin is just two colors of dark. Him the dark of storm clouds. Me, shadows on a wave.

I sunna know how much I am gonna miss him. Miss him like I miss Zef, Doobie, and Ki and Gem. I am the bull of the Tunder-Boys so tomorrow I am gonna open Tat-Tat's skin and slash up the blue writing nobody can read.

We come back from steering together to finish our stories. I'm sitting at the table in the deck house with the paints. My fingers is still making what I see into words when I hear Tat-Tat behind me, strapping the challenge knife to his thigh. He makes the words faster than me.

Tomorrow, when I beat him, I'll read his pictures and eat his story just like I ate Chandro's and Brogan's and Ivan's and Otumbe's. The bull is the strongest 'cause he's fed full of the story of all the Wave Boys who came before him.

I can't really see behind me with the kraken eyes painted onto my asscheeks, though I like to tell the other Wave Boys I can. My other eyes just tell everybody, when I show 'em, that I am always watching. It's all the stories in me looking out, watching, even if I can't see.

We'll probably do the challenge at sunrise. I think maybe I should keep my back to the sun when we do. Maybe putting the morning in Tat-Tat's eyes will—

-----------FRAGMENT ENDS-----------

THE ABOVE FRAGMENT (#0455-A) WAS FOUND AT 41.29° NORTH, 118.84° WEST BY THE SURFACE OCEANOGRAPHIC ANTHROPOLOGY EXPEDITION THAT TOOK PLACE CIRCA 5208. THE SCRIPT WAS HAND-WRITTEN ON A SCROLL OF CURED WHALE HIDE AND SEALED INSIDE ARTIFACT #0455 (SEE APPENDICES).

EXPEDITION LEADERS THEORIZE THAT THE SHAPE OF THE ARTIFACT INDICATES IT MAY HAVE BEEN CRUDELY CARVED TO RESEMBLE THE

BUST OF A FEMALE FORM, PERHAPS FOR USE AS A FETISH, MASTHEAD (SEE GLOSSARY) OR OTHER NAUTICAL DECORATION.

BONE FRAGMENTS FOUND NAILED TO THE ARTIFACT (#0455-D AND #0455-E) WERE SCHEDULED FOR FURTHER ANALYSIS BUT WERE SUB-SEQUENTLY LOST DURING A RENEWAL OF NATIVE HOSTILITIES.

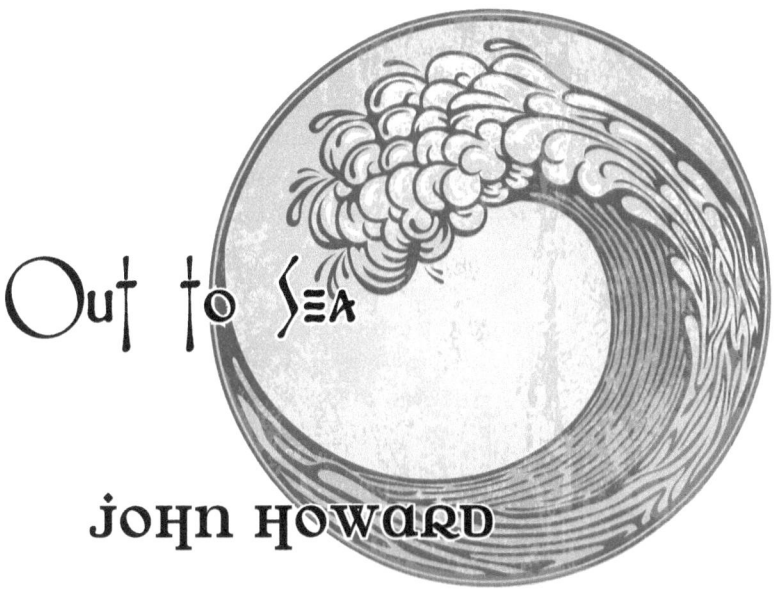

Out to Sea

JOHN HOWARD

For as long as I could remember I was aware of the islands. I could count and name all six in the straggling chain: Folta, Zhara, Ghrau, Ghelp, Laxalt, Riexa. Throughout my childhood and adolescence I never saw the islands, but knew for certain they existed. From time to time I recognized the islands as I gazed into a friend's eyes before drowning in them, or in moments when he gasped my name and shivered in my arms as we embarked on a new voyage of discovery. I grew up into adulthood landlocked, but the islands shone just off the coast, shimmering in the sunlight and as unattainable as the sun itself because of the surging waves and swift, deadly ocean currents. The islands secreted themselves at the back of my mind like an obscure place once described in an old travel guide or delineated on a worn and much-folded map. And as long as books and maps were left lingering on the shelf, neglected and unopened, the islands too were serene, dreaming in a kind of neutral zone, always looming but posing no threats. The pale blue expanses on the printed page surrounding the islands were a part of my mental scenery too, with any possible power to threaten or even just influence rendered all but void.

Over the years I told a few of the people I met about my interest in the islands. Some shared it, but most were merely sympathetic. I found one special friend who dreamed as I did, of the coast and the sea and of undertaking the short journey out to the islands. We discussed the visits we would make, reading and rereading books and literature and gazing at maps and plans. We enjoyed tracing on paper the routes we would take and streets we would explore; even the names of the bars and restaurants we would visit and the wines we would drink together.

His mouth and his tongue, his sweat and occasional tears, tasted of the salt that we knew would sting our eyes as we walked along our beach, bracing ourselves against the warm wind off the sea. Sometimes we wondered what it would be like to leave our city in the interior and make a life on the islands. One night we decided to choose one island each to make our own. Friends sitting at the table with us cleared empty glasses and bottles out of the way, and I unfolded our map. We closed our eyes tightly. And when we stabbed down our fingers on the same island, we all laughed so much that people turned to stare. Although it had been something of a game, we were both relieved that we'd made the same choice. It was a further bond. Friends gathered round and congratulated us.

In the morning twilight I knuckled my own tears away again, rubbing them out of my eyes and licking my fingers. I grimaced as the sharp taste stung inside my mouth. "We are natural islanders," he used to say. "I know it. The coastal towns are lovely, but there's the strait to cross." I had been alone again for some while before I finally resolved to take the opportunity to get close to the islands and see them for myself. One day I opened a dusty suitcase and carefully took out and unfolded the map I found under a mass of outdated guidebooks. The map split itself neatly along its folds, coming apart so easily that at first I thought I was holding several small maps instead of a single large one. But clear to see was the jagged, indented line of the coast, marked with beaches and bays and towns; and apparently so close inshore, the islands, strung out along the coast like sown seeds fallen on the stony edge of a field. The flat blue of the sea—the mere representation of it—churned and drifted as I traced with my fingers the line of brown and green smudges that was the chain of islands nested in their sea. My friends and work colleagues were kind and thoughtful. Not many showed surprise. They urged me to get

away for a rest, a change of scene, to do some exploring. It would be no
problem to take a leave of absence. I folded the map carefully away and
started to make the arrangements.

I arrived in the largest and busiest of the coastal towns at noon on a hot
and clear day. I stood under the shady portico of the railway station and
prepared to venture out into the burning streets. From where I stood I saw
the street leading down towards the bay, descending gradually through
painted terraces of houses and shops. I had bought the latest guidebook
to the town and its immediate environs, which included the three largest
of the islands: Ghrau, Ghelp, and Laxalt. I had read the book several
times and studied the maps intensely. Even before setting out from home
I had planned my route from the station to the hotel where I had booked
a sea-facing room with a balcony. As I strolled through squares and gardens filled with red and purple flowers, I already began to feel at home,
as if I were returning to my native place after a long absence. I made my
way towards to the sea, down to where the promenade followed the deep
curve of the bay.

My hotel lived up to expectation. I was courteously welcomed and immediately shown to my room. The young man who insisted on carrying
my backpack for me unlocked the door and explained where everything
was. With a smile he opened the double doors onto the balcony and in-
dicated that I should step outside. He followed me and drew down an
awning made from a heavy and rough-textured cream-coloured cloth.

"Why, this is a terrace, and not just a balcony," I said. "Will I be able to
eat my meals out here if I want to?"

He smiled again and nodded. I followed him back inside and gave him
a silver coin. "Thank you."

I had pulled out my mobile phone along with my wallet. The lad noticed it and pointed. "That won't work here. In the whole town, I mean.
Or over on the islands either." With a last smile he closed the door behind
him and I was alone in my room.

τнε sky was τall and εмpτy: I couldnʼτ gazε up inτo any parτ
of it without having to shade my eyes against the sun. Behind me the
town flowed up against its hills. Pastel buildings, brick and stone walls,
gardens and lawns—all spread out like a cloth, with one bite taken out

of it as if the sea had once risen up and swept away a crescent-shaped section of land.

At regular intervals on the stone promenade there were wooden benches set under concrete shelters or canopies. I sat down and gazed over the beach and out to sea. It was calm at that moment. I had read that the tides were minimal, scarcely varying from day to day and season to season; it was the currents and surges that ran between the mainland and the islands that were the greatest danger. Their ferocity and unpredictability often made travelling between the towns and the islands difficult and hazardous. It seemed that it was impossible to swim to and from the islands: even though they were not far offshore, no-one who made the attempt had ever succeeded. Only a few visitors would now even consider trying. My book explained that there were no bridges, even though it would be possible to link the islands together like pearls, and then to connect the closest of the islands with the mainland. I found that daring engineering and architectural schemes had been proposed and planned, but there was no evidence that any of them had ever been started.

I had decided that there was no point in coming to the town unless I also actually visited at least one of the islands. I looked up and away from the people on the beach, and out to sea. Between the distant headlands of the bay, I could see the three local members of the chain of islands. Silhouetted against the hot sky and floating on the iridescent sea, the islands solidified themselves from coloured shapes on a map into living stone and soil. It seemed that none of the islands had any large towns or villages; their permanent populations were small and scattered, but when visitors did find their way over to the islands, they were welcomed and fussed over. I read that many permanent residents were visitors who had never wanted to leave.

As my eyes grew accustomed to the glare I made out several tiny black specks, bobbing up and down in the swell of the sea. Although large motor boats were used to transport supplies, equipment, luggage, and almost everything else deemed necessary for life to the islands, they very rarely carried visitors. Anyone wishing to make the journey out to the islands negotiated their fee with one of the many rowers who kept their boats moored at a reserved part of the quay at the bottom of some steps leading down from the promenade as they waited for passengers to ferry across to the islands.

At breakfast on my terrace I drank glass after chilled glass of freshly squeezed fruit juice. The previous night after dinner I'd wandered back out into the town and found my way to a bar in one of the squares, not far from the rowers' quay. I must've drunk nearly two bottles of the spicy red wine produced on the hills above the town. Towards the end of the evening a man who looked only a few years younger than me asked to sit next to me at my table in the crowded barroom, and I remember offering him my bottle to fill his empty glass. He accepted, and we started talking. He had done much more research than I had.

"I'm a visitor here, too," he said. "I'm going out to one of the islands tomorrow. Probably Laxalt, I think. At least, I hope so. I finally arranged my fare with a rower this afternoon. I've been longing to come here for years, and I'm longing even more to get out to an island. I'm not afraid."

"Why would you be afraid?" I asked, more to listen to his lilting voice than actually get an answer. "Why would anyone?"

"Well, perhaps 'afraid' isn't quite the right word. But wait until you look for a rower—your rower. It's strange. Although I've heard about the hiring of the rower and his boat, and the ferrying across, how it all takes place, I never really believed it. Once we knew, I didn't have to work at it at all, only to agree the fee."

"What if you hadn't?"

He thought for a moment, before draining his glass. "In that case I don't think I would've ever come to this town. You're here too, you should understand."

We left the bar together and strolled for a while through the starlit streets and gardens, but I was alone by the time I arrived back at my hotel. We must have taken leave of each other, but I couldn't remember everything. I had a good feeling about him and the evening, though.

Now, sitting under the creamy awning on my terrace, I drank coffee and ate warm rolls broken open and spread with soft cold butter. I glanced at the guidebook I'd put out on the table: I planned to read parts of it again, and I also wanted to use it as a conversation opener when the young man came back to clear the table and take away the remains of my breakfast. He smiled as he worked. I told him what I recalled of my conversation from the night before. As I watched him stacking plates on his tray, a memory of my friend clearing another table in another place and era pushed itself forward, and I reached out for his hand. At the last second I took the book instead. If the young man noticed, he didn't show it.

"I can tell you that fewer come back than are ferried out to the islands," he said. "I was born in this town and have been out to visit several times since I was old enough. It is visitors like you and the man you talked to who have to decide what to do and then hire a ferry for the right price."

I walked up and down the promenade above the rowers' quay. I tried to act casual, as if I were just wandering around, taking in the sun and the fresh salty breeze blowing in from the sea. But I'm sure no-one else on the promenade who took any notice of me would have been fooled.

I leaned on the marble parapet near the steps and gazed down at the quay. Then I noticed my acquaintance from the bar making his way carefully down the steps. At the bottom he looked up at me, shielding his eyes. I thought he'd seen me and was waving; I saluted him back. Perhaps I saw him nod and smile, but the sunlight was strong and I might have been mistaken. He walked over to where two rowers were standing by their moored boats talking. He spoke to one of the boatmen and they shook hands. My acquaintance handed the rower his suitcase and was helped into the boat. Then they rowed away from the quay. I followed their progress as the boat became smaller and smaller, before finally shrinking into a black dot which was lost against the bright green and brown of one of the islands. As I stood there in the hot sunlight I suddenly felt an empty yearning, as if I'd just lost another close and dear friend.

The rower who'd remained on the quay pointed at me, and when he saw that I'd noticed him, beckoned me down. He was slim, taller than me and much younger, wiry and muscular. He wore a white shirt unbuttoned almost to his waist, and with the sleeves rolled high up over his biceps. His skin was tanned by the sun, but looked smooth and clear: not the skin of someone who spent his working days outside in fresh air and sea spray. As we shook hands I felt his strength and the power in his arms.

"You want to go to the islands, one of them out there."

"I think so, yes."

"You do."

The rower looked me up and down. It was the old feeling of being flayed out of my clothes. My mind cycled through the usual imaginings.

After long moments he smiled and nodded, and held out his hand again. I hesitated to take it.

"What will it cost?" I asked.

"What do you wish to pay?"

I did a quick mental calculation. If I left the hotel tomorrow, and then travelled straight home again after my return from the island.... I named a sum. He nodded, and we shook hands again.

"Come here this time tomorrow," he said. "And you will find out if you wish to pay."

The rower turned away before I could ask what he meant. I gazed at his broad shoulders straining the fabric of his shirt as he walked back to the edge of the quay.

The next morning I packed my backpack and checked out of the hotel. The young man I'd seen on my first day escorted me out into the street. I felt like someone who had been dismissed and had to be shown off the premises. But he beamed at me and murmured something about hoping I'd had a good stay and wishing me a safe journey in the future. I wandered out to the rocky fields at the edge of the town until it was time to make my way to the quay and meet my rower. Below me, white and pastel buildings glowed in the sun, and the subdued buzz of activity floated up to me in the still air. I ran my hand over rough stones and felt the stored warmth seep into my fingers. I gradually circled back down through the crowded streets as the time of my appointment grew closer. The weight of the backpack slung across my shoulders was negligible: it felt much lighter than when I'd first packed it.

When I reached the promenade I paused at the top of the steps leading down to the quay. There were several boats moored at the quay, with their rowers standing beside them. Some were chatting to each other; others were talking to prospective passengers. A boat was just drawing away; for a moment I thought it was my rower, but then I saw him standing next to his boat by the edge of the sea. There was a young couple, a man and a woman, talking to the rower nearest the bottom of the steps. The man and the rower shook hands, and the woman started to cry and tug at the man's arm. Then, as he tried to get into the boat, she put her arms around him, trying to stop him leaving. He disentangled himself as tenderly as he could, taking his rower's offered hand to help him into the boat. I was about to walk down the steps when the woman rushed up them and pushed past me. She was distraught and sobbing. I tried to take her arm, but she shook me off and ran on across the promenade and disappeared into one of the narrow streets that opened onto it.

My rower took my backpack and put it down next to the single passenger seat. Then he held out his hand and guided me as I stepped carefully off the quay and into his boat. I think I could've managed without him: the swell of the sea was so gentle that it hardly seemed to be moving. But I couldn't decline the offer of his hand.

"Did you see that woman just now?" I asked.

"That happens sometimes. There can be children too, mainly the older ones. It's best when men arrive here alone. You are alone."

His tone of voice irritated me for a moment. How did he know I was alone? I swallowed, remembering. What did he care? Well, my rower almost certainly didn't care. He was going to do his job and fulfil his part of our bargain—that was all. I dug my wallet out of my pocket and counted out the fee we had agreed on. He took the gold coins without a word.

"You are in my boat—you must want and be able to bear the cost."

"What do you mean?"

"I will row you across."

"Yes, I know, but—"

"You are one of us."

My rower sat down in his seat and pushed the boat away from the quay. Then he took both oars and began to row, surely and steadily, out to sea.

THE TOWN WAS STEADILY SHRINKING INTO THE HORIZON BEHIND us when I realised that I didn't know which island he was taking me to. We hadn't discussed it or agreed anything. I remembered from my map that Ghrau was the largest; for some reason I'd always assumed that I'd go to that island.

"I've forgotten to ask," I said. "Which island are you taking me to?"

"Don't know yet. Wait."

"Surely I need to arrange somewhere to stay?" I didn't mention anything about a return passage. "I talked to a man who thought he'd be going to Laxalt. Maybe the rower who took him is a friend of yours?"

"Laxalt is a good place. Now do be quiet. I must find the current."

So far the sea had been as smooth as a sheet of glass. To my left and right (or, rather, port and starboard, I corrected in my thoughts, smiling to myself) I saw the sea and sky merging in a darker blue haze or mist. I turned to look at the islands. But they seemed no closer than they had from the shore. I couldn't tell which one we were approaching. And back where we'd come from I saw the sun-washed buildings and trees of the town, nestling under the line of brown hills rising behind it. The boat seemed to be hardly moving at all, despite my rower's labours and the gentle swelling of the sea. I wondered what he meant about finding the current. I thought that'd be the last thing he'd have to concentrate on.

Suddenly he began to row faster, and the boat started to pitch and roll, as the swell also increased. Spray started to fly into my face. For the first time I heard waves lapping against the side of the boat. My rower grunted with exertion and sweat dripped off his forehead. I found a handkerchief and wiped the salt water off my face.

"Don't do that," he shouted. "You may swallow the sea but not wipe it away!"

The boat continued rocking in the surge. I began to feel a little sick. We were now going round in circles. My rower seemed to be making it happen rather than trying to fight it. Then I leaned over the side and vomited up what felt like every meal and drink that I'd enjoyed since arriving in the town. The sea swept the stinking stuff away and I felt better. I licked my lips and swallowed the salty water that blew into my face. The burning sensation in my throat started to ease, and I leaned over the side again to scoop up some water in my cupped hands. I rinsed my face and swallowed; as I did so I saw my rower grinning. He let go of the oars, and the motions of the boat calmed. My rower slid the oars out of their rowlocks, and pushed them into the sea. I watched him as if in a trance. Then he reached forward towards me and grabbed my rucksack. He threw it into the sea. It was carried away by a strong current that now ran past the boat, even as we seemed to be becalmed, motionless. The oars were swept away by the current as well. I opened my mouth but no sound came out. I couldn't form any words. Still grinning, my rower leaned forward again and grasped my forearms. His grip hurt. I cried out in surprise and pain. I swallowed more seawater.

"You can bear the cost," he muttered.

Then he pitched us both out of his boat and into the sea.

MY ROWER EMBRACED ME AS WE SLID BENEATH THE SURFACE.
I swallowed freezing water, gulping and gasping, losing bubbling air from
my lungs as I fought against my rower and the desire to scream. The water
pressed in on every inch of my body, swirling around me and invading
wherever it could. My rower still gripped me. I wriggled and fought, but
couldn't loosen his hold. My clothes were peeled off me by my rower or
by the sea. Then I was on my own. I thrashed around, trying to rise back
towards the surface, but I couldn't make any headway against the current.
The billowing silver sky above me tilted away and the water grew darker
all around me. I swallowed more water; but now it didn't taste of salt and
wasn't quite as cold as before.

I thought I saw my rower swimming away, slim and lithe, darting like
a smooth fish. I couldn't remember how deep the channel between the
mainland and the islands was; numbness closed in on my arms and legs
as my head seemed to blow up like a balloon expanding out of control.
I blinked again and again as a dark wall rushed up at me, and became
a floor then a ceiling. My chest and head throbbed with pain. I think I
touched bottom in a cloud of sludge and broken plants; debris swirled
around my knees as I waded through the mud.

The water became steadily more viscous. Now I floated just above a
smooth road, sand drifting across its white and red patterned flagstones.
I glided past the massive bases of enormous broken pillars, the ruins of
the bridges that once connected the islands with the mainland and long
since thrown down and drowned. I still wasn't moving under my own
strength. Once I saw a skeleton. There were a few gold and silver coins
scattered around it in the yellow sand. I reached for my wallet, but my
fingers touched nothing except slick skin.

My rower asked a question for the first time, and I answered: Yes. Air
I didn't know I still held bubbled out of my lungs, up in front of my face
as the silver sky rushed towards me and broke apart. The sun burst in my
eyes, warming my wet body.

DRY HANDS, STRONG SUNTANNED ARMS, ROLLED ME OVER ONTO
my back and then pulled me to my feet. I felt the pleasant sensation of
fabrics against skin—my clothes were as dry and warm as the sand of the
beach. I was led away from the sea endlessly throwing itself against the

sand, too tired to care. They led me to where a flight of steps, cut into the steep rocky slope, ascended from the beach. At the foot of the steps, in the sand, a wooden chair had been planted.

My rower said, "Sit down." He placed my backpack next to the chair, easily within my reach.

I looked at my rower and then all around me. Two sets of footprints trailed back to where I had been lying, next to where my rower's boat had been beached just beyond the reach of the waves.

"This is Ghrau," he said.

A shout of welcome drifted down on the soft breeze. A moment later a man stood in front of me and offered me a glass of chilled amber wine. Condensation dripped from the heavy pale green crystal. I drank it gratefully.

And now I sometimes take the battered old guidebook down from its shelf, or examine the worn and fragile map of the town and offshore chain of islands. I count and name them: Folta, Zhara, Ghrau, Ghelp, Laxalt, Riexa. I drink the cold clear wine of Ghrau and look out over the silky sea to the distant town, its windows glittering in the sun. I remember the currents as well, and look for the rowers at work. Occasionally, when we welcome a new visitor, I carry one of my chairs and a glass of wine down to the beach. And I still remember my rower's words to me before he set off back down the beach and climbed into his boat to row back to the mainland: "You are one of us."

Keep the Aspidochelone floating

Chaz Brenchley

"Well, then," she said softly, menacingly. "Give me one good reason—one—not to kill you. Here and now."

I don't take prisoners, she was saying, *I don't collect ransoms. The living are too much trouble.*

There were heavy splashes from astern, as the captain—the *former* captain—and his officers went overboard. No trouble at all.

I said, "There's only one ocean. One. All the waters of the world, all intermingled, all *talking* to each other, and they're under us right here, right now. Listening to you. Weighing you, weighing me. Is that good enough? Big enough?"

"It should be," she said. High sun glinted off the pocked blade of her cutlass. Another splash came from aft; I didn't look around. Down below, someone screamed: thin and hoarse, I thought it was a man. Or had been.

Her eyes didn't flicker, her blade didn't twitch. I was counting on that. She was solid: sure of herself, sure of her crew. Nothing to prove.

"It really should be," she said again. "Enough. But—you don't buccaneer. No one ever called you Pirate Martin. Did they?"

"No," I said. "No, they never did."

"No. And I don't carry passengers. So…"

The blade was like liquid sunshine in her hand, hot and ready. She'd do this herself if she had to; God knew, she must have had practice enough. She really didn't want to, but she thought she'd do it anyway. She'd be famous, maybe: the one who put Sailor Martin down, the one who sent him to the bottom at last.

That's why she didn't want to. It's not the kind of fame a person looks to carry, even on land. Out here, on the attentive waters—well. If she was hesitating, that was why.

Unhurriedly, I said, "I can cook, though."

Now I'd surprised her. She blinked, took her time, said, "You can?"

"Yes, actually. I can cook for you." Not buccaneer, but feed her and her crew: that, yes. Nothing in that to sear my conscience or darken my long story more than it was dark already. I wouldn't be feeding prisoners, conniving at their capture. What my new shipmates did to those they took—a swift blade and a splash astern—would be on their souls, not mine. I was comfortable with that.

I'd be hanged regardless, if we were taken.

I was tolerably comfortable with that, too.

"Good, then." Her cutlass slammed back into its sheath, and she turned towards the poop. "Help my people get this mess cleared away, I want to round Dog Point before sunset. You're ship's cook, but I carry no idlers; you're starboard watch, and you'll scrub and stow and haul like any of them."

"Aye aye," I said, "cap'n."

FOR ONCE IN MY LIFE I WAS ABOARD A NAVAL FRIGATE, RATHER than a merchantman; for once in my life, I was on the passengers' mani-fest, rather than the crew's roster. I'd come aboard at Port Herivel, seabag on my shoulder and my name like a whisper rolling up the gangplank and across the deck before me: *Sailor Martin, that's Sailor Martin; he'll be luck for us, good luck in tricky waters…*

The captain welcomed me to his poop deck and his table, would per-haps have given me his cabin too if I hadn't insisted on bunking in the gunroom with his junior officers.

"Those pipsqueaks? Unbreeched boys, I warn you, they'll keep you up half the night demanding stories."

"That's my intention," I said cheerfully. "Perhaps I can teach them something. Youngsters listen to me."

He grunted and didn't argue, for whatever brief good that did him. Not half an hour later, I was followed up the gangplank by a woman in black veils and her two servants, one a dusky matron and the other a boy.

I stood by the taffrail and watched while the captain and his first lieutenant went to greet her. After a minute, the captain called for his steward and there went his cabin after all, gifted necessarily to the lady. He took her through to view her accommodations; her servants followed with the baggage; the first lieutenant came thoughtfully up from the afterdeck to join me.

"Who is she, Number One?"

"Florence, Lady Hope. Says she's sister-in-law to Sir Terence Digby, king's man at Port St Meriot. That's barely out of our way, and we're only running cargo anyway; the old man said we'd take her. Between you and me, I don't believe he likes the idea, but…" A shrug said the rest of it: that even the navy bowed to politics, and a wise captain did nothing to aggravate the civilian power.

For a little time, I thought of reclaiming my seabag and treading spry down to the quay again, seeking another ship. I knew Sir Terence, by more than reputation; I knew why the king had sent him to Port St Meriot, and why he'd gone. I knew he had no family, in or out of law.

But I was ever curious, it's my besetting sin and why I can never quit the sea. I held my tongue and settled into the gunroom, amused the lads and tried not to interfere too badly with ship's discipline while I kept a weather-eye on the lady and her people.

She herself kept her cabin, didn't join us for dinner, rarely showed abovedecks and never without her veil. She was in strict mourning, seemingly. Gunroom gossip said it was for her husband, or else her lover: either way, the man who had brought her from England and then had the discourtesy to die of yellow fever, leaving her with no alternative but to fling herself on the charity of an unfortunate but obliging relative.

Her boy had little enough to do, and was apparently glad—at first—to have the freedom of the ship. I found him everywhere, from the lower hold to the higher rigging, gambling with the idlers or racing the mid-shipmen from deck to masthead and down the shrouds again.

After our second day at sea, though, I saw him mostly in the company of the boatswain. Who was a bully, as are so many of his calling; and the boy looked less than happy now, red of eye and bruised of spirit, bruised of body I suspected as he slunk about, obedient at the big man's heels.

Well. No doubt that would be a lesson learned. No doubt he'd find it useful. Myself, I spent my time in pursuit of the abigail as she laundered smallclothes in a barrel of fresh water, stood over the cook in his galley, sat to her needlework high on the foredeck in the late of the day.

Her name, she said, was Delia. Tall and broad-shouldered as her mistress was—convenient, she said, for fitting dresses—she was good-natured and open with it. Firm of purpose, knowing her own mind, finding her own course in life and cleaving to it. Free to do that, serving her mistress because she chose to: "I was never slave. I wouldn't have stood that. A person should be free. If she ain't born to it, she should take it."

As she spoke, her eyes roved the ship, the crew, the set of the sails, the horizon. I didn't need to keep watch myself; I could depend on her to do it for me.

No surprise, then, when the look-out hailed the deck: "A ship! Hull-up, two points off the starboard bow!"

Really he should have seen her sooner. I rather thought Delia had, though from the foredeck we could make out only the scratch of her masts on the skyline. She was adrift under bare poles, so the man had some excuse, but even so I thought he'd probably face a whipping come Sunday, when his officers would have time to attend to it. A warship with a skeleton crew such as ours, reduced by disease and desertion, too few to work the ship and man the guns at once: she needed fair warning above all, to close with friends and keep her distance from any threat.

I should probably have said something to the captain, that first day. Too late now. Captain and first lieutenant both were halfway up the shrouds, telescopes in hand, to see for themselves.

Before their polished boots hit the deck again, I could see the first smoke rising from the other ship, a greasy smudge against the sky.

"She looks to be a whaler," the first lieutenant confided, while his captain paced the windward side of the poop alone, considering. "A derelict, in trouble. We'll go to help. It's our duty."

Duty could bring a rich reward, salvage-fees on a vessel full of sperm-oil and ambergris. I held my tongue. Nothing about this captain impressed me, from his own indecision to the quality of his officers to the manners of his crew. I wouldn't interfere now. I distrusted even his ability to run away.

Even the wind was a conspirator, lying handsome off our aft quarter; in less than an hour we were drawing alongside. Even in his cupidity, the captain wasn't entirely stupid. He'd had the guns loaded and run out, so that we had at least the appearance of a wary warlike vessel in His Majesty's vigilant navy. Every officer bore a loaded pistol, every man went armed.

Even so, that was just routine. The ship was really not expecting trouble.

Even so, I was still exploiting my privilege, lingering on the poop with the officers of the watch, just to see what happened.

What happened first was that Delia swung up the companionway to join us. There was no sign of her mistress, nor their boy.

Delia might be free but she was a woman, a passenger, a servant. The captain merely stared; the first lieutenant moved to evict her as swiftly as he might, as rudely as need be.

"Madam, by all that's holy, you may not—!"

She forestalled him, with a swift nod of her turban'd head towards the other ship. Where a plain red flag had broken out astern, and a boil of men erupted from below.

"My God, sir, they're pirates! Hard aport! All hands, bring us about!"

Delia said, "I'm afraid you'll find that my man has cut your steering chains." Her man, she said, not her boy. I pictured her supposed mistress, as tall and broad of shoulder as she was herself, veiled in solitude. And wondered, a little, what the boy was up to.

The man at the wheel cursed, as it spun freely in his hands.

"Belay that order! All hands to the guns! Fire as they bear!"

"Unfortunately," Delia said, "I don't believe your guns will fire. I'm afraid my boy has been fooling about in your magazine since we boarded, mixing powdered glass into all your gunpowder. He's a skittish lad, so you may be lucky; but if he's done his work properly..."

The first lieutenant tested that, jerking the pistol from his belt and levelling it straight at her face at no more than two yards' distance. She simply stood there, waiting.

He pulled the trigger. There was a flash in the pan, a sullen smoke, no more.

He flung the pistol furiously at her head. She ducked, and when she straightened she had a cutlass in her hand, drawn through some cunning slit in her skirts.

She was just in time to meet his blade with her own. She was a big woman, but even so: a hanger with a man's weight behind it should have been enough to finish her quickly. Somehow, it was not. They fought from leeward to windward, and when they came bloodily apart at last it was she who stepped back and he who slumped boneless to the deck.

That the captain and his other officers had only stood and watched, transfixed—that said all that was necessary about the ship's command. By the time they saw their brother officer fall dead, it was too late to recover. A man in skirts came bulling up from the afterdeck, with his veils thrown back and pistols in each hand; grapnels were already flying across the rail to drag the doomed frigate closer, while the pirate crew came swinging aboard on ropes.

There was fighting down on the quarterdeck, but none up here now. Everyone waited for the captain; what they saw at last was his sword-belt hitting the deck as he let all slip.

And that was the battle, more or less: how His Majesty's frigate *Milford* fell to a pirate queen, with never a shot fired in anger.

And how I found myself eye to eye with her, shortly afterwards; and, "Will you spare the boys?" I asked.

"Perhaps. If they swear to follow me, and if I believe them. Boys can be taught. Don't waste your time pleading for the men. You might be better served by pleading for yourself."

"Perhaps, but I don't plead. Ever. You know my value, you know what I am. You choose to keep me, or you don't."

"Well, then..."

And so I found myself ship's cook and standing a watch, everything next worst to a pirate true. I saw the boys I'd slept with herded over onto the bait-ship, where no doubt they'd be tested and tested. I watched, and wished them luck, and hoped that some at least might survive, for a while at least.

One boy remained, as Delia took possession of her new flagship: the lad she'd brought aboard. I saw him come up from below, scrupulously cleaning his knife. A little later, I saw men carry up the bloodied ruin of what had been the boatswain.

Well, small blame to the boy for that. I remembered the screaming, and still blamed him not at all; I had a fair view of what he'd done, as the men swung the body overboard, and still not. I never did like bullies.

The boy came up and glanced at me, and seemed surprised; turned to his captain with a questioning glance, "Why's he—?" and won the only proper response, a quick cuff to the ear.

"He's our new cook. And you're his galley slave, till I say otherwise. Get below, the pair of you, and see to the crew's dinner."

His name was Sebastian, he said. That was the most of what he said for a while, caught in a fit of the sullens as we scrubbed and chopped. He held our captain too much in awe to disobey even my commands let alone hers, but he was bitterly resentful. He really didn't understand why I was still alive, let alone why he should be set under me.

Matters eased between us when I contrived to let him think that he was really there to watch me, to stand by with that good knife of his in case I tried to poison his captain or set the whole cursed ship aflame.

After that, it was easy enough to get him talking. He was barely twenty yet and mightily pleased with himself and the wild tangle of his life, bubbling over with it, spilling stories. He'd been a stable boy in Jamaica and then tiger on his lady's curricle, until he was snatched in a tavern and pressed into service on a buccaneer. Twelve years old, stolen for his pretty face and given the same choice that faced those boys on the bait-ship today: swear fealty to a pirate and knuckle under, or die.

Sebastian had sworn, smart boy, and survived. Longer already than most pirates did; and somewhere in that lucky life, he'd fallen in love with it. Like any boy he could be vicious and fearful, passionate and sentimental by turns, hungry for adventure and hungry to sleep in the sun. Playing cabin boy to a pirate crew had fed each of those urges and more; serving Delia had brought him to the point of worship, her total devotee. I could have found no simpler way to win his heart myself, than to let him talk about her.

I hadn't planned to win his heart at all, I hadn't planned to stay—one cruise, one port, I'd be away—but even after so long at sea, the sea can still surprise me.

So can a boy. Even after so long, so many boys.

I had him stir the porridge for loblolly, not to let him ruin his precious knife hacking at the navy's salt beef, harder than the barrels it was kept in. In the end I fetched a mallet and a sharpened caulking-iron. Between my pounding and his giggling, we agreed that it was wondrous condescension on her part, that she would eat this with her men; and that let me ask, "How does she come to lead a crew of men, white men, in any case?" There had been women freebooters, there had been black freebooters; probably there had been black women; but not as captain. I was sure of that.

"We elected her, of course. It's the tradition." Then he pulled a rueful face and went on, "I think it was a joke. Our last captain was no use, he lost us too many prizes and sailed us into trouble, time and again. We were hiding out, hungry and afraid with the navy at our heels and hunting. Delia had been the captain's doxy, that's why she was aboard. She was sensible, someone to listen to. Even so, it was a joke. We wanted rid of the captain before he got us all hanged, but you never call for a vote unless you know who's going to win it, and there were too many men who wanted to. That's dangerous. Nobody dared stick his neck out until Double Johnny got drunk enough. He called the vote, the captain asked who stood against him—and Johnny named Delia. Because he thought it was funny, or because it was a measure of how much we despised the captain, or because he was so drunk and the rum so bad hers was the only name he could remember, hers the only face he could make out. I don't know. I think it was a joke.

"But he named her, and when the captain had quit laughing, he asked if she would stand. And she said she would. He already had his hand on his cutlass, he knew just how this would go: of course he'd win the vote, and then he'd kill her, and then Johnny, and that would be that.

"Only he lost the vote. We all hated him that much, and we all loved Delia. So we voted her in. And then he tried to kill her anyway, but she was ready for him. She had a loaded pistol in her skirts, and she blew his head away.

"I think we thought she'd stand down after, and let us have a proper election for a real captain. Only she didn't do that. She took it on herself to be a real captain. She found us safe harbour and led us to a prize; and then we wouldn't have let her stand down if she'd wanted to. She's hard on us, but she's kept us alive all this time; and now we have a warship," unthinkable bounty. And he might want to give all credit to his captain, but he still did keep a little for himself, how clever he'd been, playing servant all those days while he quietly sabotaged the gunpowder and never gave himself or his companions away.

He wanted my applause, so I gave it him; then I traded stories with him. Soon enough his eyes were bugging out, as he finally understood just who I was. Or thought he did. He'd have known it sooner if he'd listened to the crew of the *Milford*, but he was a boy: full of himself and his own daring, listening at first to nothing and nobody but his captain. And then to nothing and nobody but his own sorrows, once the boatswain had him. I had apparently entirely passed him by. I might have been wounded, if I didn't understand him all too well.

Still, he made up now for that neglect. I was famous, all around his limited little ocean. He'd heard the common stories about Sailor Martin and wanted to test them, to hear them again from the source. *Did you really...? Is it true that...?*

He was a boy, he could readily be squashed at need. For now I talked more than I ordinarily do, I told him more than I was entirely comfortable with. I wanted an ally, perhaps a spy, certainly a bunkmate. He was still pretty; he'd do.

Pʀeᴛᴛʏ ᴀɴᴅ willing ᴀɴᴅ ᴛʀᴀiɴᴇᴅ, ᴀꜱ iᴛ ᴛuʀɴᴇᴅ ouᴛ. Bᴇᴛᴛᴇʀ than willing, awed and grateful. I had worried that the boatswain might have killed his pleasure in the act, but one night's careful negotiation took us past that. Gentleness was a revelation to him; so was anything that didn't directly marry my cock with his arse. Soon enough he was melting-hot under my hand, far past caring how roughly I handled him. He was rough himself, with the unexplored strength of the young; making me grunt was a triumph, apparently. Even if it cost him extra chores in the morning.

I took cheerful advantage of his body, day and night, this way and that: any excuse to fuck him at any opportunity, any excuse to heap work onto his wiry shoulders. The more I left to Sebastian, the more I could sprawl at my ease on the foc'sle on a bed of coiled rope in the sun. The captain didn't mind, so long as she and the crew ate three times a day; and she'd been light on crew even before she had to divide it between two ships. Really, feeding those she'd kept on the *Milford* was no burden. Not to me, at least. Sebastian grumbled, but even he didn't seem too outraged.

Our consort, the *Nymph Ann*, showed herself to be a true old whaler by her lines, when she wasn't pretending. She'd probably never been much of a pirate, but she'd made a good bait-ship. Now she offered a good shakedown to new crew, those navy boys. From my rope throne I could watch them being put through their paces, up in the rigging and around the deck, swabbing and holystoning and hauling sail. I saw one of them flogged on a grating, two dozen strokes of the cat; next day I saw a rope slung from the yard-arm and thought I was about to see one hanged.

And so I did, nearly—except that they hung the boy up by his heels and just let him dangle, for punishment or amusement or I know not what. For a while he writhed and begged shrilly, loud enough to carry across the water, while the old hands laughed at him. Soon enough he fell quiet and only hung there, and they grew bored and left him.

They might have left him too long, he might have died, if a boy can die of a blood-flood to his brain; but he saved himself at last, pointing and squealing, trying to cry out as a good boy should.

Someone looked, and called a proper warning to the ship's master at the wheel. He responded with a bellow that sent hands swarming up aloft; I suppose one of them must have taken the time to cut the boy down, if only because he was in the way of the fore course's falling.

The *Nymph Ann* veered close on our starboard, within hailing distance.

"Whale, cap'n! The boy saw her blow!"

"Where away?"

"North and two points east. If he could see her, the boats can reach her."

The captain hesitated, but only for a moment. Then she nodded, yelled her approval, started yelling orders to our own crew.

A simple cruise makes a decent shakedown—but hard sudden work, the chance of danger and the chance of profit makes a better. Pirates and whalers are close kin, half of them have been the other thing at some time; we had enough experience between the two vessels, maybe enough boats too.

What boats there were went overboard, and collected crews to row them. Harpoons came from the *Nymph Ann*, cables from our own locker, courtesy of His Majesty.

"Sailor Martin: do you whale, if you won't buccaneer?"

"I've served," I said, "on a whaler."

"Take a seat in the gig, then. Pull an oar, if you can't throw a harpoon."

I could, but not as well—I was sure—as the lean tattooed creature crouching in the bows of the gig as we pulled away. The whale must have shown again, because voices called down to us: directions, exhortations, blessings on the day. Nothing excites a crew like first sight of a blow.

Nothing is harder than to catch sight of your whale from a little boat on the swell. We rowed to where we thought she had been seen; our ships were no help, having to work up against the wind, soon left behind.

We rowed and craned our necks around, seeking and seeking. We were a fleet of three, the ocean is desert-vast, and whales can swim far and far underwater; I thought we were safe to lose her. I thought we had lost her already. It was almost a relief. Our crews were learning their work, whaling or pirating or both together; and Sebastian was in *Milford's* other boat, and if we found no whale then he was at no risk. That sat more easily in my mind and on my stomach. I hadn't expected to worry for him, but—

"There! There she is! She's logging!"

She was; and she was a cruel unlucky fish, that we should find her adrift, asleep in the water, almost impossible to spot from a boat unless you came right on her, as we had.

Once spotted, a logging whale is easy to spear. We coordinated by voice and eye, gathered all three boats together, hit her with three harpoons at once.

She dived straight down, our cables whipping out hard and hot, fit to take a man's arm if he tried to grip one. But she couldn't stay down long, she couldn't go deep, she'd had no chance to breathe; soon enough the cables slacked as she rose and breached.

Rose and breached and dived again, and now she was dragging us, and what could three cockleshell boats, two dozen men do against such a monster? This was the perilous time, when a boat can swamp or turn turtle, when a whale can turn against a crew, a fluke can splinter planking, men can die.

We hauled on the oars, legs braced: backing water until the shafts bent and our shoulders popped, until we had to yield or something broke. Then we let her pull us, until we'd recovered enough to strain again.

We worked her and worked her, each boat in turn or all together; she hauled us hard, worse when she stopped diving and only swam because she needed the air. Our little boats sheared through the swell, flew off the peaks and slammed back into the troughs, again and again. I never thought they'd survive; I never thought we would. It's always a surprise after a Nantucket sleigh ride, to find yourself and your mates intact.

If you do.

I watched Sebastian's dory when I could, when spray wasn't cutting at my face like knives, when the gig wasn't flying or smashing down into the whale's wake or tossing so hard that we could do nothing but hold on. We lost oars, we lost sight of anything outside that eggshell, we lost hope; we never lost the whale though I thought we must at any moment, the rope would break or the boat would break or the harpoon's barbs would tear free of her blubber and strand us in mid-ocean.

None of that. She slowed, the world lost its madness, the sea settled back beneath us; we recovered what oars we could and backed water one more time.

You can brace and look about you, both at once. Heaving, I turned my head and looked and looked. There was a dory, there were men in it, braced as we were, bending their oars against the whale's pull. Salt spray blinded me and I had no hand free to wipe my eyes; sun was setting, and I had no good light; I had no breath to bellow his name. Nothing to do but haul and wait, haul and wait until that fish at last stopped fighting.

Then, when she lay floating, as still as we had found her, wheezing in great bubbling salt-stink gasps; then we could call from boat to boat. I held my tongue, having nothing useful to say, but youth is loud; I heard Sebastian exult at finding himself alive yet, nothing worse than wet and sore.

I heard him call my name across the water. I heard him hushed peremptorily, hoarsely: "Quiet, lad, no chatter now. You'll start her again. Who has a lance?"

From beyond the dory, no answer. I wasn't sure if there was still a boat.

Our own harpooner fumbled in the shadow of the bow, found a lanyard, pulled it in. Blessedly, it hadn't snapped in the fury of the whale's wake or any of the impacts of the boat on water. At the end of that rope rose a long iron shaft, cruelly bladed. Once that had been in the gig with us; I hadn't noticed it go, being too busy keeping myself aboard. Lucky it hadn't taken one of us with it, or at least an arm or so. A whaler's lance is wicked sharp; it needs to be.

The dory had apparently lost its own. Poor whale. The harpooner stood in the bows as we rowed slowly in beside the floating monster. She was aware, I think, that we were coming; her fins stirred, but feebly. No danger of Sebastian's voice starting her now. I thought she was utterly overdone, we'd exhausted her beyond recovery. Even so, she had sent one boat, eight or nine men to the bottom; and all whales are female, like ships, but this one truly was. A bull would have been half as long again, maybe twice the weight. More spermaceti in its head, more ambergris in its belly, more oil in its blubber—but twice the power too, many times the temper. Never mind boats, full-grown bulls had sunk ships in their time, in their fury. I doubt we would have survived a bull, any of us.

The dory pulled up beside us at the whale's flank. Sebastian didn't risk his voice again, so recently scolded, this close to the monster's shadow. He didn't risk standing, either, let alone the leap I was half dreading: from one boat to the other, his to mine. I saw an arm wave wildly, that was all, and knew him in the murk—and, God save me, I did wave back.

And then very suddenly needed both hands for holding on again, because the harpooner plunged that vicious lance in through the hide of the whale, deep in, probing for lungs or heart or anything that mattered. The great beast spasmed, though she lacked the strength to surge beneath the water. Perhaps she only shrugged in pain; perhaps she meant to swamp us. One small eye caught the last of the sun, gleaming in the vast dark bulk of her head, making her seem more intelligent than she was. Perhaps.

That little movement raised a wave that forced us from her side. Our harpooner left his lance jutting from her flank, preferring to let go than dangle, ridiculous and at risk. By the time we'd baled and caught the oars and pulled ourselves back in, the dory had our place and a man there had the lance.

A man? No—a boy. Sebastian, of course: on his feet and taking a man's task, wanting to impress me. Pulling the lance free of her flesh's suck with one swift draw, that sweet unsuspected strength resolved into grace in shadow; letting the dory's drift carry him a yard down her flank before he drove it in again, power and spring and determination, knowing himself under my eye, coiled at the heart of my anxiety.

Again she flung herself about in the water as that vicious needle struck deep into her innards. Again, her wash forced the boats away. Sebastian was too slow to let go, too young to understand the need or else too focused on twisting the blade, probing for her heart, wanting to be the one who slew her cleanly. He found his platform suddenly gone altogether from beneath him; I saw him hang by both arms from the dipping lance's shaft, and then I saw her roll him underwater.

And then me, me too, as though her one movement had carried us both down. I swear, I never chose to dive. There I was, though, swimming through the dark in quest of him. Something on her hide glowed phosphorescent, like moonlight trapped in water; weed or living creature, I couldn't tell, but by that faint illumination I found his shadow as he sank.

Of couse he couldn't swim, what sailor can? Apart from me, of course. Rumour says that I could log like a whale and drift like a derelict and never need to shift a finger in effort, that the sea would bear me up.

Rumour is an ass. In this and many things. I swim because I learned to swim, the way I learned to handle boats: with work and time and practice.

I swim for the same reason that I sail, because I love the sea, not it loves me. Because it is dark, because it is salt, because it is deadly. Because it is bitter, and because it is my heart.

Dark, but not obsidian; deadly, but not mortal. Not necessarily mortal.

Bitter, but not unbearable. I saw Sebastian, by the grace-light of the whale's hide. I struck down and reached him, found him still clinging to the shaft of the lance. Desperation or good sense, whichever, I had cause to bless it now. If he'd let go, he'd have sunk; if he'd sunk far from that gentle light, I never would have found him.

He wasn't about to let go now, even though I'd found him. I wasn't about to allow him. If he ceased to clutch at the lance, he would clutch at me instead; then we'd both sink. I have seen men drowned by their friends, and I didn't mean to join them.

The whale meant for both of us to join them, but I too can be dark and salt and deadly. The beast had rolled deliberately, I thought, to hold Sebastian under the water. His eyes were screwed tight shut, so he was no trouble to me, if no help. If he'd been looking, if he'd seen me, he'd have lunged, I think. I didn't even touch him. I only laid my own hands beside his, and twisted that lance as sharply as I might.

Poor thing, she'd been trying to shake the boy loose and shed the pain. Now here it was again, worse than before; what could she do but roll up to the air again, and breathe, and suffer?

Sebastian's death-grip was tight enough to fetch him out, no chance of shaking loose. I hung on by grim purpose, through the wrenching tug of that roll; and there we were, breaking back into the world, gasping and coughing and holding on, still holding on as we dangled and kicked above the surface of the ocean.

And there was the dory, seeing us, pulling back to the whale's side: giving us something to drop into, if Sebastian would only let go.

At least his eyes were open now. He stared at me, wild, frantic—and then twined his legs around my waist, a death-grip too late to do harm, and swung us both back and forth.

Working that lance-head in the whale's innards, back and forth…

Finding something, I know not what, but something that mattered. Slicing into it. Bringing one last brutal spasm from the beast, and then a groaning stillness.

The dory came back for us again, and this time I let go, this time it was my turn to practise my death-grip on the boy, wrapping my arms around his shoulders so that all my weight hung from his determined hands.

He laughed in my face, and held on that one last second, long enough to kiss me. Then he let go, and we fell.

Bruisingly, into the crowded boat: oar-handles and benches and other men contributed all their share of bruises, but mostly mine came from Sebastian. He seemed all elbows in my grip, and all deliberate, and all delight. Wet lithe muscled boy, once again exultant and alive; I had to cuff him hard to make him let go, and then again just to calm him. He spat blood and grinned dizzily up at me, settled between my legs there on the boat's boards in the awkward cramping space between the rowing benches and other men's feet, and said, "What now?"

Said it to me as though I were captain, as though the decisions were mine. It ought not to have been true—but the dory fell silent, as though all the men there were waiting on my answer. Across the water I could hear the silence in the gig too, matching.

Into that delicate moment, dying or dead, the whale let rip an abrupt and tremendous fart. Which shattered the tension nicely, throwing us all into gales of laughter; and in the subsiding cheerful chatter that followed, I took an easy charge.

Got a rope around the whale's tail, not to lose her in the encompassing night; joined both boats together with another, for the same reason; said, "We'll just sit out the darkness, lads, and wait for the captain to find us in the morning. She'll come. She'll have to: can't hardly handle one ship without us, let alone two."

"How's she going to come, then, if she can't—ow!"

I suppressed my boy handily, amid another ripple of laughter, and asked who had rum or hard tack in their pockets, tobacco still dry in a pouch, anything to share around to see us through the waiting.

Later, we sang; later still, we slept, those who could, sparing only those on watch. Sebastian could most likely sleep through a hurricane; I hoped to have the chance to prove it, another day, another voyage. For now I cradled the slumped weight of him, felt the slow seize of stiffness in my joints, learned that it is possible for a man's parts to be both numb and excruciatingly painful, both at once.

When he woke, he was youthfully, outrageously limber. Also he was youthfully and outrageously heedless, teasing me and disturbing everyone, knocking men out of their slumbers as he mocked and stretched, making the whole boat rock as he scrambled to his feet to peer into the dawnlight for his beloved captain.

In the end I pitched him overboard, left him to squawk and splash for a minute before I let a man thrust out an oar for him to snatch at.

As we hauled him in dripping over the gunwale, he was still squawking, but not in protest now. He'd swallowed too much water to be coherent, or else he was just too angry—but he was a good boy, he kept pointing and making noise until we turned, until we looked, until we understood.

The sky was pearling to the east, the other way, the way I'd pushed him. Westward was still dark, but it was too dark. Not sky-dark, not even storm-dark: a rising arc of shadow split the night, cut away the stars. Now, in the hush of experience, I could even hear the sounds of surf breaking against rock.

I had not thought we were that close to land, but the whale had hauled us far and far, out of all reckoning.

"Good, then," I cried, pounding Sebastian between the shoulder-blades as though it were his achievement, as though I didn't just enjoy pounding the lad. "Landfall will make our wait more comfortable; there'll be water, sure, and green timber to raise smoke, to tell the captain where we are. Out oars, lads, and haul away. We'll haul our catch to dry land, and be dry ourselves…"

SOMETIMES I AM WRONG AND WRONG. EVEN NOW, EVEN STILL: wrong and wrong and wrong. We came ashore in the false dawn, with our false hopes high; and found ourselves cast on a hard rock, hard and bare and empty. No trees, no habitation and no water. One of the hands talked of an island he'd seen rise overnight, a seething volcano building itself in fury from below; but that had been far to the east, half a world away. There were no such stories here, save the ones he told. In the end I sent him to the high bleak peak of this rock, to keep watch for the captain. He'd have no way to signal her, but she should come in any case, as soon as she sighted land.

If she were anywhere on our trail, anywhere near, she'd come. Even if she knew what little comfort this place offered, she'd still come. Any sailor would. We love the sea, and turn to land like a needle to the north. She'd know to find us here, sure as storm.

Meantime—well. There was no fresh water, and no timber for a fire except what we'd brought with us; and no sailor would ever burn a boat. Even so, more than one hand sat on the ridge-rock shore and dangled bare hook-and-line into the tugging sea. Hope springs eternal, and you can always eat fish raw; and it was always possible that the captain wouldn't come.

That was a possibility we didn't talk about. Every man held it private, in the back of his own skull, with all that that implied.

To one boy, it didn't occur at all. Sebastian was full of excitement, empty of doubts. As full as he needed of rum, perhaps, that too: I thought the men had been topping him up, for his reward for being first to cry land or just for their amusement.

He was a happy drunk, happy and confident and trusting, almost impossibly pleased with himself. He couldn't keep still, but he didn't want to walk. The rock felt rocky under sea-legs, and his triumph floated large and alluring just offshore; he wanted to row around the whale's corpse and relive the whole adventure, show me the jutting lance and tell me how clever he'd been, how kind I'd been to come after him, how wonderfully we'd worked together.

I didn't mind, so long as he did the rowing. One lean lad shifting a heavy gig: the work of it would burn the rum out of his bones and maybe even still his restless tongue. Also, we'd find a privacy on the water that I hoped to celebrate, in the whale's shadow and down between the benches, doubly out of sight from shore. The men would speculate wildly and mock cruelly when we came back to them, I hoped with every justification in the world...

Sitting in the stern, manning the tiller, I got to watch his face as he pulled: all strain and anxiety until he had her moving, until his confidence came back. Then concentration, the determination to do the thing well, not to catch a crab, above all not to splash me more than he could help; then awe at the simple size of the thing, his achievement, the tales he could tell as we came into the windshadow of the whale. A more simple smile, when he looked at me.

An unreadable expression, when he looked over my shoulder at the island at my back. He had no breath spare, but his eyes were speaking for him. I twisted around, and saw a sea-cave rising broad and high, just a little way along the coast from where we'd come to land.

"That," I said, turning back to the boy, "looks big enough to shelter the *Milford* and the *Nymph Ann* too. You may have found our new hideaway, lad."

"Oh, I didn't…"

The protest was breathless and instinctive and utterly meaningless; he thought he did, I could read that all through him. The mighty adventurer, slaying beasts and leading us to treasures. He was almost unutterably pleased with himself.

"You were the first to see it," I said, feeding his imagination happily. "We'll call it Sebastian's Cave—"

"—Sebby's Cave, they'll call it, only you call me Sebastian. You and the cap'n—"

"—All right, Sebby's Cave, but we still won't go in there till we have torches. It's dark, and anything could be hiding out already."

"I want to go now." A dead whale, a tale told had lost all its attraction suddenly, in the face of an adventure not yet lived. It would be the same with me, I thought: right now I was all the world he lived in, as the captain had been before me; sooner or later, I would be a tale told.

It was a boy's life, that was all. Sooner or later, perhaps he'd be a man.

I felt unutterably old, and played that hand as I had to: "I know you do, but we'll still wait. You don't want them calling it Seb's Folly, because it's where you went to die. It looks like a mouth, half-open, ready. Just pretend you can see teeth hanging down, and wait till we have lights. Now row me round to the other side of this fish."

He pulled a face, but then he pulled the oars. Still a good boy.

Still a boy: he sulked, and complained about the stench of it. I laughed, and said, "You should be used to that, sleeping down below. You should *get* used to it. Wait till we flense this fish, before you worry about smells." *Then wait till we fry it*, but I didn't say that. One step at a time. Little by little, let him learn. "Now ship those oars, and come here."

Time and tide, the movement of small vessels on great waters. Sex in the scuppers. It's all one.

While I had his clothes off, I gave him his first swimming lesson. Unless the whale had done that, and all I had to do was reinforce it. All I wanted him to learn was not to panic—which made it really a lesson in trust, which started as it had to, with trusting me. "Let go of the gunnel, Sebastian. Just let go. It's perfectly safe. I'm here, and I won't let you sink…"

Eventually I had him with his arms hooked over a floating oar, kicking furiously for shore. Soon enough, I thought he'd trust himself; sometime after that, he'd learn to trust the water. And probably start calling himself Sailor Sebastian, thinking himself immortal, *the sea will hold me up*.

At the moment he was all effort, more splash than surge, and that good oar was all that held him up. I paced him in the gig, one slow stroke and then another, easy work. I was ready to pluck him out if he exhausted himself entirely, but I thought the whole crew ought to thank me if I brought him back weary to the bone. He could sit in the sun with his good knife and make himself useful as well as decorative, pick limpets from the rocks, give us all something to chew on while we waited for the captain.

We couldn't make smoke to guide her, but oh, she was good. Not four bells in the afternoon watch, and there was a bellow from the peak, a wildly waving figure, our watchman running and slipping and sliding down the long slope, risking bones and softer parts to bring us news.

"I'd have sent the boy up to you," I murmured, once we had him safely gathered in, "if you'd only waited."

Sebastian just looked at me, and went on sharpening his knife. I grinned. "Go on, then. What did you see?"

"She's coming, she's there, she'll be with us by sundown…"

"No. What did you *see*?" There were other ships in these waters, and few of them were friends to us.

He saw the point, nodded, stuck to his guns despite: "Two ships, mast-high. One warship and one whaler, I rate 'em—and don't tell me I don't know the *Nymph Ann*, for I do."

"She might have been gathered in by a king's ship. Which might have sunk the *Milford*, if the captain made a fight of it. If she could. Or the king's men might have taken both, hanged everyone, might be coming now to hang the rest of us."

If they were, there was little enough that we could do about it. Still, we all trooped to the peak to watch the ships' approach. Of course they were the *Milford* and the *Nymph Ann*, that was clear soon enough; we had to wait to see the scarlet shock of the captain's flag, to be as certain of her.

WE HAD HER gig; WE HAD TO ROW OUT TO FETCH HER. Sebastian insisted on pulling an oar, only so that he could lay claim both to the whale and his cave, before any other hand got the jump on him.

Cap'n Delia could manage him, better than any of us. Better than me. She gave him everything he deserved, in due order: praise and encouragement; mockery; a stinging slap to the head when he wouldn't subside.

Finally, after she'd seen all that we had to show her, after we'd brought her to land, she said, "Well, then. There's work to do. Food and grog for all you marooned lads and the lads who came to save you; Martin, see to that. Use the galley on the *Milford*; people will be busy on the *Nymph*. She still has all her try-works from her whaling days, but they're down in the ballast, largely. Someone wriggly needs to haul them out. Sebastian, that's you, and those boys we took from the navy. You'll be in charge down there, but that's not an excuse to slack. I want everything out and set up tonight; you don't get your grog until it is. Don't drink the bilge-water meantime. Sorry, Martin, but we need to boil down that fish before it starts going bad. You'll be on your own today."

THAT WAS NONSENSE, OF COURSE, AND SHE KNEW IT. You're never alone in a ship's galley. Even with half the crew on another ship and half the remainder ashore, with the watch reduced to a bare skeleton few, there's always someone with time on their hands and oil on their tongue, hoping to wheedle a jot of rum, or else a handful of soft tack and a dip of it in the slush.

I had company, then, and I could put them to work, but I did still miss my boy. Which was unexpected and curious, interesting to watch in myself, not easy to understand. Not easy to shrug off. Boys are like deep-ocean swell; they come, they go, there's always another on the way.

This one—well. Apparently I wanted to ride the wave awhile.

I could do that. I could afford the time. That's something I've never been short of.

A HASTY dINNER fOR All, THEN, AS EACH MESS Of MEN WAS relieved in turn. No time for the salt meat to soften, so I gave them hasty pudding. When every mess had been fed, I watered rum for the grog and took that up on deck to serve it out. Last in line, as ordered, came the boys: sodden and stinking, exhausted, elated. Arms around one another's shoulders, leaning into each other even before the rum hit them.

Last of all was Sebastian, proud of his command and proud of their work, determined to show me. I'd seen it all before, but still: for his contentment, I let him row me ashore one more time, a lamp in the gig and fires on the shore to guide us. Not till after I'd dunked him in the sea one more time, though, in the tropical sunset glow. I called it a swimming lesson, and forbore to fetch the scrubbing-brushes.

The men had roamed all over this rock-bubble island while I was busy, and found no beach. Some way down the coast from Sebby's Cave, though, the rock shelved out almost level, like a lip. Here they'd hauled the whale ashore already, secured her carcase with rocks and ropes, drained the spermaceti out of her skull and begun to flense her carcase. Come morning, they'd open her belly for the ambergris; in the meantime, no reason not to start rendering the oil out of her blubber.

The *Nymph Ann* was too old to have try-works built into her deck, all bricked about for safety, as the modern whalers did; so the great iron pots had been set up ashore on tripods, with empty barrels stacked behind and slow fires already lit below them. Those would burn night and day now, until we ran out of either blubber or barrels, depending.

"See, these are the blanket pieces, these long strips we cut straight off the fish. I did one myself, this one I think," nice boy, honestly laying claim to the least of the stacked strips, the shortest and most ragged, "till Twice Tom took the flensing-knife off me. Then we cut 'em into blocks, the horse pieces, I don't know why they're called that; and then they're sliced down for the pot. Bible leaves, Tom says these sheets are called. He wouldn't let me cut those, he says I'll take my hand off…"

He was likely right. I was grateful to Twice Tom, and impatient to quiet my boy, to stop him bubbling over with what I already knew. I knew too well what the bubbling pots would smell like, all too soon; I'd sooner be back aboard before then, or at least on the other side of this island. Besides, the reek of rendered whale-oil clings to clothes and hair even worse than the smoke of a smudge-fire, and I'd only just washed him.

I kissed Sebastian, then, to silence him, and guided him away uphill. He was too tired for the long haul back to the ship, it'd only make him quarrelsome if I tried to take him far from his triumphs; too tired to sleep, he could yet be charming company if I only flattered him a little and taught him a little. The island offered no softness, but we'd contrive.

"Sailor Martin."

Hers was the one voice I couldn't ignore. She was sitting alone in a blaze of starlight, halfway up the slope; I swallowed my sigh, settled on a rock below—the perfect courtier, attentive and obedient and not threatening her status—and tugged Sebastian down at my feet, let him settle against my legs, played with the damp straggles of his hair while I waited to hear what was on her mind.

"I had a look inside that cave," she said, "after the men's dinner, before my own." I knew it; her lamps had been lit from my galley fire. "It's not as deep as I've seen them, but it's even higher inside than it is at the mouth. It'll take both ships with ease, even at the height of the tide, and not a sign to see outside. I wouldn't want to be caught in there in a storm, mind, but if we need to duck a king's ship, that's the place. Hell, I don't think this rock is even on their maps; it's not on mine." And hers, of course, had been the king's before. She'd have nothing more recent or more reliable than the *Milford*'s charts.

"That's good news," I said, which was true, but irrelevant: good news for her, of little interest to me, not what she meant to tell me.

"Yes. Somewhere to run to. All we need now is a reason to run." Here it came. "The *Nymph Ann* doubles very nicely as a whaler, and now we have an honest cargo to prove it. We don't need to take it to Port Royal and let those thieves bilk us for a tenth its value; we can head for Port St Meriot and deal openly for once. Only, not with me on the bridge."

Well, no. News of a black woman pirate captain might have spread through the islands already; even if it hadn't, news of a black woman whaler captain would still raise too many questions. It wouldn't be believed.

"The master can stand in for you," I said.

"He can—but so can you. Everybody knows you, everybody trusts you—and you know Sir Terence Digby. I thought we might pay a call. Word on the water is he's giving a ball."

Likely he was. Everything in its season, and this was dancing weather. Light muslins damped with sweat, candlelight on gold brocade, military boots and dainty slippers, scents of jacaranda and musk in the fevered air.

I understood her perfectly. I said, "I still don't buccaneer."

"You don't need to. You only need to be there, in port, visible. Master of a whaler with her holds full to bursting. Of course he'll invite you to his dance. Of course you'll ask to bring your chosen men: your mate and the surgeon, the specktioneer and the skeeman. A couple of likely boys you think the navy might like to look over. That's your part, all I'm asking. We'll do the rest."

I could imagine the rest. She'd be in the kitchens, with a few more men: fresh fish from the harbour, perhaps, or vegetables from market, rum and sugar syrup from the hills, something. And all Sir Terence's guests in all their glitter, the finest jewels for a thousand miles—and no prisoners, no hostages. She wouldn't change her customs on dry land. The cream of the navy would be at that ball, all the senior officers and most of the young hopefuls; why would she ever leave them living behind her, knowing her face now and hot for revenge? They'd scour the ocean till they ran her to ground. Better to hew a hundred heads at a stroke, leave the navy and its government rudderless and adrift, leave no one to come after her.

"That's not what I signed up for," I said mildly. "I'm the cook."

"You are. And, for the moment, a man of mine." If that was a warning, it was pleasingly oblique: no threat, simply an observation of what was owed and owing. "Think about it. We'll be days here, salting that fish down."

She rose and left. I'd have stood to see her off, but Sebastian had fallen asleep with his head in my lap. For a long time once she'd gone I only sat there thinking, watching the stars wheel slowly around the sky while the moon dallied with the horizon.

Whalemeat for breakfast—of course!—with biscuit-crumbs fried in the grease. The crew gorged, men and boys together; the only one not groaning as he rose was Sebastian, and only because I'd rationed him.

"Oh, why?"

"Swimming lesson later, and I don't want you seizing up with cramps. You've eaten enough. The cap'n wants to move the *Nymph Ann* into your sea-cave first, then the *Milford* after, see if they both fit. Go climb the mainmast, see if you can touch the roof as she ducks under."

He went off happily enough, knowing that if he went up aloft on either vessel he'd be raising sails rather than fooling with the cave roof. The master was a disciplinarian with a ready rod, and the captain was probably worse; and half the men were ashore wrestling with the whale, so it'd be a lean crew managing some tricky sailwork. In honesty I thought it'd be easier to put the men in boats and tow the ships in, but there was pride at stake all around.

Pride has never been my problem. I cleaned up in the galley and then went on deck to watch the *Nymph Ann* through the cavemouth. Looked for my boy but couldn't spot him: not high in the cross-trees, he was probably hauling ropes down below. No matter. Even a vigorous swell couldn't lift the whaler anywhere near the roof; the master kept her on a perfect line and she headed slowly into ship-swallowing darkness.

The *Milford* would be next, but not me. I've headed often enough into damp uncertain nights, I didn't need another. The little boats were all busy, ferrying the working crew from the *Nymph Ann* back to the *Milford*; I gave Sebastian—and everyone else, but I did hope that Sebastian at least was looking—an object lesson in the confident swimmer's entry to the water. One neat dive, down and down into the measureless ocean; I could almost see the island from its underside before the water threw me up again, up and out like a breasting dolphin, vigorous and free.

I swam ashore and dried off in the sun, walking over rocks. First to the try-works, just to see how the men there were coming along: to stand upwind of the seething pots and counsel care with the ladle there, count the barrels filled and sealed, count the exposed ribs of the flatulent giant carcass.

And then away, up the rising curve of the hill that was the rock that was the island; and soon enough down again, to a high cliff-edge that I sat on with my feet hanging over. And leaned down to look and no, not a cliff after all, the mouth of another great sea-cave. And I thought about that, and the stars in their slow shift last night, and the way the moon had seemed to drift on the horizon; and I was almost expecting Sebastian's hail when it came, in that way that lovers do anticipate each other. I was almost commanding it, indeed, that way that lovers can reach out in extremis.

I said, "The captain let you go, then?"

He sat contentedly at my side, swinging his bare heels above nothing: utterly trusting, utterly vulnerable, soon to be utterly betrayed. "She said the men at the try-works don't want me and nor does she, and there's no point leaving more than a watchman on an empty ship, so she sent me to find you."

"Uh-huh." He was, I guessed, my bribe or my persuader, a little of both; she held him in her gift, and offered him to me. He was ignorant but willing, sweet and savage and desirable. I was something close to desperate, even this close to the sea. Normally, properly, that's all that matters; but nothing was quite normal now.

"Go back," I said, holding my voice steady with an effort that I could only hope he was too young to hear. "Go to the captain and say I sent you, tell her this: that Sailor Martin says there's a storm in the offing and a king's ship nearby. Tell her to bring back all the men she can, and stand by. She may need to move both our vessels out to open water, but she shouldn't do it yet. Just be ready. Tell her that. You take an oar and help to ferry, get everyone aboard if you can. Tell her that we'll watch the try-works, keep the fires going, feed the pots. Just the two of us, we can manage that between us. Leave the gig with the *Milford* once you've got them all aboard, and come back with the bumboat. Then we can get to the cave when we need to, to bring word of the storm or the king's men. Tell her that."

He stood, straight and slender at my side; he stared around the long horizon; he said, "I don't see a storm. Or a ship."

I said, "Sebastian. Which of us is a green brat, and which of us has been at sea for ever?"

He grinned. I waited, and soon enough I saw that smile slip as the weight of what I'd said, the reality of it sunk into his head.

I nodded. "Tell her nothing is immediate, but it'll blow up fast when it comes. She needs to be ready now. She should fetch the look-out down, if she doesn't want to maroon him. I'll keep watch. Go."

This time he went, urgent and easy, trusting me as he trusted the rock beneath his feet, as he trusted his captain too.

Τhere was a look-out high on the mound of the hill, watching all the wide ocean. He too would have seen nothing, neither storm nor ship. That didn't worry me. He didn't have my name. The captain might flog him just on my word, that something was coming. It wouldn't be just, but no pirate looks for justice.

Besides, I didn't think he stood in too much danger of her whip.

I sat brooding on the brow above that sea-cave, waiting for something to show. Too long, I thought I'd waited, before at last the sea seethed and surged below me to speak Her coming. She was late, She was slow on Her own behalf. I guess it takes time, all night and half the day, for the heat of slow fires to scorch through a shell as thick as rock, as hard.

Her head was as massive as a ship itself, thrusting forward like the ram of some unimaginable galley before it rose clear of the water on a neck too long, too monstrous. Her eye might have stood for the rose window of a cathedral, if those were ever glassed in black, a single untraced lens.

She looked right at me; I could see myself reflected in that glossy horror, just as a diver sees his own self rising in the stillness of a pool before he breaks it.

I thought She didn't even need to eat me; Her eye would swallow me down.

She'd need to be faster than this. I was already running, while She deliberated. Over the rise of Her unthinkable shell and then down, down to where smoke smudged the air, where the bumboat rocked in the water, where nobody yet knew anything.

Where a figure stood waiting—and a second, rising to stand beside him. Two men, two: and neither one slim as a willow, neither one rushing to meet me…

I was coldly, painfully breathless; it took time even to gasp, "Where's Sebastian?"

"Cap'n took him. She said he's your boy, and you're cook; it's his duty to polish the ship's bell, she said, and he could do that while we all waited for you. Is it coming, then, that storm o' yourn?"

She knew, then. Not the facts or she'd have one ship out by now and be working for the other; but she knew something, not to trust me, something. She was changing her habits after all, using long-established custom to hold one boy hostage. For now, for this little time I had...

Not long enough to take the boat and row that little way, to find any useful truth to tell her. Not long enough to do anything but get there, whichever way I had.

I turned my back on the bewildered men, left them to their smoky fires and seething pots—not long!—and ran again.

Along that flange at the water's edge and up the shoulder of Her shell, to the high edge above what we had taken for a sea-cave: where our two ships lay in companionable stillness, where their crews had gathered in secrecy and darkness. Where I had sent them, to a cold destruction. Where the captain held Sebastian, but would not hold him long. One way or the other.

Straight to that high edge, and straight over.

I have dived into water so still I could see myself come at me. I have dived into the steady swell of the deep ocean, where nothing but myself disturbed the water for a thousand miles all around.

This was...not like that. Even as I went, I could see how the sea's surface bent and stretched below me like a mill-race at a sluice, as great things shifted out of sight.

Down and down I went, purposeful as a hurled knife. As I plunged through the broken surface, I felt the water's familiar grip, tight as a sleeve closing about me; but I could feel the first slow tug of dreadful currents too.

Too fast to be seized, I went down and down, as far below as I had been above; and further yet, far enough that I really could see Her underside this time, the plastron of Her shell. Clad in barnacles and weed but unmistakably floating, more like a vessel Herself than an island; and here came Her flippers, ponderously unfolding to pull Her down below the surface, to cool that fierce hot spot on Her back.

Unfolding from behind those great arches we had taken for cave-mouths, that I'd only understood late and slow, and too late now. What must it be like within the shell there, on board ship and still not understanding, knowing only that the great cliff of the cave-wall was moving, lurching forward, crushing one ship against the other and both against the inside of Her shell, heedless as a man crushing snail-shells underfoot?

What must it be like in the captain's head, thinking *he knew; Sailor Martin saw something, knew something, sent us all into the ships exactly for this, because he knew…?*

Never mind the captain; I was looking for my boy.

Either one of the ships might have been lucky, might have been popped out like a bottle from a cork—but I'd have seen the shadow of her overhead if she was, parting company from the vastness of the turtle, bobbing away. I did look, up into the brightness of the sea-sky.

No ships, no. The great broad blade of Her flipper, undelayed by whatever ruin She had wreaked on its way—and here came the first fringes of that ruin, splintered timbers and twisted ironworks, heading for the bottom.

Timbers and ironwork and a boy, floundering, frantic. Sebastian, with the ship's bell on a rope around his neck, a terrible brass weight to drag him down, sounding his knell for him as he went.

The captain hadn't even bound his hands or feet: just belled him and thrown him overboard, as soon as she felt the trap close about her. Let him struggle as he would, the bell would bear him all the way, irresistible. That was a cruel touch, one last vengeful fling at me, though I ought never to have known it.

Except that I was here, and down he came towards me; and she had taken his good knife, of course, but I had mine. I caught the bell first, and severed that rope with a slashing cut; then I caught my boy.

And shook him hard, and held him until he remembered his lessons, not to panic, not to flail about; and then held him and kicked for us both, kicked for the surface.

We were too deep, too short of air. Even I don't have gills, to breathe salt water; and I couldn't breathe for him. His mouth was closed yet, but his eyes were bulging; he couldn't last. And there were men in the water all around us, not all of them broken or dying yet, dead yet; and those jagged plunging timbers, those were a danger too, though the men were worse; and—

Men in the water and a woman too. Of course she'd never learned to swim, the captain; of course she had weights of her own beneath her skirts, weaponry and harness and whatever else she chose to carry against ill-chance, gold and more. Here she came, easy to know in the chaotic waters with her skirts puffed out around her like a jellyfish, like a ship's bell…

Like a bell, yes. Yes.

Easy to know, easy to reach. Poor Sebastian was dragged by his neck again, though this time it was my arm curled about him; and I dragged him below the margin of his captain's skirts and thrust him upward, past her kicking legs to where the billowing fabric still trapped a bubble of air.

Just a bubble, but enough: enough for him, for now. I held him by the body, and felt it as he gasped, as he breathed and breathed.

Then pulled him free of those entangling skirts, and didn't let him see her as she fell below us: faster now, with that last buoyancy stolen from her, dwindling into the dark. He didn't need that face in his memory, those mute curses on his mind. He barely knew what I had done there, only that I'd found him air from somewhere.

Air for him. None for me, and I can't breathe water—but I can hold my breath longer than most, and think while I do it.

And look around, and see the vast bulk of the ancient turtle sliding by, and act against all obvious good sense.

Tow my boy *towards* that surging shadow, not away.

Perhaps he thought that I was mad at last, mad for lack of air perhaps; he tried to kick against me, to pull me back.

He had no chance of that. I took a tougher grip and towed him on, into the currents of Her passage.

Turtles use their front flippers to drive them forward. Their back feet do quieter work, acting as vanes against the water. I wouldn't have risked this if She was coming at us, but that lethal front flipper was past already.

Besides, we were committed now, caught in the turbulent suck of the water She threw back. Rolled over and tossed about, I clung and kicked and maybe prayed a little; and saw what I was looking for, a break in a mighty wall, a gateway not quite blocked by the massive limb protruding through it…

You can trap air in a skirt, until it leaks out in a thousand streams of bubbles. You can trap air in a bell, and it won't leak; make a bell big enough, you can lower a man to the sea-bed and have him breathing all the way.

How much air can you trap in a cave, if your island takes a dive?

Enough, there'll be enough.

I hauled Sebastian in, and the water flung us up, and there was air; and even a hint of light, that same phosphorescence that had clung to the whale. Enough to show that we floated in a chamber where half the wall was rigid shell and half was shifting leather, the obscene leg of the thing. It looked like seamed rock, but no rock ever moved with such purpose, this way and that like the rudder of a ship under steerage-weigh.

Everything about Her was slow and mighty; She had no reason to heed us little things. I helped Sebastian pull himself out of the water, up onto a ledge of Her leg, and found just strength enough to follow.

Then we lay against each other and only breathed awhile, painfully, gratefully.

When he spoke at last, his voice sounded strange in that strange space, distant and muffled and hollow all three. He said, "We, we're inside it. Aren't we?"

"Her," I said. All ships, all whales. All giant turtles, seemingly. It felt right. "I suppose we are."

"Like Jonah."

"Something like Jonah. Not swallowed, though."

He thought about that, then said, "What happens now?"

I didn't know, but lying's easy in the dark. I said, "She won't stay down long. When She rises, we'll go out and see where we are, who's about. There'll be someone to signal, or land we can reach. We'll be famous, shipwrecked mariners who survived Leviathan, like St Brendan survived Jasconius."

His head was on my thigh, wet and warm and welcome. He sounded sleepy, like a child; he said, "You're famous already."

"I am, I suppose. Not for anything particularly praiseworthy. Just for surviving, mostly; and here I am again. Doing that. And here you are, doing it right alongside me."

"I'll be a part of your story." No self-deception there. The fact of it, the act of it, the being with me: that could only ever be temporary, in the nature of the thing. He knew. But the story of it, that goes on for ever.

"You will," I said, toying fondly with his ear. "And you'll tell it yourself, to Sir Terence Digby yet; he'll invite us to his ball, and we'll dress up fine and dance all night," and take no prisoners and do no harm and perhaps Sir Terence could find a berth for him, some other life that he could love, not buccaneering. And perhaps I'd be there with him for a while, be a part of his story, however briefly told. "It'll be a masked ball, naturally. You can go as a pirate boy, you'll like that. Yo ho," I said, "Sebastian."

contributors

Chaz Brenchley has been making a living as a writer since the age of eighteen. He is the author of nine thrillers, most recently *Shelter*, and two fantasy series, *The Books of Outremer* and *Selling Water by the River*. As Daniel Fox, he has published a Chinese-based fantasy series, beginning with *Dragon in Chains*; as Ben Macallan, an urban fantasy, *Desdaemona*. A British Fantasy Award winner, he has also published books for children and more than five hundred short stories in various genres. His time as crimewriter-in-residence on a sculpture project in Sunderland resulted in the collection *Blood Waters*. His first play, *A Cold Coming*, was performed and then toured in 2007. He is a prizewinning ex-poet, and has been writer in residence at the University of Northumbria. He was Northern Writer of the Year 2000. Chaz has recently moved from Newcastle to California, with two squabbling cats and a famous teddy bear.

Nathan Burgoine lives in Ottawa, Canada with his husband, Daniel. His previous short stories appear in *Fool for Love*, *Blood Sacraments*, *Tented*, and *Boys of Summer*. He has nonfiction works in *I Like it Like That* and *5x5 Literary Magazine*. He has listened to the ocean at both sides of Canada.

Brandon Cracratt lives with his partner and a black cat in the historic district of Tucson, AZ. His stories have appeared in several anthologies, including *Look What I Found, WTF?, Scribing Ibis*, and *Night Gypsy*. He has also written plays, screenplays, articles, and is currently at work on his first novel.

Jonathan Harper lives in Northern Virginia and received his MFA from American University in 2010. His writing has most recently appeared in *Chelsea Station* and *DefenestrationMag* as well as the anthologies *Homewrecker: An Adultery Reader, Wilde Stories 2008* and *The Lost Library*. In 2012, he received a residency at The Writer's Colony at Dairy Hollow. He is currently at work on a short story collection.

John Howard was born in London in 1961. His fiction has appeared in several anthologies and the collections *The Silver Voices* and *Secret Europe* (2012). He is also author of a novella, *The Defeat of Grief*. His collaborations with Mark Valentine appeared in *The Collected Connoisseur*. He contributed essays to the books *Black Prometheus: A Critical Study of Karl Edward Wagner, Fritz Leiber: Critical Essays*, and *The Man Who Collected Psychos: Critical Essays on Robert Bloch*, all edited by Benjamin Szumskyj. He has reviewed genre books for a wide range of magazines and society journals for thirty years.

Alex Jeffers's short fiction has appeared in many magazines and anthologies, including several edited by Steve Berman. *You Will Meet a Stranger Far from Home*, a collection of wonder stories, is published this year. His other books are *Safe as Houses*, a novel; *Do You Remember Tulum?* and *The New People*, short novels; and *The Abode of Bliss*, a novel-length story sequence. He lives in New England, merciful and compassionate God alone knows why, and at sentenceandparagraph.com.

Vincent Kovar is a writer, journalist, playwright and professor living in Washington State. He is founding editor and curator of the Gay City anthology series and recently was a collaborating playwright on a stage version of HP Lovecraft's *Pickman's Model* and on Gay City Health Project's *The Infection Monologues*. He has previously performed on stage and in independent films such as the gay-zombie spoof *Creatures from the Pink Lagoon.* His fiction has appeared in *Hardcore Hardboiled,* edited by Todd Robinson, and in *Hot Gay Erotica,* edited by Richard Labonté. Vincent is also hard at work on a novel. He can be contacted via his website: vincentkovar.com.

Joel Lane is a British novelist, short story writer, poet, critic and anthology editor. He has twice received the British Fantasy Award. Nine Arches Press recently released a chapbook, *Do Not Pass Go.*

Jeff Mann has published two novellas, *Devoured,* included in *Masters of Midnight: Erotic Tales of the Vampire,* and *Camp Allegheny,* included in *History's Passion: Stories of Sex Before Stonewall;* two novels, *Fog: A Novel of Desire and Reprisal* and *Purgatory: A Novel of the Civil War;* a book of poetry and memoir, *Loving Mountains, Loving Men;* a volume of short fiction, *A History of Barbed Wire,* which won a Lambda Literary Award; and assorted erotic tales involving Vikings, werewolves, sea sprites, faeries, and the thirsty undead. He teaches creative writing at Virginia Tech in Blacksburg, Virginia.

Matthew Merendo grew up in a small suburb twice-removed of Pittsburgh, Pennsylvania. He is a Taurus who does not like long walks on the beach, small children, or large bugs. He does not like large bugs, either. He does, however, enjoy the color purple, beach scenes when viewed through the windows of a gorgeous beach house, and snow. He firmly believes that one day the world will know how many licks it takes to get to the center of a Tootsie Pop; he believes it is more than three. This is his first published short story.

Damon Shaw grew up in Orkney and moved to the Canary Isles by way of London and a career in acting and set/puppet design. Despite now living on an island only forty miles long, he is still not close enough to the sea. He has been published in *Icarus, Daily Science Fiction,* and has work forthcoming in *Bull Spec* and in another forthcoming Lethe Press anthology, *The Lavender Menace,* amongst other places. Visit him at damonshaw.livejournal.com.

EDITOR

STEVE BERMAN has visited two oceans and many lakes. He does not care for the beach. While safe on dry land he has written a novel, *Vintage*, and edited over a dozen anthologies, including the two-time Lambda Literary Award finalist *Wilde Stories*, an annual series showcasing the finest gay speculative fiction of the prior year. He resides in southern New Jersey, which features a lot of coastline.